THE HOLY SINNER

Thomas Mann

THE HOLY SINNER

Translated from the German by

H. T. LOWE-PORTER

VINTAGE BOOKS

A DIVISION OF RANDOM HOUSE

NEW YORK

First Vintage Books Edition, October 1983
Copyright 1951 by Alfred A. Knopf, Inc.
Copyright renewed 1979 by Alfred A. Knopf, Inc.
All rights reserved under International and Pan-American
Copyright Conventions. Published in the United States
by Random House, Inc., New York, and simultaneously
in Canada by Random House of Canada Limited, Toronto.
Published in the United States by Alfred A. Knopf, Inc.
in 1951. Published in German as *Der Erwählte* by
S. Fischer Verlag GmbH, Frankfurt am Main,
copyright 1951 by Thomas Mann.

Library of Congress Cataloging in Publication Data
Mann, Thomas, 1875-1955.
The Holy Sinner.
I. Title.
PT2625.A44E75 1983   833'.912   83-5895
ISBN 0-394-71741-4 (pbk.)

Manufactured in the United States of America

CONTENTS

THE HOLY SINNER

Who Rings?

THE RINGING of bells, the surging and swelling of bells supra urbem, above the whole city, in its airs overfilled with sound. Bells, bells, they swing and sway, they wag and weave through their whole arc on their beams, in their seats, hundred-voiced, in Babylonish confusion. Slow and swift, blaring and booming—there is neither measure nor harmony, they talk all at once and all together, they break in even on themselves; on clang the clappers and leave no time for the excited metal to din itself out, for like a pendulum they are already back at the other edge, droning into its own droning; so that when echo still resounds: "In te Domine speravi," it is uttering already "Beati quorum tecta sunt peccata" into its own midst; not only so, but lesser bells tinkle clear from smaller shrines, as though the mass-boy might be touching the little bell of the Host.

Ringing from the height and ringing from the depths; from the seven arch-holy places of pilgrimage and all the churches of the seven parishes on both sides of the twice-rounding Tiber. From the Aventine ringing; from the holy places of the Palatine and from St. John of the Lateran; above the grave of him who bears the keys, in the Vatican Hill, from Santa Maria Maggiore, Santa Maria in Foro, in Domnica, in Cosmedin and in Trastevere; from Ara Celi, St. Paul's outside the Walls, St. Peter in Chains, and from the house of the Most Holy Cross in Jerusalem. And from the chapels in the cemeteries, from the roofs of the basilicas and oratories in the narrow streets come the sounds as well. Who names their names and knows their titles? As when the wind, when the tempest rakes the strings of the æolian harp and rouses the whole world of sound, the far apart and the close at hand, in whirring, sweeping harmony; such, translated in bronze, are the sounds that split the air, for here everything that is rings for the great feast and high procession.

Who is ringing the bells? Not the bell-ringers. They have run into the street like all the folk, to list the un-canny ringing. Convince yourselves: the bell-chambers are empty. Lax hang the ropes, and yet the bells rock and the clappers clang. Shall one say that *nobody* rings them?—No, only an ungrammatical head, without logic, would be capable of the utterance. "The bells are ring-ing": that means they are rung, and let the bell-cham-bers be never so empty.—So who is ringing the bells of Rome?—It is *the spirit of story-telling*.—Then can he be everywhere, hic et ubique, for instance at once on the Tower of St. George in Velabro and up in Santa Sa-bina, which preserves columns from the abominable Temple of Diana? At a hundred consecrate seats at once?—Of a certainty, that he can. He is as air, bodi-

less, ubiquitous, not subject to distinctions of here and
there. He it is that says: " All the bells were ringing";
and, in consequence, it is he who rings them. So spiritual is this spirit and so abstract that grammatically he
can be talked of only in the third person and simply re-
ferred to as "It is he." And yet he can gather himself
into a person, namely into the first person, and be incarnate in somebody who speaks in him and says: "I
am he. I am the spirit of story-telling, who, sitting in
his time-place, namely in the library of the cloister of
St. Gall in Allemannenland, where once Notker the
Stammerer sat, tells this story for entertainment and
exceptional edification; in that I begin with its grace-
abounding end and ring the bells of Rome: id est, report that on that day of processional entry they all together began to ring of themselves."

But also, in order that the second grammatical person should come into its own, the question runs: Who
art thou then, who saying I sits at Notker's desk and
embodies the spirit of narrative?—I am Clemens the
Irishman, ordinis divi Benedicti, visiting here as Brother,
accepted guest, and envoy from my Abbot Kilian of
the cloister of Clonmacnoise, my house in Ireland, that
I may foster the ancient relations which since the days
of St. Gall and St. Columbanus obtain between my
house and this strong citadel of Christ. I have on my
journey visited a great many seats of pious learning
and abodes of the Muses, such as Fulda, Reichenau,
and Gandersheim, St. Emeran in Regensburg, Lorsch,
Echternach, and Corvey. But here, where the eye laves

itself in evangeliaries and psalters with such priceless
illumination in gold and silver on purple, with decora-
tion in vermilion, green, and blue; where the Brothers
under their choirmaster intone more sweetly than ever
elsewhere heard; where the bodily refection is excellent, not forgetting the cordial little wine which is
poured out with it, and after table in the cloisters one
can exercise so agreeably round the fountain; here I
have made my station for a somewhat more spacious
time, occupying one of the always ready guest-cells
into which the highly estimable Abbot, Gozbert of his
name, had thoughtfully put an Irish cross, whereon one
sees figured a lamb in the coils of snakes, the arbor vitæ,
a dragon's head with the cross in his jaws, and the ec-
clesia catching the blood of Christ in a chalice, whilst
the devil tries to snap up a bite and sup of it. The piece
witnesses the early high standard of our Irish arts.

I am deeply attached to my home, St. Patrick's nook-
shotten isle, its meadows, heaths, and moors. Its airs
blow damp and mild, and mild too is the air in our
cloister of Clonmacnoise, given as it is to training disci-
plined by a measured asceticism. With our Abbot Kilian I am of the well-tried view that the religion of Jesus
and the practice of ancient studies must go hand in
hand in combating rude ways; that it is the same ignorance which knows nothing of the one and of the other,
and that where the first took root the other also flourished. In fact the height of culture reached by our
brotherhood in my experience quite considerably sur-
passed that of the Roman clerus itself, which is often

all too little touched by the wisdom of antiquity and among whose members at time a truly lamentable Latin is written—if also none so bad as among German monks, one of whom, to be sure an Augustinian, lately wrote to me: "Habes tibi aliqua secreta dicere. Robustissimus in corpore sum et sæpe propterea temptationibus Diaboli succumbo." That is indeed scarcely tolerable, stylistically as well as also in other ways, and probably such peasantly rubbish could never flow from a Roman pen. Altogether it would be mistaken to believe I would speak ill of Rome and its supremacy, whose loyal adherent on the contrary I profess myself. It may be that we Irish monks have always held to independent dealings and in many regions of the Continent have first preached Christianity, have also acquired extraordinary merit in that everywhere, in Burgundy and Friesland, Thuringia and Allemannia, we erected cloisters as bastions of the faith and of our mission. That does not mean that we have not since early times recognized the Bishop in the Lateran as head of the Christian Church and seen in him a being of almost divine nature, in that we consider at most only the site of the divine resurrection as holier than St. Peter's. One may say without untruth that the churches of Jerusalem, Ephesus, and Antioch are older than the Roman, and if Peter, at whose unassailable name one does not gladly think of certain cockcrows, founded the bishopric of Rome (he did found it), the same is indisputably true of the community of Antioch. But these matters can only play the role of fugitive comments at the margin of truth: that, firstly, our Lord and Saviour (as it stands in Matthew and may be read there, though indeed only in him) summoned Peter to be his vicar here below, but the latter transferred the vicariate to the Roman bishop and conferred on him the precedence over all the episcopates of the world. We even read indeed in decretals and protocols of early time the very speech which the apostle himself held at the ordination of his first successor, Pope Linus, which I regard as a real trial of faith and a challenge to the spirit to manifest its power and show what all it succeeds in believing.

In my so much more humble quality as incarnation of the spirit of story-telling, I have every interest that others like me shall regard the call to the sella gestatoria as the highest and most blessed of elections. And it is at once a sign of my devotion to Rome that I bear the name of Clemens. For natively I am named Morhold. But I have never liked the name, it strikes me as wild and heathenish, and with the cowl I put on that of the third successor of Peter, so that it is no longer the vulgar Morhold who moves in the girted tunic and scapular but a more refined Clemens, who has consummated what St. Paul to the Ephesians so happily called the "putting on a new man." Yes, it is no longer at all the body of flesh which went about in the doublet of that Morhold, but rather a spiritual one which the cingulum girds—accordingly, a body which makes not quite worthy of sanction my earlier statement: id est, that I am the "incarnate spirit of story-telling," namely that it is "embodied" in me. I do not care for this word "em-

bodiment" so much, since (of course) it derives from
the body and the fleshly shape, which together with the
name of Morhold I have put off, and which in all ways
is a domain of Satan, through him capable of abominations and subject to them, though one scarcely under-
stands why it does not reject them. On the other hand,
the body is the vehicle of the soul and God-given reason, without which these would be deprived of their
basis; and so one must regard the body as a necessary
evil. Such is the recognition fitting to it; one more en-
thusiastic we owe it not, in its urgent need and its repul-
siveness. And how should one, in act to relate a tale, or
to retell it (for it has already been told, even several
times, if also inadequately), which abounds in bodily
abomination and affords frightful evidence to what all
the body gives itself, without fear or faltering—how
should one be inclined to boast overmuch about being
an embodiment!

No; for the spirit of story-telling, having concentrated itself in my monkish person, called Clemens the
Irishman, has preserved much of that abstraction which
enables it to ring from all the titular basilicas of the city
at once; two instances of the fact I will cite straightway.
Firstly, then, it may escape the reader of this manu-
script, and yet it is worthy of remark, that I have inscribed it with the name of the place where I sit, namely
St. Gall, at Notker's desk, but that I have not said in
what times, in the how-manyeth year and century after
our Saviour's birth I sit here and cover the parchment
with my small, fine, scholarly, and decorative script.

For there is no fixed term, and also the name of our Abbot here, Gozbert, does not furnish one. For it repeats itself all too oft in time, and, when one would cite it, turns quite readily into Fridolin or Hartmut. If one ask me, teasingly or maliciously, whether I myself indeed know *where* I am but not *when*, I answer pleasantly: there is truly nothing to know, for as a personification of the spirit of story-telling I rejoice in that abstraction, the second instance of which I now give.

For now I begin to write and address myself to tell a tale at once frightful and highly edifying. But it is quite uncertain in what language I write, whether Latin, French, German, or Anglo-Saxon, and indeed it is all the same; for say I write Thiudisch, such as the Germans speak who live in Helvetia, then tomorrow British stands on the paper and it is a Breton book that I have written. By no means do I assert that I possess all the tongues; but they run all together in my writing and become one—in other words, language. For the thing is so, that the spirit of narration is free to the point of abstraction, whose medium is language in and for itself, language itself, which sets itself as absolute and does not greatly care about idioms and national linguistic gods. That indeed would be polytheistic and pagan. God is spirit, and above languages is language.

One thing is certain: that I write prose and not little verses, for which on the whole I cherish no exaggerated regard. Rather in this respect I am in the tradition of the Emperor Carolus, who was not only a great lawgiver and judge of the nations but also the protector of grammar and an assiduous patron of correct and limpid prose. I hear said, indeed, that only metre and rhyme can result in a strict form, but I would like well to know why this hopping on three or four iambic feet, resulting to boot in all sorts of stumbling in dactyls and anapaests, with a little light-hearted assonance of the end words, is supposed to indicate the strict form, as against a shapely prose with its much finer and less obvious rhythmical laws. If I were to begin with:

> There was a prince by name Grimald,
> He had a stroke that laid him cold.
> He left behind twinn children fair—
> Aha, was that a sinful pair!

or something in that kind, would it be a stricter form than the grammatical and dignified prose in which I now present my tale of grace, that many who come after, French, Angles, and Germans, may dip into it to make their little rimes?

So much by way of preface; I begin as follows:

Grimald and Baduhenna

THERE was once a Duke of Flaundres and Artoys, by
name Grimald. His sword was called Eckesachs, the
Terrible. His Castilian war-steed was named Guver-
jorss. Securer in God's favour seemed no prince than
he, and bold ranged his eye over lands his by death and
inheritance, with fat cities and strong citadels, and
rested, stern with self-respect, on his meiny and squire-
shaft, with runners, cooks, kitchen-boys, drummers and
trumpeters, fiddlers and flautists. He had also his body-
servants, twelve boys of distinguished birth and gentle
manners, among them two sons of Saracens. The Christian lads were forbidden to tease the latter about their
idol Mohammed. When with his wife Baduhenna, that
lofty dame, he paced to the church or the festal board,
then these pages sprang by twos, handfast, in coloured
stockings before them, setting their feet crosswise and
becking with their heads.

His native stronghold, where Duke Grimald chiefly
held court, was Chastel Beaurepaire, and lay on the
heights of sheep-feeding Artoys, looking from afar as
though turned on a lathe, with its roofs, terraces, out-

works, and ring-walls reinforced by towers, a very refuge such as a prince well needs: against savage foes from without as well as against evil notions of his own subjects; yet indeed most habitable and pleasant to the senses too. Its kernel was a towering donjon keep, square, with inner rooms of great splendour, the like of which however were hidden not only in the dwelling-tower itself but also in the course of the walls in many a special building and inner ring as well; and from the great hall of the keep a straight stair went out into the court and garden sward, where surrounded by walls there stood a spreading linden tree. On the bench that went round it the ducal pair liked to sit of a summer afternoon on cushions of fine phelle silk from Aleppo and Damascus, while the court sat round at ease at their feet on carpets spread by squires on the well-tended sward; and they listened to many a true and many a de-ceiving tale of player folk who, picking their strings, related of Artus, lord of all Brittany, of good-weather King Orendel, how he suffered bitter shipwreck in late autumn and became thrall to the ice-giants; of the combats of Christian knights with strange, frightful people in such remote lands as Ethnise, Gylstram, or Rankulat: folk with heads like cranes, with eyes in their foreheads, web-footers, pygmies and giants; of the ex-traordinary dangiers of the magnet-mountain and the outwitting of the griffins for their red gold; of the battle for the faith of St. Silvester with a Jew before the Em-peror Constantine; when the Jew murmured the name of his God in the ear of a steer and the animal fell dead

to the ground. But Silvester invoked Christus, and the
bull rose on his legs again and in thundering roar proclaimed the superiority of the true faith.

All this only by way of illustration. At other times
they gave each other cunning riddles or carried on free
conversation full of cortoisie and wit, so that much
merry laughter of mixed voices, lords and ladies, filled
the air.

For my part I have to laugh, because some might
think in the great hall above there burned of evenings
smoking torches of straw and pitch-pine for light. Oh
no! Rings hung from the roof thick bestuck with flickering candles, and wall candelabra held bunches of candles with tenfold gleam into the room. There were two
marble chimney-pieces where aloes and sandalwood
burned, and broad carpets covered the stones; on occasion perhaps the Prince of Kanvoleis or the King of
Anjou—bien soi venu, beau Sire!—being guests of the
Duke, there were strewn branches and green rushes and
flowers. At table the Lord Grimald and his Lady Baduhenna sat in chairs with cushions of Arabic achmardi,
opposite to them their chaplain. The musicians sat at
the foot of the table or else at a separate little table and
the court at square tables let down from the walls, covered with white, and four squires for each table handed
golden beakers and gay silk napkins and they carved
kneeling. Fit was the food for court: heron and fish
and lamb cutlets, and birds caught in snares in the
woods, and fat carp. With each dish there was sauce,
pepper and agrass (by which I mean fruit sauce), and

diligently, their faces red as fire (for they drank too, behind the doors), the pages filled the beakers with wine and mulberry wine and red Sinopel and spicy "clear drink," that is to say claret, with which with the greatest pleasure and frequency the Lord Grimald wetted his gorge.

But I will not further celebrate the good life on Beaurepaire, though it were indeed untruth to conceal that the presses were bursting with linen and damask, silks and velvets of rare sort, otter-skins, and also fine sables; that the stands and cases glittered with Azagoger fine-ware, such as bowls hollowed out of precious stones and gold goblets. The drawers scarcely held the supply of spicery with which the air was scented, the carpets and couches strewed: herbs and woods, amber-gris, theriac, clove, muskat, and cardamom; that in se-cret treasuries were bestowed many a golden mark from the Caucasus, wrested from the claws of griffins; thereto jewels and wonder-working stones unset, as carbuncle, onyx, chalcedony, coral, and whatever else they are called: agate, sardonyx, pearls, malachite, and diamonds; that the magazines and armouries were crammed with priceless weapons, shirts of chain mail, harsenières and shields from Toledo in Spain, harness for rider and steed, trappings, harness, saddles, and bell-bridles; the stables, penfolds, kennels, and cages were full to over-flowing with horses and hounds, game lures, falcons, and talking birds.

But enough of such pæans! Though it were no small thing to align and keep in grammatical sequence such

encomiums as these! In most courtly fashion, it is clear,
did the Lord Grimald and the Lady Baduhenna pass
their days, admired by all Christendom round about,
richly besene with all the good things of the earth. So
it goes in all the tales and then goes on to say: "Only
one thing was lacking to their joy." The life of man
follows well-tried patterns, but it is only in words that
it is old and traditional; in and for itself it is ever new
and young, though even so nothing may remain to the
teller save to give it the old words. Only one thing then,
says he, perforce, was lacking to make their happiness
complete: that was children—and how often one saw
the pair kneeling side by side on velvet cushions, wringing their hands to heaven for that which was withheld!
Not only so; but in all the churches of Flaundres and
Artoys each Sunday prayers rose from the chancel to
God for this boon, yet He seemed ever to deny His ear
to the plea; for both were already forty and still de-
layed the hope of posterity and direct succession, so
that one day belike the dukedom would be torn insun-
der in strife of contending heirs.

Was it because the Archbishop of Cologne, Utrecht,
Maastricht, and Liége entered the lists with solemn
masses and supplicating processions? I so believe; for
after long hesitation by the Almighty the ban was at
last lifted and the princess looked forward to maternal
joys—joys, alas, destined only to be quenched in the
tortures of a childbed whose agony bore witness to the
lingering misgivings of the All-Wisdom on the score of
her hopes. For woe! The dame was not to recover from

the twins which with inhuman shrieks she bore to the
light of day. Her own light failed, and Duke Grimald
was made a father only to find himself at the same time
widowed.

How strangely does providence mingle for us mortals joy and sorrow in one cup! The Archbishop, un-
favourably affected by the doubtful success which his
pressure upon the Almighty had brought about, left it
to the Bishop of Cambray to hold the exequies in the
cathedral at Ypres. When now the stone slab covered
the vault where the Lady Baduhenna kept her cold
childbed, Duke Grimald returned to Beaurepaire to rejoice in what was given him, after in due form mourning what had been taken away. The swaddling-pair,
death's dearest scions, lad and maid, his flesh and blood,
heirs of his house, they were his bliss in bane, and were
the bliss of all the burg, wherefore together they were
called Joidelacourt, meaning joy of the court, for more
charming infants truly the world never saw, and no
painter from Cologne or Maastricht could have painted
more beauteous with paint: so pure of form, flowed
round by all sweet airs, with little hair like down of
chicks and eyes at first all full of heaven's light; seldom
crying, ever ready with angel smiles that melted one's
heart, not only for others but also when they looked at
each other on the chiffonier, clapped hands together,
and said "Da, da!"

Joidelacourt, of course, they were called only in common and in flattering jest. In holy baptism, bestowed
by the chaplain of the castle, they received the names

Wiligis and Sibylla; and though younker Wiligis, who clapped so much harder while saying "Da, da" than did his sister Sibylla, was the chief person and heir, yet on her too, as on her whole sex, fell a gleam from the glory of the Queen of Heaven and with tenderer eye did Duke Grimald regard his daughter than the so important and quite as handsome son. His son would be a knight like himself, doughty and bold, made for the women, when after jousting he would wash from his body the rust of his sweated armour; made for the claret too, yes, one could tell that. The sweet strangeness of tender womanhood, endowed from above, takes hold quite otherwise of the rude heart of man, even the fatherly one; and thus the Lord Grimald called his son only young sprig and monkey but the wee girl "ma charmante" and kissed her while he only patted the boy and gave him his finger to hold.

The Children

WITH what care now the noble little children were reared by women of experience, whose brow and chin the coif embraced! These fed them with sweetened gruel and pap, bathed them in bran-water and rubbed their bare gums with wine that the milk teeth might come through more easily and quickly and grace their smiles. They did so, readily, without much puling and the teeth were like pearls, though very sharp too. But as the twain were now no longer in swaddling-bands, no more the tenderest of newcomers here below, the sweet light they had brought with them from above passed as cloud-shadows pass; and they grew darker and began to take on more earthly shape, though the very most graceful, I must say. The down of young chicks on their little heads turned into smooth brown hair that contrasted quite charmingly with the unusual foreign yvorie pallor of the fine-fine little faces and the skin of their growing bodies: clearly an inheritance from distant forebears, not their parents, for the Lady Baduhenna had been white and apple-red and Sieur Grimald was vermilion-hued in the face. The chil-

dren's eyes, whose rays at first were azure, darkened
deeper and deeper into black with a blue depth, seldom seen and almost uncanny, if also no longer heavenly—which is not to say why some little angels should
not have such night-blue eyes. Also they both had a
way of looking sidelong out of one corner as though
they were listening and waiting for something. Whether
for good or ill I cannot tell.

At seven, the time of losing the first teeth, they got
chicken-pox and as they scratched the pocks a mark remained on the forehead of each, a scar and a flat hollow,
in exactly the same place and the same shape, namely
like a sickle. Their silken brown hair fell over it but
the Lord Grimald sometimes in playfulness or wonder
stroked it back from their brows, what time the coiffed
women, as they did daily at a fixed hour, brought the
children before his footstool, as he sat with goblet of
claret ready to his hand. The nurses with bent heads
smiling withdrew for several paces down the hall in order not to disturb by their lowly proximity the pleasure
of the noble family. Or they remained standing by the
door and let the children go to their sire, Sibylla in her
little shot-silk gown (or whatever one calls a pattern
artfully woven with gold thread), Wiligis in his velvet
smock bordered with beaver, the hair of both on their
shoulders. Wiligis by precept and training knew well
to bend the knee: "Dieu vus sal, dear Herre wert," said
they in little voices somewhat hoarse with alarm. And
then the father chatted and jested with them, called
them gent mignote de soris and sweethearts, asked how

their day went, and commended them at length to the
Saint Esperit, clapping Willo and kissing Sibylla. He
told them: "Be good children!" They answered in uni-
son, with their hoarse little voices: "May God reward
you!" and went away backwards from him as custom
bade, while the women hurried towards them from the
door and took their hands, the outside ones, as they
were holding each other's.

They were ever handfast wherever they went, at
eight and at ten years, and were like a pair of dwarf
parrots or love-birds, together day and night, for from
the first they had shared a bedchamber high up in the
tower where the little owls flew hooting and where
their bedsteads stood with straps of salamander-skin on
which the cushions lay and bedposts of twisted snakes.
The upholstery under the cushions was palmat. Of the
coiffed women who still for company and serving slept
by them on pallets, they often inquired: "We are little
yet, aren't we?"—"Two little turtle-doves, high-born
and fine."—"And shall be small a long time, shan't we,
n'est-ce voir?"—"Yes, suerement, sweetnesses, a long
time yet."—"But we want to be little always on earth,"
they said. "We have made it up like that, when we cosy
together. We shall then easier become little angels in
hefen. It must be very hard with belly and beard and
bosom to turn into a little angel when one dies."—"Oh,
little silly, que Dieu dispose! And He will not have it
that one remain for ever a child, whatever you may
have made up. Deus ne volt."—"But if we chastise ourselves, and not sleep for three nights long but only pray

that God keep us little?"—"Hark to the sweet simplicity! My faith, you will fall asleep and sweetly grow in
sleep."

And so it was. I do not know whether they tried the
scourging in earnest; I would like to think that the
nurses' words refrained them. But by little and little, as
the years passed over castle and country, foliaged and
fallow, ice-grey and then again green with may, they
came to be nine and ten and eleven, two buds which
would unfold, or even if they would not, yet were
about to, no longer small, but young-young things,
pretty as pictures their pale faces, with silken brows,
lively eyes, thin nostrils which visibly quivered, and
long, somewhat arched upper lip; in body quietly shaping according to their destinies, not yet rightly in pro-
portion, but rather like young hounds whose paws are
too big; thus when Wiligis in the morning, high-
spirited from sleep, nude like a pagan god, his sickle-
mark in his tumbled hair, jumped about the wooden
bathtub before his bed, whereon swam rose-leaves, that
by which he differed from his sister, his male part,
looked too large and developed compared with his slender yvorie-toned body. The sight makes me in a way
sad. So childlike fine and wise on top the little head
on the slender shoulders and then low down such a
thumper! But the nurses clucked their tongues respect-
fully and made great eyes at each other, saying: L'espoirs des dames!" As for the maid, she sat, a bud scarce
yet half open on the bed's edge, the sign on her forehead
quite plain since her hair had been drawn back for the

night; almost darkly she looked out of the corner of
her eye on him and his admiring womenkind. I know
what she was thinking. She thought: "I will—l'espoirs!
Mine is the sweetheart. That damsel who has to do with
him—j'arracherai les yeux and take no poen for it, I,
little daughter of the Duke!"

There had been assigned to her a noble widow, a
Comtesse of Cleves, with whom she sang the psalter in
the window-seat and who taught her the embroidering
of stuffs of costly wool. The younker in his turn had a
gouvernail named Eisengrein, Cons du Châtel, that is to
say count of a fortified castle in a lake with moats wide
and deep and a high look-out over the sea, for the castle
stood down in the plain, where it was called Rousselaere
and Thorhout, quite near the sea. (Take care and note
this water-castle, near the sounding seas! It will have its
bearing on this history.) Thence came the Sieur Eisengrein, a foremost in the land and leal vassal, to Beaurepaire expressly to be lord-in-waiting to the younker,
and his maistre de courtesie. There was given to him
also for the grosser services the squire Patafrid. But
though the Lord Grimald had always because of the ra-
diance from on high preferred the maid before the son,
and the more the bud unfolded the more tender and
gallant he grew, though the more, as the younker grew
up, the gruffer to his son, yet he was right fatherly
mindful of the good breeding of the heir and gave order that he become un om de gentilesce, afetié, bien
parlant et anseignié. So from those two he learned
knighthood and fine morality. From Patafrid he learned

(whether with especial pleasure or not) to leap on his horse without the rein and from Master Eisengrein how when riding for pleasure in light attire one lays légèrement one leg foremost upon the horse. With the principal squires he had to fight a joust in iron armour from Soissons and learn how one aims with the spear at the four nailes on the opponent's shield, whereupon Patafrid to pleasure him would fall from his horse and give surety. He learned too how one hurls the short gabylot as well as to use the long lance in running up. With his gouvernail and the falconers he rode to the hawking in the greenwood, learned to fling the well-schooled bell-falcon from his hand and whistle so skilfully on a blade of grass that all the wild game thought to hear the cry of their own kind.

What know I of knighthood and venery? I am a monk, at bottom ignorant of all this and even somewhat fearful. I have never confronted a boar nor heard in my ears the crashing horn at fall of the stag, nor brought in the game and as master of the chace eaten the tidbits roasted upon coals. I merely behave as though I could actually say how the younker Wiligis was brought up, and put words to the telling. Never have I swung a gabylot in my hand nor thrown the long lance under my arm; nor yet "leafed"—blown on a leaf—to deceive the wild things; this very word for it which I use with such apparent ease I have just picked up. But so is the way and the spirit of story-telling which I embody that all it tells of, it pretends to have experienced and to be at home in it. The buhurd too, the joyous tourney young

Wiligis practised on the soft valley bottom at the foot
of the castle hill with gentlemen and squires, when in
full career host assaults host and each seeks to force the
other from the field, while the ladies sat on wooden bal-
conies round about, either mocking or applauding their
gallants. This rough-and-tumble too, I say, is at bottom
quite beyond me and rather offensive than otherwise.
Yet am I able to run on and tell how Willo with his host
pressed forward, clods flying, the handsomest fifteen-
year-old one can imagine, on his dappled steed, without
armour save the neck- and shoulder-piece of light chain
mail, which framed his fine pale boyish face, in tabard
and doublet of red Alexandrine silk; and how one and
all courteously avoided him, let him seem to thrust
through the whole opposing troop, because he was the
Duke's son; and how the ladies congratulated Sibylla,
his sweet sister, who laughed and breathed quick upon
his victory.

That it was a sham triumph consoles me somewhat
for speaking with such sham fluency of matters which
are none of mine. But even from a sham triumph one
gets hot too, and hot and proud because they had been
so courteous to him came Wiligis back to the castle and
stood before his sister, who in her turn knew quite well
that he had won by common consent, and in spite of
or because of that, was just as hot and proud as he.
Would you know how (in celebration of the day) the
maid was clad: she was arrayed in a gown green as
grass, of Azagoger velvet, very wide and long and vo-
luminously draped, and in front where it hung in wide

folds one saw the lining was of red silk and the under-petticoat of white. Round her yvorie throat it fitted close and was sewn like the wrists with pearl and stones which lower on the bosom came together to form a broad ornament. Thick set with precious stones was the girdle too and the virgin crants on her flowing hair consisted as well of little rubies and garnets, red and green. Many a maid might be taken with envy at this description of the Duke's child, and also because of the length of her lashes, between which played the blue-black eyes; further because I, my own eyes monkishly downcast, record that under velvet and gems her bosom rose and fell, nor may I be silent upon the extraordinary beauty of her hands—hardly smaller they were than her brother's, but altogether fine-boned, with pointed fingers, on some of which sparkled rings, one each on the upper and the lower joints. Slender she was, with lovely line of hips, and just as with him the upper lip began far forward under the little nose and was arched, the thin nostrils quivered just like his.

"Ah, lord and brother," she said, as she freed him from the chain-mail head-piece and smoothed his dark hair, "you were glorious, when they had to let you thrust through the whole troupe! How your legs stood in the stirrups at the attack, that I saw with joy. Yours are the most beauteous young legs of any here. Only mine, in their different kind, are just as beautiful. Insonders thrill me your knees when you gambol and give the animal your thigh."

"Glorious," he answered her, "are you, Sibylla, quite

of yourself and with no buhurd at all! My sex, it must
bestir itself and do something, to be glorious. For yours
one need only be and bloom and is already glorious.
That is the most general difference between male and
female, aside from the more particular."

"We envy you," said she, "your differences, admire
them and are covered with shame, because we are
broader in the hips instead of in the shoulders, and in
consequence have too large a belly surface, also a much
too ample derrière. But this I may say, that even so my
legs are high and slim, leaving nothing to wish in this
respect."

"That you may," he returned, "and you must not forget that we in our turn look on your differences if not
with envy, yet with sweetest pleasure. Even the word
'envy' might be in place, for where is our flowering-
time? We have nothing either here or there, only somewhat of strength at best to hack ourselves out of our
disadvantage."

"Say not that you have naught! But let us sit down in
the window niche and causer cosily a little about the
buhurd of today, how comic Count Kynewulf of Nie-
derlahngau, named Weewight by reason of his small-
ness, looked on his huge black mare, and how Sir Kala-
mede, fils du comte Ulterlec, when his steed stumbled,
came to lie under his horse, whereat Dame Garshiloye
of the Belfontane almost lost her senses."

They did as she proposed, sat, with their arms in velvet and silk across each other's shoulders, on the bench
in the niche and anon leaned their comely heads to each

other. At their feet, head on his paws, lay their Anglo-
Saxon hound, a pointer, Hanegiff by name, a very lovable creature, white, black only round one eye and both
ear-flaps. He shared their sleeping-chamber and slept
there always between their beds on a materas stuffed
with horsehair. The view through the window was over
the roofs and battlements of the castle and down upon
a street in the valley, bordered with flowering shrub-
bery and meadows where flocks of thick-fleeced sheep
moved leisurely and slow. Sibylla asked:

"You had eyes of course for Alisse of Poitou in the
silly gown she showed off in, half of silk worked
through with gold and half of phelle from Nineveh,
with the skirt embroidered in colours. There were many
who found her most stately."

To that he said:

"I had no eyes for her supposed stateliness. I have had
eyes alone for you who are my female counterpart on
earth. The others are foreign, not equal in birth like you
who were born with me. She of Poitou, I know, makes
herself so fine for men like the giant Hugebold, and for
such bean-poles as Sir Rassalig of Lorraine, twice as
tall as I am, and not much thicker than a lath. Since
shadow of beard darkened my lip, many a lady makes
her eyes melting when she looks on me. But I turn her
the cold shoulder, for no one fits me but you et plus n'i
quiers veoir."

She said:

"The King of Escavalon has addressed a letter to Grimald our lord, and sought of him my hand in marriage,

who now am man-ripe and he still unwived. I know it
from my maistresse, the von Cleve. You need not start,
for the Duke has mildly denied him and told him I am,
though man-ripe, still too young, unripe as queen even
for so small a kingdom as Ascalon, and he should look
round among other the princes' daughters of Christendom. Indeed not on your account and that we may yet
stay together hath our lord refused the King. Rather
'will stay a while,' he wrote, 'sit at table with both my
children, my daughter on my right, my son on my left,
not with the lad alone and then only my priest besides,
opposite to me.' That was the ground of his refus."

"Let it," he said, as he gave himself to playing with
her hand and looking at the rings on it, "be whatever
ground it like, if only one does not part us in our sweet
youth before the time of which I will not know when
it will come. For of us two no one is worthy, neither of
you nor of me, worthy is one of the other, since we are
wholly exceptional children, high of birth, that all the
world must behave lovingly dévotement to us, and born
together out of death, each of us with our graven sign
on our brow, they come of course only from chicken-
pox, which is no better than croup, measles, or mumps,
but the origin of the sign does not signify, tout de même
it is the pale little hollow that is important. When God
will have lengthened the days of our lord and father
dear and good up to the furthest measure of humanity,
as it may please Him to do, then shall I be duke over
Artoys and Flaundres, a rich and blessed land, for here
the grain waves on fat acres while on the hills ten thou-

sand and more cropping sheep carry wool for good cloths, while below, towards the sea, the flax grows so abundantly that the peasants, as I hear, in clumsy joy dance in the taverns and the land is bestuck with splendid cities as your hand with rings: Ypren is joyous, Gent, Louvain, and Anvers stuffed full of wares, and Bruges-la-vive on the deep sea-bay where ships overladen with treasure from oceans south and north and east ride ceaselessly in and out. The burghers go in velvets and furs, but they have not learned to leap free-handed to horse nor to aim with the lance at the four nailes of the shield, nor yet to ride a buhurd, therefore they need a duke who protects them, and that am I. But you of all maids best who alone are fit for me, I will, while they throw their caps in the air, lead by my hand among them as sister-duchess."

And he kissed her.

"I like it better," said she, "when you kiss me than when our dear and worthy lord scratches my neck and cheeks with his rust-coloured moustaches. How much must we be glad from our hearts if he came visiting us, as may any moment happen."

For often, that is, when they so sat cosily chatting of many things, Duke Grimald might come to them, not to keep them company, but rather with harsh words to drive away the younker and chat with the maid.

"Fils de duc Grimald," he said, "do I find you here, young puppy, with this sweet child your sister? That you affect her is to be praised and I praise it that you give her your best strength and stand by her and enter-

tain her as well as a young stripling can do. But so
long as I live, trust me, I am her protector before all
others and still man enough to take it upon me, and if
you flatter yourself that such a precious child is closer
to the brother than to her sound and sturdy father, then
you may expect a couple of smacks from me. Allez
avant and away from here! Go shoot at the target with
Master Patafrid! The Duke will have a chat with his
little daughter."

And then he sat down beside her in the niche and
courtisiered her, old knight that he was, in a way a
monk can but uneathe imagine.

"Beau corps is yours," thus he spoke, "and what the
frensche call florie, the bloom that rests upon you, you
have of late most increased in loveliness. Hélàs, the time
is tender to youth, making it daily blossom sweeter,
whereas it more and more uglifies the old, takes the hair
from the skin of the head, and strews grey in the snout.
Yes, yes, the greybeard must feel shame before the
youth, for age is repulsive. Meanwhile, pourtant, dignity has to make up for beauty, and you, my dearest,
must not forget that Grimald is your father, to whom
you owe affection and thanks, that he brought you into
the world, and so early lost his precious consort. As for
thee we must see that you soon hold the wedding feast,
for many sweet signs speak for thy nubility. I think
only of thy happiness. But truly, as for me, the first
comer is not the best, and not only you must he please,
but I must give you to him, and, faith, I grant thee to
no one so easily, old knight as I am."

Thus, or the like, Sieur Grimald when he sat with
her in the window-seat; I repeat it, as well as a monkish
understanding can.

In the next year, when the children were sixteen,
came for young Wiligis the celebration of his knighthood—but what can I know of such a thing? I know
that in the world's mouth it means for the younker to
gird on the knightly sword. That Duke Grimald gave
his son, and dubbed him knight amid vivats and ta-ra-
ra, after solemn high mass in St. Vaast, at Arras in the
citadel, in the presence of many kindred and knights,
and afterwards he strode between his children, leading
his son with his right hand and with his left the virgin
maid, before the eyes of the jubilant quemune down the
perron d'honneur from the lofty tower. The new-made
chevalier, used to wear only the short hunting-knife at
his hip, had to take care lest the immense sword which
now hung from his belt in front get between his legs.
But to both children came the thought that after all
how much nicer it would be if only they two, hand in
hand, paced down the ramp and the father were not
between them.

But now that Wiligis had been duly knighted, Sibylla
was in her turn in all eyes of age and ripe for marriage,
and there were ever more suits from proud princes of
Christendom, who might well venture the offer. In part
they wrote, in part sent noble wooers to Beaurepaire, in
part they came themselves to woo. The old King of
Anjou brought his son Shafillor, who forsooth was but
simple. Count Schiolarss of Ipotente, the Gascon Duke

Obilot, Plihopliheri Prince of Waleis, as well as the
lords of Hainhault and Hespaye, they all came and
made themselves fine with sable-bordered garments and
ermine, and flowery addresses which they read in part
from a sheet. But the Lord Grimald rejected them all,
for to no one did he grant Sibylla, yes, he was scarcely
able to dissemble the anger and hatred he felt against
the wooers, and with his nay-word let them all, however fine, ride back again into their domains. And that
caused much ill will round about the courts of Christendom.

But young Wiligis had at near this time a frightening
dream from which he woke his whole body wet with
sweat. He dreamed his father hovered over him with
legs spread out behind in the air, copper-red in the face
with rage, with bristling mustachios, and silently threatened him with both fists as though he would straightway take him by the throat. The dream was incom-
parably more frightful than it sounds in words and for
sheer dread lest he dream it again he did so for the second time—the same or even more frightful still—the
very next night.

The Bad Children

FOR seventeen years Duke Grimald outlived his wife Baduhenna, for that term and not less; then he came to her under the stone in the cathedral at Ypres, and on the stone they both lay, stiffly chiselled, as Christian spouses, their hands crossed before God on their breasts. For this prince since the decease of his wife had been increasingly given to excess of claret and one day he got as dark copper-red in the face as Wiligis had seen him in the dream, and after that yellow: the Foule Fiend had tapped him on the temple and he was dead of a stroke—for the moment only on his right side, so that he could not move the limbs and also he partly lost his speech and could only blow words like bubbles out of the left-hand corner of his mouth. But his doctor from Löwen and the Greek Elias whom he had sent for, neither of them concealed from him that the Foule Fiend might easily strike him again before long and then he would inevitably be dead on his left side too.

They said this in order that he might still be in time to bestow his kingdom; by their warning they put him

in mind and he sent for the best in the land, kinsfolk,
man and servant, to commend to them his soul and his
children and admonish them upon their leal oath if now
death was to be his company. When now they all, cousins and liegemen, together with his children had gathered round the bed where he lay, very much disfigured,
one eye shut and his cheek hanging paralysed, then he
spoke to them as well as he could:

"Seigneurs barons, hear my words as though I spoke
them with both lips, whereas I can only shake them out
of one corner of my mouth, that may ye pardon. Me
hath death seized, he already blows over me the cornure
de prise, to flay the noble stag in the grave. With the
tap of the Foule Fiend has he paralysed one side of me
and can any minute fall me entirely, that my physicians
beyeah in so many words and thus display their healing art. So now I am to take leave of this abode for
worms, and this evil wolf's gorge, into which we were
cast by Adam's misdoing and which I will still rail at
since I must leave it and hope through the will of God's
martyr wounds to enter through the porta paradyses,
where me the angels will tend, both day and night,
whiles ye still a lytel must abide in this garden of
worms. Therefore about me no unseemly haviour!
But be mindful, seigneurs barons, of the hour when you
did put your two hands together between mine in the
oath of fealty. Do the same now to my son when I am
quite dead, and put your hands between his even though
it seem to you matter for laughing that he should protect you, since the stripling needs your protection in-

stead. Grant him that, cousins and sieurs, as true men,
and keep faith to my house, both in urlag and in peace."

When he had thus taken leave of the gentlemen of
his lands he turned to Wiligis and said:

"You, son, have the least of all reason for lamenting;
crown, sceptre, and land, which fell to me as heir, these
I hand on to you by my death, if also most unwillingly;
and you will enjoy mickle honour in this wolf's gorge
out of which I now depart. Small concern do I give myself on your account, but so much the more for this
lovely child and sister thine. Too late do I see that I
have ill managed her future and I overwhelm myself
with reproaches on her account. Vere, vere, thus should
a father not bear himself! Also as concerns you, I know
I have made myself to some extent guilty in that through
over-great nicety in choice of a spouse for this sweet
child I have created much ill will in the courts round
about our house. Not otherwise can I atone than by giving the best fatherly counsel now at my end in presence
of my land barons so long as I can still speak out of my
left side."

And he said to his son all that his own father had said
to him, as is the usual thing and all that he thought fitting to say in such an hour.

"Be leal and true," so he said, "not greedy for treasure, yet not of all too free a hand, humble in pride, af-
fable, yet exclusive and strict, mindful of the knightly
code, strong against the high, and mild towards them
who beg at the windows for bread. Honour thine own,
but also shalt thou make strangers dependent and oblig-

ing to you. Choose the society of wisdom and length of days over that of young fools! Above all, love God and deal according to His justice. So much in general. But as my own soul commend I to you this your lovely sister, that you behave towards her as knightly brother and go not from her side until you have found and indeed as soon as possible a husband of equal birth, which I by my sinful niceness have made hard. The princes who have already asked for her, neither the Count Schiolarss nor the Prince Plihopliheri nor any of the others, they will not return, for I was far too inhospitable to them for that. But there are yet many Christian realms whose heads till now have not sued for her, and her beautiful eyes, black with a blue gleam from beneath, her charming nostrils, the blosme on her body, not forgetting the rich dowry I have left for her, will soon make many a noble wooer draw nigh, with that I trost myself. But you too must take care to wed without delay and beget a son on whom you one day in dying can bestow the domains of Artoys and Flaundres. Here stands many a cousin in whose eye I read that all his hopes dwell upon the failure of the direct line. So I speak, because to the dying one must grant a true word. At the courts which I have sinfully affronted you cannot ask. But there are truly so many more, in Brittanye, Parmenia, Equitania, Brabant, and the German lands. But now the left corner of my mouth is sore from speaking and I must rest. God keep you from sorrow. Ade."

After the Lord Grimald had spoken thus, he lived only

a few days more; then the Foule Fiend tapped him for
the second time on the temple and he was quite dead.
Stiff and yellow, like the waxen candles which burned
at the sides of his lofty bier, he lay in the castle chapel in
ducal state though also quite indifferent towards it, as
towards earthly life altogether, belonging to the eternal; until they brought him to Ypren in the cathedral to
join his wife, and monks spoke litanies for his soul beside him through the night. But now I cry Woe alas!
over this night, when the Lord Grimald was scarce
dead; as a corpse still present, though put to rest, gone
hence and as father no longer between the brother and
sister. For according to Valande's wicked counsel and
to his abominable pleasure which they mistakenly held
to be their own, in that same night the brother slept
with the sister as man with wife, and their chamber
above in the donjon keep, round which the owls circled,
was so full of tenderness, defilement, rage, and blood
and sin that my heart turns over for pity, shame, and
anguish and I may scarcely tell it all.

They both lay naked under their covers of soft sable
in the pale gleam of the swinging lamp and the scent of
the amber with which their beds were dusted—they
stood, as fittingly, far apart, and between them, coiled
round like a snake, slumbered Hanegiff, their good
hound. But they could not sleep, they lay with open
eyes or only sometimes shut them perforce. How it was
with the damsel I do not know, but Wiligis, o'er-
wrought by his father's death and his own life, groaned
under the scourge of the flesh and under Valande's spur

until at last he held out no longer and slipped out of his bed, went round Hanegiff on his bare foot soles, gently lifted Sibylla's cover and came, the godforsaken one, with a thousand forbidden kisses, to his sister.

She spoke jestingly, albeit with voice unjestingly choked:

"Lo, my Lord Duke, mickle honour you show me with your unexpected visit! What gives me the privilege of feeling your dear skin near mine? A joy would that be to me, if only round the tower the little owlets would not so awfully screech."

"They always screech."

"But not so awfully. That may be why your hands cannot rest but must so strangely wrestle with me. What means, my brother, this wrestling? How have I thy sweet shoulder at my lips? Why not? It is dear to me. Only you must not aim to part my knees one from the other; for they shall altogether and unconditionally remain together."

All at once hound Hanegiff set himself on his haunches and gave lamentable tongue, he began to howl up to the roof-tree, just as when a dog bays at the moon, long drawn out, heart-breaking and from the bottom of his heart.

"Hanegiff, still!" cried Wiligis. "He will wake the household. Beast, be quiet, lie down! O devil-beastie, if you do not stop I will make you dumb!"

But Hanegiff, afore always so biddable, howled on.

And the younker just as he was, half crazed, sprang out of bed for his hunting-knife, seized the dog and cut his throat, so that with a throat-rattle he stretched his limbs in death; threw the knife on the body, whose blood the sand of the floor drank up; then he turned drunkenly back to the place of another shame.

Oh woe for the good and lovely dog! To my mind it was the worst that happened this night, I rather pardon the rest, unlawful as it was. But I suppose it was all of one piece and was not more blameworthy here than there: a spewing of love, murder and passion of the flesh, that may God pity. At least it makes me pitiful.

Sibylla whispered:

"What have you done? I have not looked, but pulled the cover over my head. It is so still all at once and you are rather wet."

He said breathlessly:

"So far so good. Anaclet, my body-servant, is leal and true. He will make order early, scratch a hole and hide him, and destroy all signs. Us may no one ask. Since Grimald is dead, no one, sister-Duchess, my sweet other-I, beloved."

"Consider," she breathed, "that he died but today and lies stiff below in state. Wait, the night belongs to the dead!"

"Out of death," he babbled, "were we born and are his children. In its name, sweet bride, give thyself to thy death-brother and grant what minne covets as minne-boon."

And they murmured what one would no longer understand and is not even meant to be understood:

"Nen frais pas. J'en duit."

"Fai le. Manjue, ne sez que est. Pernum ço bien que nus est prest."

"Est-il tant bon?"

"Tu le saveras. Nel poez saver sin gusteras."

"O Willo, quelle arme! Ouwe, mais tu me tues. Oh shame! a stallion, a buck, a cock! Oh, away and away! O angel boy! O heavenly friend!—"

Poor children! Glad am I that I have naught to do with love, the dancing will-o'-wisp above the marsh, the sweet devil's torture. So they went on to the end and wreaked Satan's lust, who wiped his mouth and said: "Now it has happened. Could just as well be again and often." For thus it was he was used to speak.

In the morning young Anaclet, blindly devoted to his lord, set the bedchamber in order and fetched away unseen the body of leal Hanegiff. But how outward alone was this order and how disorderly things were with the erring pair, the charming young folk, to whom I will so well, without being able to excuse them, and who truly through lust were fettered far closer still to each other than ever—out of all bounds they loved and that is why I cannot quite rid me of well-wishing for them, God help me!

Of course it is said: "When the bed has been gained the right is obtained," but what was here obtained but unright and topsy-turviness to make one giddy? According to rule, the bed-lying goes before betrothal and wedding; but here it would have been madness and delusion to think, after the bed-gaining, of betrothal and marriage, and Sibylla, no longer maid, might not next

morn bind up her hair and put on wifely snood; but
must still wear the lying crants which yet by her own
brother had been torn, when she paced at his hand before the subjects of the land at the Lord Grimald's bur-
ial and the ceremonies of the oath-taking. Before Arras
on the mead were many splendid tents set up, with
particoloured velvet roofs (when one drew off the
leather cover that protected them in rainy weather),
and poles, more than the forest has trees, were planted
round in the plain, hung with shields and rich banners.
Many an old knight there put his hands between the
hands of the sinful young Wiligis and bent low before
the maiden Duchess, who by rights must have buried
herself in dust and ashes. But she held the strange view,
and spoke also in this sense to her left-hand spouse, that
one who had belonged only to her own brother had not
become a wife in the common meaning but rather was
still a maid and wore with right the garland.

And so they lived on and on in unlawful wedlock,
moon by moon, and there was no talk of either looking
to marry, as the father had prescribed. Too ardently
they clung to each other, paced to the board hand in
hand as ducal pair, and the pages sprang before them.
But the latter were already winking one eye, even the
Saracens, and as Hanegiff's mysterious death had not
gone unmarked, there was a whispering at court which
sometimes broke out in loose talk. For the Sieur Wittich, a knight with crooked shoulder and loose mouth,
said at table Duke Wiligis would certainly one day be
famous for catching the unicorn if it went to sleep in his

chaste sister's lap. Then the foreign pallor of the young mistress turned a shadow paler, and her brother forgot to hide in time his fist under the table: all saw it on the cloth, the knuckles quite painfully white as it was clenched.

The Sieur Eisengrein

Now when some months had passed over the land, the
Duke remarked a great bewilderment and dismay as
well as a pining in his beloved; and her habit, which she
shared with him, of sometimes looking sidelong out of
the corners of her eyes as though listening, grew constant and permanent, so that she now never seemed able
to look otherwise at all, and also her lovely lips were
parted with dread.

"What is it with you, nearest and dearest, precious
friend, you only one, what frightens you?"

"Nothing, no matter."

Then he found her flung across a table, her face buried in her arms, quite dissolved in tears.

"Sibylla, sweetheart, now you must tell me all. I can
no longer bear your distress and cudgel my brains for
its reason, which I find not, upon which, do all I can, I
cannot come. Now I implore you, confess it to me!"

"Ah, fool," said she with sobs, her face scarce lifted
from her arms. "Ah, stupid, sweet at night but utterly
stupid by day! What are you asking? Yet there is only
one thing which can so fling me into despair and hellish

fear, but you do not think of it. O Willo, how could you hide from me that from one's own brother one can really be made a wife and become a mother? I did not know it and never thought it was possible. But now it is clear as day, or if not yet quite day, then must it very, very soon be rumoured, however wide and draped and flowing the garments, and we are both, we are all three lost!"

"What, and you are—"

"Of course and indeed I am. Why ask? So for long have I been, and bear in extremity my secret and thy fruit. E! Deus, si forz pechiez m'appresset! Willo, Willo, if you knew that a maid could be with child without husband and marriage just from her brother, then you have done very ill by me and yourself and our child as well, for which there is no place at all in God's wide world except in my love. For I love it already, in its abjectness and its innocence, beyond everything, although, poor thing, it is our punishment. But as I did not know that one's body can be blest from one's brother, I mean curst, so also I did not know one can so love one's punishment. Nothing will I do henceforward but pray that God bless our child, though both of us should roast in the fires of hell."

Pallid, trembling, the poor wretch stood there, sank down beside her on his knees and mingled his tears with hers. Her hands he covered with kisses, seeking pardon, pressed her wet cheek to his, and his voice, still breaking with youngness, sounded piteous with weeping.

"Ah, poorest, dearest, best beloved," so he wept,

"how is my heart torn for your sake because of thy extremity and my great guilt! Forgive, forgive me! But can you even forgive me, what helps it and whom? Had we never been born, then this lawless and homeless child would not be, which takes away from ourselves the ground under our feet and renders us both unpossible in the world. For thy sake, beloved, it rends my heart, although in all your despair you are in a measure better off than I. For you can love our punishment with mother love, whereas I cannot love at all but only curse. What a contrary fate! Twenty years and longer had Baduhenna in lawful wedlock with Grimald to wait for us. Yet we were straightway so cruelly blest! Is sin in such haste to bear fruit? I did not know that sin is so fearfully fertile, not I. And then the sin of pride: that it will straightway bear fruit, truly and in faith I have not known that such was its way. But pride, my dearest, poorest thing, was our sin, and that in all the world we would hear of no one else but just of us very special children. Yet some guilt, with all respect be it said, the Lord Grimald, now laid to rest, bears too, not only because he begot us, but also because he was too knightly to you, my sweet, and in jealousy often drove me from your side—that drove me to your bed.—But ah, what helpeth all that? However the guilt be portioned out, lost and ruined are we both, our portion here shame and yonder hell-fire!"

And he wept afresh without words.

Then she left off weeping and said:

"Duke Wiligis, I like not to see you so. Since you

could be a man by night, only too well, then be one
also by day. This womanish wailing helps us not out of
our plight, which is so frightful that sooth nothing can
help us out of it; yet something or other must happen,
be it only with regard to our child the innocent and
damned, this poor fruit of pride, for whom a status must
be found on earth and in heaven, even if we are lost
both here and there. So pluck up your heart, be a man
and think."

He, thus admonished, dried his eyes and cheeks with
his kercher and responded:

"I am ready and set store by being a man, as well by
day. I have wept with you and said much of all sort
about apportioned guilt and ill-apportioned fruitfulness.
But one can very well at once weep and consider, and
mingled with my talking I have silently considered a
way out, or, since there is scarcely such a thing for us,
then what conclusions must be drawn from our cruel
and comfortless state. They can only be harsh, but they
must be drawn and indeed we cannot draw them alone,
save by one way, that we fling ourselves all three
straight down from the highest louver of our donjon
into hell. Is it your view that we should each for himself do so?"

"By no means. I have told you that for the little one
I here cherish a place must be found on earth and in
heaven, not in hell."

"Then we must tell; and even though the words are
unwilling to pass those lips, which in bed so fatally
cling together, we must force them to confess it all. I

have thought of whispering it all, groaning and stammering into the ear of our priest in the confessional, for him to give us counsel from heaven. But that must come in the second place, for meseems worldly counsel is here more urgent than priestly. Now I know in my lands a wise and goodly man, the Sieur Eisengrein, Cons du Châtel, my gouvernail and maistre de courtoisie, of whom I learned venery and light riding and the rules of chivalry. And in other ways too he gave me much good upright counsel, and I did not so greatly care for him, just because he was so stout and upright; and because I knew that our father, the lord Grimald, often called him to counsel. But aside from the fact that his very great uprightness rather weighed on my spirits, my confidence in him was always as solid as his own person. He has ice-grey eyes that look out with shrewdness and goodness from under thick bushy brows, a short grey beard; and he steps out strongly in his cote armour, whereon is embroidered the lyoness that he bears in his shield, suckling a lamb at her teats, the symbol of power and Christenity. To him shall we confess in our extreme need. He shall draw the hard conclusions from our state and be counsellor and judge what shall happen to us unblest ones in this world. If I send my Anaclet to him in his waterburg with urgent summons, he is sure to come."

It is unbelievable how comforted Sibylla was for the moment by this proposal. Nothing was thereby altered or improved in the desperate case of the brother-sister

pair, but to the unblessedly blest maiden it seemed even
so that by the mere sending of the squire a way out of
their misery was already found; and just so it seemed to
her all-too-loved brother as well; so that with heads
erect and hand in hand they paced to table behind the
pages springing before them. And they had not deceived themselves as to the Sieur Eisengrein's fealty: for
not two weeks had passed, during which the unblest
little fruit in the maiden's womb had fed and waxed
apace, when the knight rode with Anaclet across the
drawbridge of Beaurepaire, had himself unarmed in the
court, and mounted to the chamber where the sinners
in hope and trembling awaited him.

He looked just as Wiligis had described him from
memory to his beloved, and wore on his cote armour
the lyoness suckling the lamb. Stout and stocky he appeared, saluted with fatherly respect, and asked after
the Duke's commands. But the latter spoke with small,
stammering voice:

"Dearest Baron and gouvernail, I have naught to command, rather I and this lovely sister mine have only to
ask, yea, to beseech you, for advice and wise guiding;
that out of the state and uttermost bredouille in which
we find ourselves, you may draw the conclusions which
our anxious youth does not know how to draw. For the
bredouille is of such a kind that our honour is as good as
lost except and unless God illumine your fealty with
good counsel and teach you to resolve us to our deliverance. Behold us here!"

And thereupon both, as they had made up beforehand, flung themselves before him on their knees and
with tears stretched up their hands to him.

"Dear noble children," said the knight, "for God's
love, what do you? This kind of greeting would cause
me embarrassment even were I your equal. I beg you,
make an end of this scene! But you, Duke, give your
will words, against which I will never act! If it has to
do with revealing to me your distress—well then, I am
your servant, and what of counsel I can dispose, be assured that of it you shall dispose. Then speak!"

"But we will not rise," answered the youth, "before
we have disclosed ourselves, for one can by no means
do that standing."

And right knightly did he take the speech upon himself for both, so that Sibylla need say nothing but only
kneel beside him with head bent low—said it all out as
it was, and as it was hard to say, even kneeling, stammering and sometimes quite losing his voice the words
fell from his reluctant lips, and the Sieur Eisengrein
had often to bend his ear, out of which grew a great
grey tuft of heres, to understand the boy's words.
When at length he was silent, the old hero behaved
quite splendidly. Not enough can I praise him and must
here expressly thank him for his bearing. That was a
whole man! He did not raise his voice to cry shame, he
uttered no curse nor fell back in his seat, but only said:

"How bad, how bad is this!" so he spoke. "Oh, dear
noble children, how bad! Here you have quite actually
slept with each other so that the brother's fruit waxes

in the sister's little belly and you have made your blessed
father on both sides a father-in-law as well as a grand-
father, all in a very irregular way. For what you, damsel, there nourish is the Lord Grimald's grandchild in
all too direct line; and however he set store by unbro-
ken descent, this is so much too direct that inheritance
can no longer be talked of. I see you weep, because you
fear shame which threatens you. But whether you really
understand what you have set going in the world, that
would I well like to know. The greatest disorder have
you set up and a bafflement of nature, that she knows
neither out nor in, no more than you yourselves. It is
God's will that life shall breed life; but you have made
it so that it has overlapped and have made with each
other a third brother-sister, or however one is to call
this sleeping life. For since the father is brother of the
mother, he is uncle to the child, and the mother, since
she is the father's sister, is its aunt and fantastically carries her little nephew or niece about in her womb. Such
a disorder and confusion have you unthoughted brought
into God's world!"

Wiligis, who had meanwhile stood up and helped his
sister to rise, said in answer:

"Gouvernail, we see it. We see it all ourselves, but
much better with help of your words, in its whole evil
meaning. But now, lord, for God's love, find us some
counsel, for it is unspeakably pressing! Soon comes the
time when my sister must lie down, and where shall she
recover of the child, without revealing that we have
overstepped? As for me, without wanting to step be-

fore you, I am considering if I should not in the mean-
time for the sake of restraint live far from here, and outside the country."

"Outside the country?" asked the Sieur Eisengrein.
"That is, Lord Duke, very gently put, for in the outlying kingdoms of Christendom under such circumstances as these there will be no place for you. Let me
consider!"

And he bethought himself a while with very concentrated mien.

"What I have to advise, I know," said he then. "But
I give the advice only on condition that you promise
beforehand to follow it without delay or dicker."

They said:

"We do."

"You, Duke," said the knight, "should straightway
bid all who govern your land, young and old, kinsmen
and serving men and those who gave counsel to your
father, in short all the best of the land, that they come
to court, and give us to know that for the sake of God
and your sins (I say sins and not sin) you have resolved
to take the Cross upon you and journey to the Holy
Sepulchre.—Then ask of us, and request, that we all take
the oath of fealty to your sister, that she administer the
land as long as you are away, be it even for ever. For
travel and travail are close kin and it is possible you do
not return but on the journey give up the body which
sinned against God in order that your soul may come
the easier to Him. In such case, which I would half welcome and half mourn (in truth more mourn), the oath

would be so much more necessary in order that she be
our liege lady. In presence of all the barons shall you
commend her to my lealty and care, which will be
bound to please them, for amongst them all I am the
richest and most looked up to, since to me belong all
the flax-fields round Rousselaere and Thorhout, for all
which the glory belongs to God alone. Home to me and
my wife will I take the maid, and I vow to afford her all
such easements that without any noise she bear her
niece or nephew. Take note, I do not advise that on account of her sin she renounce the world, give up her
possessions, and shut herself up in a cloister. By no
means. Penance for her sin and shame will be afforded
far better facilities if her goodness and her goods remain
together and she can welcome the poor with them. If
she has no more goods, then there remains to her only
goodness, and what good is goodness without goods?
About as little as goods without goodness. Good seems
to be, rather, that she keep goodness and goods, for thus
by means of the goods she can accomplish the goodness.
Is my counsel agreeable to you?"

"It is," answered the youth. "You have with strong
hand drawn the conclusions from our state, harsh as
they must be and mild as they may be. Everlasting
thanks!"

"But what," asked Sibylla, "will become of my dear
punishment, my brother's child, when I have borne it
under your protection?"

"That is a later question," answered Sieur Eisengrein, "and we will cross that bridge when we come to

it. A great deal of advice have I already given you on the spot. You may not demand that I resolve at once everything that is put before me."

"Certainly we do not," they both assured him. "So much already, good sir, have you resolved and are truly like the lyonesse at whose teats we lambs drink."

"Yes, you are certainly proper shorn lambs," said he, not without bitterness. "Even so! And now to work! Duke, send out messagers! In all haste must your will and request be told to your gentlemen. You have, we have all three or four no time to lose!"

Dame Eisengrein

How often indeed in telling this tale about the bad children have I had to think on another brother-sister pair: on our master divum Benedictum, son of Euprobus, and his dear Scholastica, how they lived so sweetly and saintly together in the valley of Sublacus until Satan by basest guile drove them thence. For he brought seven passingly beautiful hetairas to them in the cloister, whereby some of his pupils (not all, but a goodly number) yielded to sensual lusts. Then of course the brother and sister fled, and betook themselves, accompanied by three ravens, upon a toilsome wandering; bearing all out in love with each other, converting all the heathen whom they still found, flinging down altars to false gods, and the saint himself amid Scholastica's applause destroying the last temple of lyre-playing Apollo. For my part I call that Christian love of brother and sister inseparable and angelic. And I have to tell of such a sinful love! Should I not rather in all pious detail recount the tale of Benedict and Scholastica? No, of my own free choice I rather elected this one, because the other witnesses only to saintliness, but this one to God's immeasurable and incalculable loving-kindness. And I confess myself guilty of a weakness—not for the sin (the heavens forfend!), but for the sinners, yes, I venture to believe that our master too, though he fled the valley of Sublacus on account of its pollution, would not have withheld from them some pity. For together with his dear sister he might undertake a painful pilgrimage, but my young sinner (and I well see that it was inevitable) must part from his fellow sinner—when they both from infancy all too passionately clung to each other, and evil lust had only knitted them closer together, which should not increase my sympathy, yet it does—and quite alone with his squire Anaclet betake himself upon that godly pilgrimage into the unknown, a travel so beset by travail and loured on by dangiers that his return was a matter God-given and unknowable.

They were deadly pale and trembled in all their limbs when they took leave of each other. "Ade, farewell!" They spoke and dared not even kiss each other. Had they not first sinned with each other, then they might have kissed, but then indeed had Wiligis not had to travel. He said:

"The little one, our third brother-sister, I would fain have seen with my own eyes. I cannot help imagining it as enchanting."

"God knows," she replied to him, "what our good angel, the Baron Eisengrein, will decide about it, when we come to cross that bridge.—One thing, Willo, I promise: I will never belong to another man than you. Probably I may not, but above everything I will not."

Before that, of course, had come the meeting of the land barons on the Burg Beaurepaire and the Duke's speech to them, as planned. There had, he said, however young he was, so many a sin gathered upon his head that a journey to the Holy Sepulchre was highly needful to his soul, and for the term of his absence, be it short or long, they were to take the oath of fealty to his sister, that she should be their liege lady. But he commended her to the hand of his gouvernail, the Baron Eisengrein, to the loyalty of this best of men he commended her that he should be her aid and she rule over the land from his waterburg.

Now in the matter of the oath of fealty things were not quite so smooth and simple, because there had been some winking and inkling about how it stood between the maiden and her brother and some gentlemen were not blithe to consent to the proposal and take the maid for liege lady. But Eisengrein let it privily be known that everybody who refused to grant the Duke's wish he would challenge to a joust with long lances and short swords, and not accept surety from anyone. And as he had a body like iron and had never been thrust from his horse, so they reconsidered the idea and took the oath. But he led his ward down through the land to his citadel on the sea, with men-at-arms before and behind, and Sibylla, wan, widowed, and reft, swayed in a soft carrying-chair between two horses while the Baron Eisengrein rode beside her, armed, right menacingly looking about him with his knightly fist boldly doubled on his thigh.

That God had sent her this stout, shrewd protector, for that one must thank Him, so much suffering was still before her and so wretched she now already was. Poor soul! I am a monk and have set my heart on nothing on this earth; I am so to speak strong against good and ill and, girt with the cingulum, offer no weak spot to fate. Just on that account has the spirit of storytelling chosen me as its vessel, that I take upon me the distresses of such poor things and bring their pale anguish to honour in the telling, however much it may lack in itself alone. The parting was far too hard for the brother-sister pair. They were, with the sickle-sign on their brows and one carrying the child of the other, not equal to the parting. Pale was the maid, partly from the child, but partly and particularly because her heart was gone out of her breast, being with the traveller. And his in turn was with her, however urgently he needed it himself, to thrust through the world with Anaclet at his side, among robbers, wild beasts, quicksands, and forests ill reputed, rolling rock and raging waters, to reach the port of Massilia, where they thought to charter a ship for the Holy Land. For both the youth and the maid it was more wretched in spirit than can ever fall to my lot, girt round as I am. But a little the better of the two, that I must admit, was it for my maid; for she was to give birth, and so in a sense looked life in the face, but he only death.

Now upon the Sieur Eisengrein's waterburg, in the flatland, close to the clattering seas, Sibylla was received so well and graciously and pleasantly with as much dis-

cretion and if I may say it so much professional understanding of her state as one can well imagine. The Sieur
Eisengrein, that is, had well known to whom he was
bringing the sweet sinner: I mean, to his wife, Dame
Eisengrein, a matron whom I must praise in her own
way as much as her lord. For something quite especial
and therewith exemplary she had: if he presented such
an exceptionally firm and sturdy masculine picture, so
she was feminine through and through, by nature and
nurture, with her whole soul turned to feminine concerns—yes, except for God (she was very pious and
wore a large jet cross on her mountainous bosom) she
was interested in nothing at all but what has to do with
women's life, in the most pious, most physical sense of
the word, and thus in particular in female burdens and
needs and sacred fertility rich in pain; in arrested
menses, gravid bodies, chokings, strange cravings, childbed, solemn shrieks and writhings, tapping movements
in the belly, labour pains, birth and afterbirth and sighs
of bliss and hot cloths and bathing of the mucus-cov-
ered fruit, to be stroked smartly with rods and held by
the feet upside down if it did not at once show life by
screaming.

All this was Dame Eisengrein's passion; there could
not be enough of it for her in the castle among those
who lived there; also among the women of the flax
farms and the villages went the lady of the castle, to
stand by them in her wisdom at their hour. Six times
had she herself been a mother. Four of her children had
died very young, at which (and this surprises me) her

affliction was much less than had been her joy in bringing them forth. On the bringing forth, so it seemed to
me, was set all her store. Of her grown sons one had
fallen in struggle and strife, another lived wedded
within his own walls. So she was past conceiving. Thus
she lived, alone with her husband, and thought sadly of
the time when she might move in the heavy, honourable
state of wifehood, the white hand laid piously on the
swelling belly. High was her bosom, no more her body,
and so much the more devotedly did the fruitfulness of
others interest the brave soul; so soon as she knew of it
her blunket-blue eyes (she was a maid from Suabia)
would fill with a warm glow and a rosy red enkindle
both her good downy cheeks. For some time had that
pleasure been denied her, yes, for many moons; so she
was not a little stirred up by Sibylla's coming and the
private revelations which her husband made to her
about the maiden. How her piety reconciled itself with
the improper and quite monstrous situation of her
guest, I know not. Probably any maternity, in whatever erring way it had come to pass, was a holy blessing
and an act of God, a challenge to her solidarity with
everything feminine and her almost greedy joy in standing by.

Like a mother, only still more fervid and full of zeal,
Dame Eisengrein took on the piteous one, shut her off
straightway from the whole castle and all its inhabitants in a remote chamber, where she lacked for nothing
and where she became the dame's dear prisoner, who
visited her quite alone, fed and provided her, listened

and felt and sought to console the pale and ever more gravid one when she wept for her errant lord, the only and alone beloved.

"Ah, Mother Eisengrein, whither went my beloved, my only one, my brother? How shall I ever grasp that we are parted in this world? I shall not endure it and cannot get used to it. Do I double my sin and strengthen my damnation the more that I weep for him? Ah, the seed of his body and life I bear and carry beneath my heart, that his embraces gave me! The little owls cried, Hanegiff lay in his blood, and bloody too was it in the bed. But how passing sweet it was when he was with me, when I had his lovely shoulder at my lips and he made me not to wife but yet to woman."

"Let be," said the lady-in-waiting, "and let him go. When they have made us women and given us our own, then they are of no more use and all the rest is just women's matters. Let us be glad that we are now among ourselves, we women! We shall have a splendid child-bed and are not far from the time when I shall put you in a hot bath, it relaxes and does good. From the first pains on, and let it be only so little, I will no longer leave your side, but sleep, if must be, in the straight chair here wakeful by your bed, until you are really in hard labour. Just wait, that will be very fine and is at bottom much finer than a lytel embracing."

But Sibylla too had a bad dream, which of course she had to tell the lady of the castle. She dreamed she gave birth to a dragon who cruelly tore her womb. Then he flew away, which caused her great mental anguish, but

came back again and gave her even greater pain by
squeezing back into the torn womb.

"So one sees from that, child, you are afraid, and
nothing else. A dragon, forsooth? Splendidly we shall
come down with a fine straight child and I would it
would be a girl-child. No fear! I will have it already
and make it free and if it will not straightway cry I will
cuff it."

The Exposure

THERE was no need of that at all, for the infant which the maiden mother brought in her hour to the light of day screamed to heart's content, a boy so finely shaped and well made that it was a marvel to see, with long lashes, longish skull, brown hair, and lovely features, like the mother and also the uncle, in short so pretty that Dame Eisengrein confessed: "Indeed and deed, I had wished me a mægde, but this one here is quite right with me."

Six months had her dear prisoner sat in the chamber like a Strasbourg goose, then she came to her labour and lying-in, with the lady of the castle quite alone to aid her, for it must all come about without scandal and the midwif allowed no one in. That was hot work, for although it was the summer season, Dame Eisengrein had fanned up a blazing fire in the chimney (she held that to be good) and both their faces were swollen, scarlet, and sweating at their work under the bed-canopy.

But everything went as nature would, as favourably and regularly as though the child were not at all begotten in such sin with its own flesh and blood but as it should be with a stranger man. The women quite for-got the sin; it escaped them entirely that on this earth there was no place for this perfectly acceptable and winsome infant. When it was washed and swaddled they were both on fire to show it to the master Eisen-grein, that he might share in their joy. So then he came, summoned by the lady of the castle, looked at the new-born and spoke:

"Yes, it is a splendid babe and more princely, that I must confess, than it ought to be, seeing it was born of such great sin. In short, it is a pity, I too have eyes and a heart and deny it not. Only I ask: What shall we do with it now?"

"Do?" cried the young mother in terror.

"Would you kill it then, you Herod?" asked Dame Eisengrein.

"I, kill?" So he. "Woman, would you put on me the murder of this fine child? Dead," said he, "it came into the world, though it lives, that is the dilemma, and it has no status, even though it is here. That is the contradic-tion which you present me to resolve, and call me all sorts of names on top of it. Shall the boy grow up here in the chamber? For outside it no man's eye must see him. I have not made the gentlemen of this land swear to this maiden that she be our liege lady for now her transgression and shame to become open and my hon-our go hence with hers. But you women have brains like sparrows, with feeling only for fine plump children but none at all for honour and politics."

Then the two women wept: Sibylla wept into her

pale hands under the bed-canopy, and Dame Eisengrein, who held the infant in her arms, wet it with her tears.

"I will consider," he said, "and reflect carefully what we can best do. Only such names as you named me, I cannot permit." Then he chucked the infant a little under the chin with his finger. "Hey, you young sprig you, hey, chickabiddy, poor sinner, don't be downcast, there will some half way be found, and some sort of counsel."

But another day he spoke to his wife in the hall:

"Eisengrein, best for us to do as little as possible with this fine child but give it wholly into God's hand. He must know what He means to do with the homeless, and whether it is to live or die, let us put that in all humility up to Him. I vote that we only do just what is necessary in order to give the boy entirely into God's hand, no more and no less. Therefore I have resolved to put him out to sea, but with the carefulness with which I do it, to indicate to God that we, for our part, would be glad if He would save the child. I will put it in a little tun, I have my eye on one already, very solid and good, and this tun in a boat, which we will give to the waves. If they swallow it, so much the worse, then it was God's providence, not ours, for we have taken every care. But if His hand bear bark and barrel somewhere to shore, where people live, then may the little one be brought up there as a foundling and be glad of life in the way of the land and his rank in it. What do you think?"

"Meseems God gave you, my lord, but a harsh good

nature," so spoke the woman, and repeated to Sibylla,
sitting on her bed, all that her wedded lord had opened
to her. She held the child to her mother-breast and
wailed aloud, so that the little one was feared, lost the
nipple, and screwed up his face in bitter wailing.

"Alas and woe, my sweet punishment whom I so
love, since first it stirred within me! The one thing re-
maining me from my beloved, gift of his body, which
I cherished in suffering and in such great heat brought
into the world! O Knight Eisengrein, O monster, is this
your fealty and lealty? Ah, tu es mult de pute foi! And
did you call him chickabiddy and promise good counsel, now to fling him to the wild waves in a little tun,
but I, whether he die or live as foundling, shall in no
case ever see him more with my eyes? No, no, I cannot
bear it! Rather shall you put me too in the cask, me too
along, that the wild waves swallow us both, me and my
child, my precious pledge! Oh woe, Mother Eisengrein,
as you helped me at my hour, help me now too, for I
despair!"

"Now listen, lady mine, one must after all be reasonable," the old dame advised her soothingly. "What
kind of little cag would that have to be into which you
both could go, on the ondes so wild? The one he has
in mind, the good solid one, is much too small for both
of you. And besides, you have to govern the land as
liege lady, in your brother's stead, so it is agreed, and
what would become of him if he came back and found
you too gone with the child? Look at me, for me four
children I bore have died early, and one fell in combat,

and have I therefore lost my reason? We have had a fine pregnancy and a beautiful childbed, but that the child would have no place on earth, that unfortunately was not unknown to us. It can at most find one by sea, in so far Eisengrein is quite right. But what we must actually do, that he has only sketched out. The finer details we must think out, we women. He would just simply stick the little love-bird into the tun, but not like that, God forbid! Rather we will put under him the very best silk, of the richest sort and spread richly of the same kind over him. What else shall we put? Of red gold a sum, not less than princely, that he may be well brought up and in the best way, if God graciously bring him to land. What say you? Has Dame Eisengrein in such a way a lytel refined on Sieur Eisengrein's counsel? But if you think I am at the end of my tether, then you are wrong. For we will do the following too: we will put in a tablet, written like a letter, on it we will write, with réserve and without giving name of man and country, the connections of the babe. High of birth it is, will we write, only unfortunately things so shaped themselves that his parents are brother and sister and his mother his aunt, accordingly his father his uncle. On such account and to conceal this he has been put out to sea and the finder adjured by his Christianity (for we hope he will be a Christian) to have the boy baptized and with the money pay himself for the upbringing. He shall, of course, increase Christlike his property and make it breed. Also he must faithfully preserve the tablet and before all else make him master of the writing

art, that one day when he has become a man he can read
the whole story from his tablet. So will he learn that he
is by birth very high, yet very, very sinful, and will not
be over-proud but rather turn his mind to heaven and
by a godly life atone for the misdeed of his parents, so
that you all three come in the end to God. Then early
and late you all must tell Dame Eisengrein advised
well."

She in her bed pressed the child to her breast and
only sobbed, but said no more and thus betrayed a rue-
ful consent. And she could not quite help being pleased
with the costly silk stuffs which the lady of the castle
proposed to spread over and under the child, and also
with the assigned treasure, of twenty marks, baked in
two loaves of bread which she would lay at its feet. But
best of all was the tablet which she brought her—would
God so splendid a writing-tablet ever came my way! I
have a love of writing and good tools for it, but I am a
poor monk, and such a tablet of finest yvorie, framed in
gold and set round with all sort of gems, will never be
mine. I can only tell of it and pay myself for my poverty with prize of praise. On this fair surface, then, the
mother wrote with ink made of galls the connections of
the child, just as her hostess had said, and put down
amid tears: "Be mindful, shouldst thou live, of thy parents, whom I may not name by name, not with hatred
and bitterness! Far too much they loved each other, and
themselves the one in the other, and that was their sin
and thy begetting. Forgive them and make good with
God, by all thy life turning thy love towards other

blood and striving as knight for it at need—" She would have written more on the margin and filled every little corner but Dame Eisengrein took away the tablet.

The hour came when she took away the babe too, gently and consolingly. Only seventeen days old it was, when the lord of the castle found they could no longer give it harbourage, but rather must with all due carefulness lay it in God's hand. He had once more drunken his fill at the mother-breast and was swollen red for fullness. Then the hostess took him away and secretly, under the hands of her lord and herself, the plump little cask became his dwelling, a new mother-womb out of whose darkness if God pleased he should be born again; with dowry of silken stuffs, gold-filled loaves, and written word. Swiftly and secretly it came to pass, and when the bottom of the cask was repitched, then came a strange progress by mist and midnight from the citadel down to the sea: the Sieur himself, disguised as a carrier, urged his little horss through sand and dune grass; behind him in the care of a discreet servant the bellying casket with painted hoops, a bung-hole and iron ears at the sides; they were needed, for the bark, which lay ready on the desolate shore, had inside it other such ears and with straps the little cask was bound fast; they worked silently, while hurrying clouds now hid the moon, now let it shine. Then master and man pushed the bark with its tender little skipper into the water, and the dear Christ gave favouring breeze and current. Gently rocking, the bark pushed off, the child glided away and was in God's hand.

But from the battlements of the castle, whither she, leaving her childbed before her time, went up with the help of the mistress, Sibylla peered out by the o'erhurried moon to watch the descent as the cortège swayed through the dunes. Yes, even on the shore beyond she thought to see the men moving and the cask floating away. But when even she could not persuade herself that she saw aught, she hid her face in the bosom of her nurse and moaned: "There he flies, my dragon, woe, oh woe!"

"Let him fly," Frau Eisengrein consoled her. "They always fly and we in all our fullness of pain must look after them. Come, I will help you down from the tower into the place of your sacred childbed, for that is where you belong."

The five Swords

THE SPIRIT of story-telling, which I embody, is a shrewd and waggish soul who knows his business and does not straightway gratify every curiosity; on the other hand he rouses many more, satisfies one and meanwhile puts the others so to speak on ice so they will keep, and perhaps even grow stronger. If anybody feels he must know forthwith what became of the child on God's wild sea, his mind is diverted and occupied with other tale, which to know is just as needful to him, let it even go to his heart with grief. But that it is so sad may strengthen his hope that out there on the ondes it may go more happily, for the spirit of story-telling is not so unshrewd as to tell only sad tales.

The next news is of the sinful mother and how ill it continued to go with her. The woman had grief to bear, alsus much indeed that I know not whether my mouth be skilled to report it and do it justice in words. I feel indeed it lacks me of experience. Neither true joy nor true sorrow was ever my lot. I live as it were midway, by my monkdom cut off from one as from the other. It may be that which makes me call allegory to my aid to depict the suffering of my lady, and to say that five

swords pierced her, not less than so many. And I will
straightway explain my metaphor and call each of the
five swords by name.

The first was the spiritual anguish which beset her for
the sin she had committed with her brother, when she
felt bliss in her very flesh and blood at the thought of
it, and for the way she clung to the hope of her mate's
return.—The second was her childbed sickness and
weakness, for the recovery from the birth was slow
and hard, despite the midwife's faithful care. Her milk
struck in and gave her fever and after six weeks, which
as they tell me is the right time for women to rise from
childbed and go first to church, she was still so weak
that she could hardly stand on her feet.—Did that come
only from the milk fever? Ah, no, for now I name the
third sword: that was anxiety, dread and heartache for
the small skipper out there in the wild wind, so utterly
given into God's hand; who drank her milk no more,
and of whom she knew not whether he had been res-
cued or swallowed up by the sea. How it wounded
her, this sword!—But the fourth was a two-edged one,
thrust into her heart by so cruel a hand that I wonder
how she survived and added to her days—though not to
her salvation, or only quite at the last, which I reserve
to myself to tell. Twice indeed she sank in a swound
from this sword: once when she felt it in her heart, and
again straightway when she realized it was still there.
Yet she lived with and bore it—how? That you must
ask of her tender woman-nature, tender, yet so strong—
I cannot tell you.

Just three days, that is, before the day when, still pale, she should go to church, it befell that Anaclet, the squire, appeared at the castle with shield reversed in sign of ill tidings. What could they be? Scarcely needed he to give them words, yes, hardly needed to come with shield reversed, to be understood. That he came back alone was enough. His sweet lord was dead.

Oh, I am quite inconsolable over this loss! The mere writing of it causes me such a pang as is in truth as little granted to my monkhood as is actual joy. Very likely I am writing only to take for myself something of both human joy and human sorrow. Scarcely can I contain my tears at the sight of Anaclet's reversed shield; were it not that out on the ondes there lived some hope of compensation and of life renewed, I could not persuade my heart to slay poor Wiligis. For as it is the spirit of story-telling which rings the bells when they ring themselves, so it is he too who slays those who, in the song, die.

Dead, young Wiligis, so slender and fine! It is true he had thought nobody good enough for him, save his sister, twinn-born and just as fine as he, and had sinned with her beyond pardon. Only hardly, again, do I forgive him the murder of Hanegiff, so good a hound. But for penance he had been knightly ready, when it turned out he was not able for it. I do not know, this youth, although gifted for sin and swiftly roused to it, had probably never in the depths of his heart been very firm. All too quickly he went pale, trembled easily, and was gallant but frail. The parting from his sweet sister, his mate, had seized harshly and consumingly on his life, and for the hard crusade he was probably in his soul not well armed. Of robbers, monsters, swamps, forests, rocks, and waters he had with Anaclet surmounted much, but he had not got so far as the port of Massilia; before he came there he clutched his breast, turned his drawn face to heaven, and sank into the marshy ground, where his steed snuffled at him in sympathy. How swiftly then sprang Anaclet from the saddle! In his arms he bore him to a castle not far thence, whose lord received him hospitably and put the way-weary one to bed with all care. But his heart was broken, the second day he gave up the ghost, and when they drew the shroud over his head, however old it got this earth would never again see this quite special brother-sister countenance, these lips arched over a mouth of gravity, these eyes blue in their blackness, this quivering nose, the forehead with the sign in the dark hair, the fine-fine brows.

At the thought I suppress a tear, and I applaud the good lord of the castle for ordering that the corpse of the princely pilgrim be brought back with honour to his home. Anaclet rode a day ahead of the train and came before Sibylla with drooping head and shield reversed. She had already been near to swound when his name, his alone, was named to her. When she saw him she lost herself and sank against his arm. I am ashamed of my own tears, for they fall only out of a gentle melancholy, whereas hers was a pang that no tears soften, and when she revived a second time her eye was dry and her bearing rigid. She had herself informed by the squire what had happened to her lord and then said: "Good." This "good" was not good at all. Such a "good" is by no means submission to God's will, rather it is a word of recalcitrance and perpetual denial of God's counsel and it means: "As you choose, Lord God, I draw my own conclusions from your dispensation, to me unacceptable. You had in me a female, a sinful one, certainly. Now you will have in me no female at all but for ever a rigid bride of affliction, closed and defiant, to amaze you." God keep me from such a sword and such frozenness. True, I afford it no opening. But glad am I even so, that the tale lets me taste it and I do know in a sense how it feels.

The Sieur Eisengrein said to her:

"The bier of your brother is come and stands in the castle chapel. He has given to God his body for his soul, and you are now our liege lady. Accept my bended knee. At the same time let the warning be spoken, for your honour and mine, that when we bring him to his grave you shall show a grief such as one pays a brother and no other. Any grief warmer than is fit and proper for a sister must be sternly concealed."

She answered him back in this wise:

"For advice and subtle suggestion, Sir Knight, my thanks. I think my bearing is not such as would expose my protector's honour with expressions of too extreme a pain. You are indeed inexperienced in grief if you think the deepest would be loud. I intend now to pray three hours over the bier of my sacred brother. That

should not overpass the bounds of decency. Then with
measured mourning you may bring him to his place.
Mine is no longer here on your waterburg, and not
from this place will I rule the land. I hope further to
have a loyal servant in you, Cons du Châtel, yet I like
you not, and though you made me your liege lady, you
stand not close to me in favour, of this at this hour be
assured by me. You took from me my sweet brother-
sister child, shipped it on the savage seas and its father,
my dearest-loved brother, sent to his death—that had, I
suppose, all to be, for honour and statesmanship, but yet
I bear you a grudge for it and am weary to death of
your iron-hearted good nature. I will have you neither
to seneschal nor steward, nor will I have you anywheres
about me when I take residence in my chief city in the
high castle at Bruges on the deep sea-bight. You might,
were you about me, forge shrewd plans of policy, on
account of the direct succession, and want to marry me
off with some prince of Christendom, equal in birth to
mine; whereas only one was equal with me, for whom
I everlastingly mourn. Of marriage I will not hear, for
celui je tiendrai ad espous qui nos redemst de son sanc
précieu. Alms and fasts, watching and praying on the
bare stone, with all that is harsh and repulsive to the
flesh, so shall my life be as lady of this land, that God
may see He has in me no longer a sinful woman but no
woman at all, instead a princess-nun whose heart is dead.
Such my resolve."

It was, and remained, and was, Christ knows, not the
right one. For oh, it brought the fifth sword above the

woman's head and the land's, of which straightway.
Sibylla returned not to Beaurepaire, the place of her
youth and her sin; it lay forsaken, guarded only by a
castellan and a small troop of serjents. The princess held
court in the castle at Bruges, on the ocean bay, a strict
court where no laughing was, save when the mistress
absented herself, lying alone or in prayer on the bare
stones, between two monks. In white robe she descended, accompanied only by two women with bas-
kets, and dispensed to the poor, who called her blessed.
Joy and ease she had not for her portion, only night
masses, castigation, and short commons, and this above
all not for love of God but to defy Him that it might
pierce through and through Him and He be shaken.

So she lived some years; her beauty was not punished
by her punishment, though she would willingly have
yielded it. Often blue rings from watching lay round
her eyes, yet she ripened from year to year, preserving
on earth the traits of her dead brother, into the loveliest
of women; and that I feel was also according to her
will, that God might be vexed because she granted so
lovely a body to no husband, but remained her brother's penitent widow. And yet, as already in her childhood, many a Christian prince sought her out and offered his hand, by missives and messengers and sometimes
even in person. But each was turned away. It saddened
court and country, even God whom it was meant to
sadden, though against so much penitential abstinence
He on His side could have nothing to say. The dilemma she did not begrudge Him.

In the sixth year a most noble prince, Roger-Philippus, King of Arelat, began to importune her for his marriageable son, Roger by name without the Philipp. He was a prince such as for my life I cannot bear, a shameless fellow. Even at fifteen years he had a black pointed beard, eyes like burning coals, eyebrows arched like his moustache, and was tall, hairy, quarrelsome, gallant, a cockerel, a heart-breaker, a dueller, a devil of a fellow, to me quite unspeakable. That his father wished him well I can understand, also that he thought good to settle him as soon as possible in wedlock. The Lord Grimald's high-born and pious daughter seemed the right choice, and political considerations played a part as well, for not only did the King covet the lovely woman for his heir, but also on top of that to join Artoys and Flaundres to Arelat and Upper Burgundy, that he wanted for him above all.

So then messengers and missives, tender proposals and wooing gifts went from land to land, and King Roger-Philippus himself (with his son and stately retinue of Burgundian knights) visited the court of Bruges, where Roger straightway seduced three maids of honour but was looked upon coldly by the liege lady. She had a way of measuring his most knightly figure up and down with mocking eyes, which embittered the cockerel to his very marrow and enflamed him for ever against her so that he felt his honour lost if he were not to possess her. The whole court too, including the three ladies who had fallen the first few days, were in favour of the suit, for they all wanted Sibylla to give the realm

a duke and that there should be at length a bourne set
to her chastity. But she courteously avoided the King's
advances, said not Nay but by no means Yea, and made
condition of an indefinite period for consideration after
the Burgundians had gone home again. Thence they renewed their messages, reminders, and pleas but were put
off and on with fair words and then denials which soon
sounded more like No, only veering more to a Yes for
the sake of politeness, and always leaving everything in
the balance, to the end that father and son might finally
tire of the business.

Four years passed like this; then King Roger-Philippus gave his hand to death and must needs go with him;
so Roger of the pointed beard became King of Arelat.
By this time he had laid under obligation all the court
ladies of less than fifty and a host of burghers' daughters
to boot; yet he had never forgotten his lust after the
coy dame in the white robe who had looked at him so
offensively; and after he reached the throne the desire
to possess her chimed with a craving to increase his
realm by adding hers, as had been his father's political
design. So then barefaced threats mingled with sweet
wooing when he wrote to her and sent missives post to
the effect that sooner would he strive against her in
arms than resign her peerless self and wed another. Hers
was the fault that his realm remained without a queen
as it was hers as well that her own lacked a lord; and
against so much evil God Himself would in the end bid
him take the sword. So or in such like words the cock
and stallion. But Sibylla, to keep him in check, let her

Nay veer to the side of Yea and thus passed three more years, until his patience wore out. But at last it did: and with two thousand knights and ten thousand foot-soldiers he fell upon Sibylla's land and overran it with fire and sword.

"A moi, Baron Eisengrein! Forget that in our distraction we banished you from our court. Be mindful of the services which you paid our lord and father now in glory with God. Call up my knights, assemble my foot-soldiers, open the arsenals, stout Fieldmarshal, and hurl yourself on the impudent robber who would snatch us with bloody hand into his bed! Protect your Duchess, ordained of God!"

Thus began the "wooing war" between Burgundy and Flaundres-Artoys, so called in the mouths of the troubadours, which with varying fortunes, and stubbornly resumed again and again, was waged with great destruction for five long years.

"Give peace, lady, after so much travail to this land and offer him your hand who ever yearns for you, the suitor bold, so true and tireless ever!" But she said: "Never!"

The Fishers of St. Dunstan

I, CLEMENS, extol the works of the wisdom of God. How excellent, constraining us to amaze, does not, to him possessing some knowledge of geography, appear the fact that a connection exists between the oceanus and the North Sea: through a passage, namely, between Karolingia and Engelland, on account of its narrowness in jest called "the sleeve," also of course "the canal," although to speak precisely only a ditch dug by the hand of man should be called a canal, and not God's salt element, which having naught of the abiding calm of a canal is only too often lashed by storms and roused to wild blow of billows, thus teaching the sailor to pray. This is true even on larger and seaworthy ships, like that on which I a short time ago clave the waves. But when I think with what hazards a frail bark, an open boat, is delivered thereon, mere plaything of the waves, perhaps not even manned or only in the most strangely tender and helpless way—I shudder at the brevity of the hope that such a little ship can ever come happily to land; and I marvel at God's skill how He, when He will, knows how to steer it through dangers which He Himself has heaped up in its path. Verily, it gives occasion for the words to rise to the lips: "Nemo contra Deum nisi Deus ipse."

Islands there are in these waters, I mean where they open towards the great ocean: islands larger, smaller, and quite small, called the Normannic, probably because they lie nearer to France and the land of the Normans than to Cornwall and Sussex; and on one of the smallest of these, somewhat apart from the others and further into the ocean towards England, I am about to put myself and my reader in the spirit. It was a wave-girt little piece of God's earth, whose inhabitants to their salvation had been reached by Christianity, but who otherwise led a right primitive life, little versed in world events. They were mostly lodged in a village of scattered buildings with cattle, meadows, and kitchen-gardens, which, so far as they knew, like the whole island was called St. Dunstan, and lived on cattle-breeding, butter-making, vegetable-raising, and fishing. I betake myself thither, not in the last instance, but really first of all, on account of a capital and pious man to whom my whole sympathy belongs, and to whom I should like here to extend my thanks for the excellent services which he performed in his goodness to the history with the refurbishing of which I divert myself and glorify God. I speak of his honour Gregorius, Abbot of the cloister Agonia Dei, which, preceded by an ancient laura and cenobite settlement and belonging to the Cistercian Order, lay near the shore of the island open to

the west, and formed its spiritual adornment—as I hope
it does to this day. Of conventuals who had taken the
vows, it had within its walls hardly more than our Lord
and Saviour had disciples, perhaps fourteen, with them
a number of lay brothers who took care of the cloister
livestock; also likewise a number of children, future
Brothers, whose training was in charge of the monks of
Agonia Dei. Some of them came from other islands;
But all of them, big and little, greybeards, boys, and
grown men, on account of his goodness, mildness, uprightness, and cherishing care, looked up as to a father
with single-minded and trusting reverence to their Abbot Gregorius. For this, as the instructed know, is according to the meaning of the word.

Abbot Gregorius should be described as a man of
medium height and pleasing manners, whose full, carefully shaven face with a small mouth and a full, prominent lower lip was crowned by a bald and brilliantly
polished cranium. Curly grey hair stood up from his
temples. The dress of his order, girded with a neatly
twisted cord, through which the rosary was drawn, was
rounded out by a respectable little paunch that seemed
rather expressive of a good conscience than of a burden
on it, taking away from the Abbot's tournure none of
its ease and agility, which were remarkable for his fifty
years. That laziness and self-sparing were not in his line
is obvious at once from the fact that we find him of a
very early morning, in more than unfriendly weather
(for the clouds hung low and leaking, and a wind blew
hatefully from north-northwest) quite alone on his way

down to the beach, walking round the horseshoe-shaped
bay which cuts into the island on this side, and into
which the sea rolled its waves to break on the outlying
rocks. At his back his cloister, whose buildings veiled
by rain stood out against a strip of dark wood, the
Abbot with his habit tucked up paced along the wet
sand, setting his long staff before him, often through
all sorts of rocky and stony debris, large and small, or
even ground to powder, which lay in his path. Round
his shoulders as protection against the wet he had a piece
of felt which he held together with his hand in front; on
his head he wore a most unclerical waterproof hat with
turned-down brim such as the fishermen of the island
wore at their work. He blinked and held his head slantwise against the wind; yet again and again turned his
wet face the other way to peer anxiously out to sea.

His thoughts went like this: "Beastly, beastly; we
have a lot of bad weather on our island, but this is exceptionally contrary in view of the time of year. I am
not grumbling, but I am disturbed. How high the breakers, and here in the bay they are after all a good deal
tamed, spray up on the rocks! From time to time they
quite roll over them, and pour furiously into the brack-
ish pool on my right, so that I am forced to jump aside
with almost unseemly agility. What must it be like outside in the open water, where the fishermen, the brothers Wiglaf and Ethelwulf, now are, and at my orders!
Whoever saw me here would say that I betake me
down to the beach *despite* this bitter weather. But it is
just *on account of* the weather that I come down so

early, driven by uneasiness which causes me to make
such idle and trivial observations as this about 'on account of' and 'despite,' which in my uneasiness become
one and the same. God does not want a man to be too
calm, so He gives him unrest to discipline him, or rather
He makes him give it to himself: just as I have done by
sending the fishermen out in this weather, which after
all could not have been foreseen yesterday afternoon.
How calm I might otherwise be, without the uneasiness
I created for myself! For everything else is in the best
condition, at least a very good one, on this island which
according to the assertion of its oldest inhabitant is
named St. Dunstan, and with my cloisters back here too
—it being without question called God's Passion—and
also on the nearest, though even so far distant islands
known by this name. Only in humility can one be mindful of all this, and it means no serious temptation to
pridefulness to be its Abbot. For among the monasteries
of Christendom it is one of the least and has not even
its own chapter-house, for the cenacle must also do
duty for the chapter although a stale smell of earthly
vitaille always reigns there. Besides, only half of the
Brothers have their own cells, the others must sleep in
the common dormitory, and only I, of course, have a
spacious room for myself, of which I should not think
with complacence, but only be gratefully mindful how
smooth-like everything goes its pious and appointed
ways in our godly little foundation, and how agreeable
it is to find a bed made beforehand so that one no longer
needs to do the heavy work and clear the wilderness but

only to preserve and keep all in order. The pioneering
and clearing have been attended to a hundred years ago
and more by the Brothers of the single common life
who came here first, wielded spade and hoe and trowel,
carted stones, and while building their claustrum and
turning sandy soil into vegetable-plots, at the same time
enlightened the dark minds of the islanders and illu-
mined them with the truth of Jesus Christ. They well
knew that idleness is the slough of all temptation, therefore they devoted themselves not alone to contempla-
tion, on which moreover they could not have lived; but
laboured industriously and cleared the ground; just as I
myself see to it that my lambs, besides the preoccupa-
tion with God, are also provided with some hard manual labour and garden work to make them honestly
tired. I myself am of course too old and dignified for
that. Too old, not too dignified. The word 'dignified'
the Devil only whispers to me, to make a mock of my
humility, which even without it is always exposed to
certain dangers because I am happily as mitred Abbot
the first man on the island, over whose hand all bow
who meet me. Were these people actually in time past
converted to Christianity because an already enlightened maiden whom they would sacrifice to a dragon in-
festing the island held up the crucifix before him so that
he, after once more breathing fire and smoke from his
jaws, lay down on his side and died? It is said that all
were so impressed by the sight that they straightway
en masse acknowledged Jesus. I can scarcely believe the
story, for how should a dragon come on this island and

out of what egg did he creep? I simply cannot picture
to myself a dragon in this place who takes maidens as
sacrifices. But that is perhaps only a sinful lack of simplicity, even if, at risk of getting into the Devil's
kitchen for arrogance, it seems to me that between what
a learned man may believe and the belief of the vulgus,
a certain distinction is justified before God. In passing
I remark, indeed with some concern, that the Christianity of the folk hereabouts is not of the most sure-footed,
whether there was a dragon or not, and precisely therefore is it such a great blessing that we Brothers here
stand on guard for the faith in Agonia Dei. For what
has been gained may be lost again; indeed I have heard
that in the land of the so-called Allemannes, far from
here, Christianity had even in Roman times gained a
foothold but that the land sank back into darkness until the appearance of certain Irish missionaries who re-
kindled the light. Separation from the world by much
water has its advantages, I suppose, in that it keeps men
simple and preserves from many a confusion. But on
the other hand it is not good when great popular movements, changes and migrations, such as to my knowledge took place in former times, pass over the single
man spun round in his own thoughts and are gone, so
that, if I may so express my thought, world events do
not take him with them, but leave him inexperienced
and back in the former stage. I know very well that all
sorts of backward ways and customs obtain privily here
among the people, scarcely deserving a better name
than druidical abominations; against their getting the

upper hand our little citadel of God is the sole bulwark.
These people, because no one troubled about them, sat
among themselves always on the same spot, where otherwise, so I believe, no land on earth is inhabited by its
aborigines but all are brought by force and have driven
away others here before them, who had to find other
places themselves, be it that they found them already
forsaken or that they snatched them hard-handedly.
Thus I have heard about the Burgundians, who came
down from Ultima Thule to the Roman Wall and not
without self-satisfaction settled on the Rhenus stream,
where meanwhile they were harried by the Huns till
only a few were left. Not only that: I also knew about
Vortigern, the Breton prince, that he took seafaring
Germans to his aid against the wild Picts, with whom
then those summoned straightway made common cause
against the summoner. Angles, Augerons, Saxons, and
Jutes unexpectedly made a British kingdom, thereon
the Norman set his foot and seized it with both hands.
Yea, my knowledge, it is amazing! But, my God, instead of boasting about it to myself, I ought to keep in
mind why I am stumbling along here on my staff in all
this wind and water; and how all the out-of-the-way
and wholly useless thoughts I am spinning only arise out
of my uneasiness, due to the lack of forethought I was
guilty of, and that in turn was due to my forethought.
Like a father I was caring for my lambs: that is, I
wanted to order them a good fish meal on this fast-day,
ample for all. So I arranged with Wiglaf and Ethelwulf,
the fishermen, to go out before dawn and promised

them extra good pay if they caught me a plenty of
tasty fish. But the Devil cooked up a weather such as
otherwise only sets in with the fall of the year and
turned my forethought into the grossest lack of it. For
tempted by mammon the two trusted themselves outside the bay, who knows how far, and if at this hour
the great waves have swallowed them, then, God help
me, I am their murderer. Certainly they are seasoned
seafarers, tough as Hungary leather, who have nothing against a dance with the wild waves. But what shall
I do if they have already got them, and how face their
widows and orphans? Ethelwulf, the elder, has only one
daughter, married to a man on the next island to the
east, named, so most people think, St. Aldhelm. But
Wiglaf, his brother, struggles to maintain six, and his
wife has the youngest still at the breast. My uneasiness
about all of them is constantly on the increase. Wait!
Now I stand as though rooted to the spot and peer out
to the opening of the bar where with my still gratefully
sharp eyes I think I see a sail. My view is made easier
by the fact that it has stopped raining, if not blowing.
God be praised, it is a sail, it is Wiglaf's and Ethelwulf's
boat. They have reached the sheltering bight, one may
regard them as saved, and perhaps they are even bringing me my hoped-for fish. No, that is really too much:
hardly do I feel some hope of the men's survival when
I begin to think of the fish, though the importance of
them long since sank to nothing in face of the danger.
What a toy is the heart of man, tossed between fear and
pride! It is only so far good in that it is the virtue of

forethought which brings me back so soon to thoughts of fish.—But what about my eyes? For I seem to see *two* boats out there, close to each other, rocking on the waves. Are my eyes, generally so good, deceiving me? No, for as Christ loves me, I see one sail and two boats. Or I saw them a moment ago, for now the other seems to dissolve or be swallowed in the mist and only the sail-boat, which after all is the main thing, is still there and steers with a clearing wind easily into the bay. The seasoned sailors have such skill and practice in avoiding the rocks that on that account my concern is as naught. They come, they come. They shoot across, the sail full of wind slantwise from the back. I would be strongly tempted to shout to them with Hi! and Ho! through my hollowed hands, if that were not unclerical conduct. I see they are coming in by the tongue of land over there; they will stop where the sea makes a shallow little inlet between rock shelf and coast. I must go back to meet them, my heart full of gratitude. Scarcely would I be surprised if they also brought in a big catch of fish."

So the boat came in, the Abbot waved; the sail fell, and the men beached their bark, then got out into the water and drew it by main strength up on the sand, amid the Abbot's joyful greetings.

"Hallo, hallo, stout fellows, Wiglaf and Ethelwulf, welcome back to safe harbour! May God be praised that you've got back out of this weather! We should do well all three to kneel down on the spot and sing His praise. You see your Abbot has felt such bitter concern that he has struggled down through storm and rain. How are you? Have you any fish?"

"Hey, Master Abbot, all's well," they answered. "Fish? Nay, that's a lytel bit mickle to ask. We can talk of luck, that the fish not got us, that were a gale, lord, an' wer' coups de vent, de master can make no notion of it. One man got to draen the sea out of the boat and de udder with all his strength hold the timon and nary chance to think of nothink else."

"How they talk!" thought the Abbot. "So ordinary." He thought he was angered at their way of speaking, but actually he was only annoyed that they brought no fish. "How glad and relieved I am, that they are back, yet it is a very low plane they are on."

"Since God has saved you," he said, "I presume you men have prayed right fervently to Him in your need?"

"Yes, yes, lord, dat tu."

"And have mixed in nothing of another kind, old saws and all sorts of gibberish from early times?"

"Nay, nay, lord, how would we then?"

"Probably, even so," he thought. "On that low plane. What red beards they have, and red and seasoned are their sinewy bodies, naked to the waist. Why are they so naked and have taken off their jerkins and jackets in such weather as this?"

His eyes ran over the boat; it was painted green outside but the colour was peeling off so that the whitewash showed underneath. There were nets in it, two oars, a stake. At the back something was stowed; they had thrown their clothes over it.

"What have you got there, and what sort of heap is that?" he asked and motioned with his staff.

"Pover volc stof," they muttered. "A lord wouldn't care about it."

"Have they fish after all," he thought, "and want to eat it themselves? Or what are they hiding from me under their clothes? It is obvious that they are embarrassed. One must get to the bottom of the thing." And saying: "Oh, let me see," he came over with his staff and shoved aside their sweaty garments from what they covered. It was a little cask, handy, plump-sided, of painted staves.

"Well, now!" he said. "How do you men come to have that smart little cask in the boat? What is in it?"

"What shud be intil't?" they answered with averted faces. "Pover volc stof. There's fresh water, there is tar intil it, dram to tipple." They contradicted themselves absurdly.

"You're telling lies," the Abbot reproached them. "Speak correctly one doesn't have to; but tell the truth, that one must." And he drew nearer, felt the cask, and bent over to see the better. Then he started back and struck his hands together. Through the bung-hole, out of the inside, a whimpering came up to him.

"Good Lord God!" he cried. "Be quiet, don't stir! Not a sound, so I can listen." And bent over again. There was more crying from inside.

"Ye blessed spirits and messengers of grace," said the Abbot, no longer very loud, for his voice failed and he crossed himself several times. "Sons of one mother,

Wiglaf and Ethelwulf, whence have you this cask? For whether you know it or not, I swear to you there is a human babe inside."

"Just a baby?" they asked. That they knew nothing of, and would be disappointed if that was all. They had with their freezing hands fished the cask out of the rollers at the entrance to the bight, where a boat without crew was tossing about; they had steered up to it and made it fast and taken the little cask into their boat thinking it might hold something that could be useful to pover volc and it was no business of anyone if they laid hand of it.

"Wayte ye make no words," Gregorius interrupted them. "For every word is idle, and every moment precious. Out with the cask in a trice and up here on the beach where I will spread the covering from my shoulders. No chatter, no delay! This wonderful and heartmoving little cask, broach it straightway, on the spot! I tell you there is a living infant in it. Break in the head, be quick as careful; take your hatchet, your knife! Scratch away the tar where it is sealed. Oh, open, open!"

They did so. Fired by his zeal, they lifted it briskly on shore and like the handy-men they were, knowing how to go about things, they were quick to loosen the staves, split them, and open it up. The Abbot knelt by them as they worked and when the wrappings were loosened he reverently with murmured prayer drew out what they hid: a swaddled infant, bedded on layers of Alexandrine silk, and covered with the same, at its feet two loaves and a tablet, a most priceless one, written like a letter. The child blinked and sneezed at the light of day, dull as that was.

It was well for the Abbot that he was already on his knees and needed not to fall on them. "Deus dedit, deus dedit!" he said with folded hands. "This birth out of the wild waves is the strangest, most solemn thing I have ever seen in all my life. What does this tablet tell us?" And he seized it, brought it up to his eyes, and ran over the writing. At first what he read only vaguely penetrated his understanding; so much however he got at once, that the child's origins were at once noble and shocking.

"What did I expect?" he thought. "That it would be a baby of usual origins that tossed about in a cask on the water?" Pityingly he bent over the tender, sinful foundling. And lo, as it saw the mild face so close to his, the child's sweet little mouth shaped a smile.

The good man's eyes got moist. But at once his mind was full of business and he rose, ready for the most decisive arrangements.

"Men," he said, "this foundling, a boy, as they write here, is so blessedly formed and besides so wonderfully preserved by God in this mean little cask that it clearly follows we must undertake him, shrewdly and with discretion, for God's sake and according to His unmistakably revealed plan. Of course, this infant, still unbaptized, belongs to the cloister. But straightway and for the present, Wiglaf, you must take it to your hut, already swarming with brood and blessing, and give it to

your wife Mahaute, she has just now her breasts full of
milk, and must warm and feed it. It is true that God has
graciously kept it on live on its journey, yet for lack
and cherish it must now go in danger of death. Credemi,
what you do for the mite you shall not suffer for. His
connections are, it seems, irregular indeed, but poor are
they not, as you already see from these precious weaves
he has brought with him."

Again he sought the tablet for counsel, having already hidden it in his garments, and read the writing.
Then he picked up one of the loaves, broke it, and
looked inside.

"If I give you," he turned again to Wiglaf, "two
marks for board, once and for all, will you take the
child and bring it up with yours, as though it were your
own, only with still more care, because so soon as it is
a few years old, it shall belong to the cloister?"

Two gold marks being more than Wiglaf had ever
seen at one time, he promised.

"Away then to your homes!" cried the Abbot. "We
stand here and discuss much too long already, in view
of the child's pressing need. Wiglaf, wrap the little one
in his under-bedding—it is from Alisaundre in the Eastern lands, you know. Take him in your arms and carry
him as gently as you can! I will take the covers and the
two loaves, for the child cannot eat them. And hearken,
if folk ask you and your wife how it comes that all at
once you have seven children instead of six—though
who will notice the difference!—say you have this one
from your brother's daughter on St. Aldhelm, or how-

ever that island is called—she has borne it but she is short-winded and cannot take care of it, so you have fetched it and out of family affection would take charge of it."

"But that is all lies and fiddle-faddle," Ethelwulf now mixed himself in contrarily. "Mi dohtor isn't asthmatic at all, but hale and hearty, sound like'n apple 'n could bring up a doezin kidens if she only had 'em. Dat's hocus. You, lord, have always said we shu'd tell truth even in our common lingo."

"Must you keep on barking, Ethelwulf?" asked the Abbot, "about such a well-conceived explanation and call by such ugly name what comes so close to the truth? For the way you came in with the boat, you could, the way it looked, quite well have come from the island of St. Aldhelm and from your daughter, whom I do not know but whom you have deliberately described as exaggeratedly robust. I will tell you something. If I give you a gold mark, once for all, will you then let pass this pious lie which I told your brother and religiously hold your tongue about how we found the child?"

For a mark Ethelwulf was satisfied with no more ado.

"Wiglaf," cautioned the Abbot, "do not stumble with the child for joy over your riches. But Ethelwulf too is now right well-to-do. He has nothing against it if you, you and Mahaute, when you have eaten, after the mid-day hora, were to bring the little lad to me into the cloisters and tell me it is your brother's daughter's child; but that you will take the place of parents to it because the mother keeps her sickbed most of the time. And you

all beg me to be his ghostly father and have him granted
baptism, which he still lacks. Speak properly and nicely.
I will receive you in the circle of the Brothers and this
is no matter about which you should let your tongue
run on in the usual everyday way. The Brothers would
laugh at you. Do not say I shall crishen or dippen the
suckling. That would be unseemly. Pull yourselves together; purse your lips and say: 'Your Honour, Lord
Abbot, this new-born little child our pious relatives
have entrusted to us and beg you to bestow on him
holy baptism with your own hands that a blessed life
may be bought for him, insonders if it please you to
give him your own name, Gregorius.' Wiglaf, say all
that after me!"

And three times had Wiglaf to recite the request,
with great pains and pursed-up lips, before the Abbot
left him and he came to his hut. There he gave the infant to his wife Mahaute, ordering her on pain of a
beating never to ask after his origins but to tell people,
if necessary, thus and so, and to care for it as for her
own, if anything better. But she thought: "That for his
beatings! One must be a man to think one could keep
such a secret for long from his wife! I will soon give it
an airing!"

The Money-breeding

Now behold how God brought it to pass, and with the utmost dexterity contrived against Himself that the Lord Grimald's grandson, the child of the bad children, should come happily to shore in the cask. A strong current had driven his rudderless bark, the toy of the wild winds, through the narrows where it is only a step between the countries and down the Channel to the neighbourhood of the separate island which Wisdom conceived as a state for the stateless. Two nights and one day only had his journey lasted, and a longer one, I am sure, even a strong, up to then well-nourished child like this would not have survived. I believe he mostly slept, cradled in the surge of the billows and sheltered from them in the mother-darkness of his cask, for though when he arrived he was not quite dry, that was not from the sea. Great danger threatened his sinful life even in the last hour, from the foam-girted cliffs of the bay where his little bark sought entrance. But there the fishermen found it and could not hide their find from the Abbot. So then things went as I have related.

Mahaute, Wiglaf's wife, otherwise skinny and shrewish, was always ample-bosomed and mild when she became a mother; therefore the man despite the poverty of his hut as often as possible saw to it that she carried her load. She had milk more than enough for her own infant, ample for the newcomer, and suckled and warmed it with the gentleness which was now for a short time her portion. So the babe lay, red and satiated in ragged swaddlings on the straw beside the fisher-boy Flann, his foster-brother. But when the pair had eaten they took the child and carried it over to the cloister as the Abbot had bade them. He had kept the Brethren in the cenacle and ordered Brother Fiakrius, the reader, a monk with a velvety bass voice, to read to them another chapter out of the work *Summa Astesana*. They were listening with relish when the fisherfolk begged for admission, and my friend the Abbot showed himself rather ungracious to the interruption. "Why must they disturb us," he said, "in this edifying chapter?" But was then full of mildness to the poor people, if also surprised.

"Well, good people," he said, "what brings you three to us, with this strikingly fine child?"

Now was the time for Wiglaf to purse his lips and deliver his parrot speech about the pious relatives, his brother's ailing daughter, and the christening, and as he did so mirth spread among the Brethren. The Abbot had rightly thought they would laugh if the fisherman spoke in his accustomed rude tongue; but now they laughed just because he spoke with such refinement, though sometimes he could not quite manage it and now and then against orders said "sucker" and "crishen."

"Hark to the little man," they cried. "The tongue he has in his head, and his eloquentiam!"

But the Abbot, smiling somewhat himself, bade them not to jest and with tenderness and admiration took the little boy in his arms.

"Has one ever," he said, "on this island of St. Dunstan, seen such a well-conditioned, lovable child as this? Look at these eyes, with blue in their blackness, and this fine little upper lip! And the little hands too, in their unusual delicacy! And if I touch the little cheek with the back of my finger, it feels like foam and sweet air. There is scarce any substantia, or one from heaven. It grieves me to hear that it is a sort of orphan through the sickness of its distant mother, and I can only praise the wedded pair Wiglaf and Mahaute that they are moved to take charge of it and consider it their own. But especially it troubles me, credite mihi, that such a lovely infant has not yet been received into the Christian communion. It is high time. We will at once and all together betake us to the christening-font in the church, and I will baptize it with my own hand, and as you ask it be his spiritual father and give him my own name, Gregorius."

So it fell out, my friend did as he said, and the little lad now went by his rather solemn name, Gregorius, but usually and for every day Grigorss. Under this name he flourished among the cottagers' children and under Mahaute's hand, even after she came out of the condition of voluptuous mildness and was long since fallen into dryness and shrewishness. For Abbot Gregorius had a sharp eye on the fulfillment of her maternal duties, and let scarcely a day pass without coming over to Wiglaf's hut, to make sure of the well-being of his little spiritual son. But all the children of the fisherfolk, and they two themselves, fared better than before, for the two marks which Wiglaf had had from the Abbot helped him far over and above the small outlay for the fare of the seventh one, and though bitter poverty had till then had him in its clutches, now he was free of its grasp and could by degrees put his household upon a more comfortable footing. His labour had lain so long on the brine, in hardship had he worked it and with fishing barely appeased his family's hunger; but now all that was changed. He bought four cows and two pigs, likewise grazing for the cattle on the common; carpentered stall and sty to his hut and an extra room and sat there with his family at milk soup, sausages and greens. And he won a little garden-space and turnip-field from the community by manuring the soil, grew carrots, cabbage, and field beans, partly for their own eating, partly for market, and soon he turned to the hardships of fishing only as a secondary thing—all this through the blessing of the child.

When his wife Mahaute first saw him building the stall she flung up her hands and wondered herself to death over what he was doing there, and why, in all his poverty. But he did not tell. So when two cows came, and somewhat later two more, after that the sty and the pigs, then the extra room, then the turnip-field, at each successive novelty she marvelled at the top of her voice: "Man, are you crazy? Man, for heaven's sakes what's got into your head, and what will come of it all, and in all our poverty? God help you, man, where will you get the chinks for all this luxury? We had naught but the meagrest fare, and now we have sausages and buttermilk and are rolling in wealth! Husband, that is not straight, and now you grow carrots! If you don't tell me where the money comes from, chil be bound to believe you have dealings with the Divell!"

"Have I not," threatened her husband, "forbidden you, on pain of my belt, to ask questions?"

"It was about the child you forbade me to ask, not about the money."

"I forbade you to ask about anything," said her husband.

"I am not to be allowed to ask about anything? You hoard up treasures and conjure up horned cattle and pigs and I am not allowed to ask who helps you?"

"Woman," said her husband, "another word chil take my strap till ye and make you yell out of tother side of your mouth."

Then she kept quiet. But one night when he lusted after her weazened body she would not let him come to her before he confided in her about the child and how he and his brother had fished it with icy hands out of the ondes and thabbot had discovered it, and he had given him two gold marks to bring it up for the monastery. But whose child it was and who put it out to sea in a cask, that nobody knew.

Afterwards, when he had had his satisfaction, he said: "Ugh, it wasn't worth it! If you don't keep quiet, if you prattle it all out that Grigorss is a foundling from the sea, I'll beat you black and blue." And she kept quiet and did not prattle for many years, because she was afraid it might be all up with the sausage and buttermilk if she did. She gave the foundling no worse foster than Flann, her own youngest, and showed the Abbot, whenever he came to look after things, a flourishing pair of milk-brothers. He too acted as though equally interested in the blooming health of both lads and praised the coarse-fibred Flann not less than the stranger who was so obviously of far finer metal and whom secretly his interest concerned; not only because the lad was fine and handsome beyond all the fisherfolk but above all because the Abbot knew that he was born in great sin, for that touches a Christian very near and moves his heart to a sort of reverence.

He saw with chuckles the way the fisherman prospered from the board money. But that reminded him that he himself was bound over by the tablet to breed the child's fortune and make it grow. From the first day on he read much in the tablet; all in all a tablet has probably never been so much read as this one. Abbot Gregorius shut himself in his room when he studied in it and at first it took him no little time to ferret out of the shrinking circumlocutions the sinful truth of the child's relationships, so moving to a Christian heart; namely

that it was brother and nephew and niece of its own
parents. Brother and sister—what extremity of need!
God had made our sin His own agony, sin and cross,
they were one in Him, and above all He was the God
of sinners. He therefore had consigned this stateless little scion to His stronghold of God's Passion as a state
and status. The Abbot felt it deeply and his task was
dear to him. The first admonition of the tablet he had
already fulfilled in christening the wild scion. The second, that he should teach it script so that the boy should
one day read his tablet: that he would satisfy so soon as
the child had been brought up by the fisherfolk to a
teachable age. But the third instruction also required
following: namely to increase the abandoned one's
property, the seventeen gold marks left over from the
twenty in the loaves after he had given three to the fishermen. This caused him many scruples, for is not such
a capital sure fuel for the fires of hell, to say nothing of
putting it out at interest to make it pay for God's time?
And yet he would be so glad to do as the tablet said,
for the sake of his little son in the spirit.

Therefore he summoned the bursar of the cloister,
Brother Chrysogonus, to his study, bolted the door, and
said to him:

"Brother, I, your Abbot, have here a fairly rich capital and orphan-money in gold marks, seventeen in number; it has been given over to me for safe-keeping—not
that I should merely put it in the chest as caput mor-
tuum, but in order to make profit from it. Now it is said
a pious servant shall not bury the pound God entrusted

to him, but rather make it fructify. And yet, when one thinks twice, usury is not the Christian's business and is a sin. In this dilemma, what do you advise me to do?"

"That is quite simple," replied Chrysogonus. "You give the money to the Jew Timon from Damascus, with the beard and pointed hat, an exact and reliable man, well versed in usury. He deals with nothing but money in his bank of exchange, and has a look-round in the money world you wouldn't believe. He will send your sum if possible to Londinium in Essex, that it may work there and make profit, interest and compound interest; if you leave him your capital long enough, he will make you a hundred and fifty marks out of your seventeen."

"Is that sooth," asked the Abbot, "does he know how to milk time like that? And is he honest too?"

"There is no more pious usurer," responded the Brother, "than the Jew of St. Dunstan."

"Good, Chrysogon, then I ask you to take the orphan-money and give it to Timon with the yellow hat, into his bank. Go at once, that the money may start to grow, and bring me the receipt."

Thus the Abbot dismissed the Brother, but at the door he called him back again.

"Chrysogone," he said, "I, your Abbot, have such comprehensive knowledge that, credemi, it is not easy to carry it all about. I have many synods and councils going round in my head, which forbid the taking of interest to the priest as to the laity, or if not to these latter, yet to us of the order of the priesthood they do. So when you have given the money to the Jew, you would do well to go down into the scourging-chamber and for your sins receive a moderate castigation."

"Not so," responded the Brother. "I am already sixty, and can ill bear a flagellation even if I lay it on myself and sparingly. But you are ten years younger and the money is yours. So if there is penance to be done, you must go down into the chamber and administer it to yourself in a suitable amount."

"Go with God," said the Abbot and read on in the tablet.

The Mourner

OF such trial and transactions the boy Grigorss knew
nothing, nor of himself and his connections anything
save what the day brought forth. Among the fisher-
children, who took him for their brother as he did them,
he grew up, and also to the island folk, when they
troubled about it at all, he passed for Wiglaf's and
Mahaute's youngest. For the Abbot's fairy-tale invented
on the spur of the moment, that he was from St. Aldhelm, the son of Ethelwulf's ailing daughter, there had
been no need, or even if at first, it had been early lost to
the memory of the folk. He wore the common clothing
of his brothers, and when he was three he began to
talk like them and their parents, said: "Wat for a thing"
and "I don't keer." But from the Abbot, his godfather
and frequent visitor, he had learned to introduce the
word "Credemi" into his speech so that he said: "Flann,
credemi, I hain't stole yer marbles," so that the brothers
and sisters and finally the parents too, first as a joke but
then quite regularly, called him "Credemi." And he answered to the name.

Credemi-Grigorss was lovely to behold. His lips

seemed not made for the garbled jargon on which he practised them, his soft brown hair was unlike the bristly, matted head-thatch of the fisher urchins, his smile not like their grins; nor was his subdued sobbing when he hurt himself anything at all like their bawling. At five years he shot up tall and slender-limbed, varying more and more from the young rascals his brothers in his development in hands and feet and gait and stance; with longish head, grave and pleasing face, the mouth austere. Even so early he held his head leant to one shoulder, and with his arm bent to the other one, the eyes, hidden under their dark lashes, looked down sidewise into a dream.

At six he came into the monastery; the Abbot found the time was ripe. The good man was in haste to have Grigorss learn script—not that he wanted him to read his tablet so soon; but even so he was impatient to put the lad in a position to do so. The parting from his family seemed no great matter to them or to the boy. Of course he was only moving from the parental hut a short distance away to the monks. And still the separation went deeper; indeed, the break in his life was more significant than either side realized at the easy parting. Though he saw them at once and as much as he liked, yet from moon to moon the gap widened between them, so that the others were mostly silent when he sat with them.

He was a scholar of the cloister now; exchanged the patched smock for a sort of chorister's surplice, wore his hair thick round the ears and close shorn at the back,

was clean of hands and feet. Reading and writing he
quickly learned from Father Petrus-et-Paulus, a gentle
Brother who as scholar and poet was called Geoffrey
of Monmouth and who watched over and instructed
five or six nurslings of the Agonia Dei, with whom
Grigorss slept in a vaulted alcove. They were older than
he and already knew the script when he came, but he
overtook them soon with style and pen and to Petrus-
et-Paulus's joy was distinctly ahead of them after a year
or so, in the little arts and sciences of word, number, and
song, for the boys also sang Latin hymns which the
Brother composed and to which he struck the theorbo.
Grigorss learned this too, as well as Latin.

His speech was clean, like his feet and hands, and
soon he could no longer speak the dialect of the hut
even when he tried, this not out of arrogance. When at
eight and ten he sat with the cottagers on a visit, he
took pains out of courtesy to use their words, but they
came wrong in his mouth and seemed unnatural, so that
they all pulled a wry face, his for shame, theirs for anger because it seemed to them he mocked them. In particular his own foster-brother Flann, a fellow with a
bullet head and short neck, also eyes like husked chest-
nuts and just as round, looked at him with ill will, purs-
ing up his thick lips and even balling his fists.

That distressed Grigorss, for his feelings were friendly
and he did not like to boast but only behaved as he did
quite involuntarily. His progress was winged, it was the
joy of Peter-and-Paul as well as of the other Brothers
who taught him, and when the Abbot tested him he was

amazed. At eleven he was a well-found grammaticus
and in the following years his understanding so reached
its full strength that Divinitas became wholly clear to
him. That is the knowledge of the Divine. He turned
over a great many books; what was set before him he
dived into, grasped its essence and mastered it. At fifteen and sixteen he heard lectures de legibus, a science
which deals with the law and requires a very open mind.
But young Credemi grasped it with ease and was soon
a legiste such as one would go far to find. Yet I will say
and know how true it is, that in all this acquisition of
knowledge his mind was only half there. And I will add
what may sound puzzling, that if it was all the fine
learning that estranged him from the hut of his origins,
there were other things as well, feelings and mental
images, which sometimes even spoiled his taste for
monkish learning and for books, in that it seemed to
him not only that he was different from his kind in
fabric and pattern but also that at bottom he did not fit
with the monks and his fellow pupils either; not in his
garb, his station, or the course of his life, wherein kneeling alternated with sitting over books; that he was secretly a stranger here as there.

Was that arrogance and sinful conceit? But if he was
not proud over the success of his studies, if he considered it actually insignificant and not for his true interest and honour, what was there then that he could be
so proud of? Can a man be proud quite simply of himself, just as he is, without regard to talents, and accordingly regard scholarship as a thing for people who need

it in order to be something? Yet he was modest, courteous towards everyone, not in flattering wise but out of native good manners. At fifteen and sixteen he had grown to be the pleasingest stripling, slender of limb, the face narrow with small straight nose, charming mouth, lovely brows, the face bespeaking a gentle melancholy. The people of the island felt kindly towards him. When he went among them on errands for the cloister, to the village of St. Dunstan, they smiled in his face as they spoke to him, and behind his back they spoke of him—and he listened, with reluctance yet with a strange eagerness too. He would stand talking with a man and at the same time listen behind him where two others were speaking about him, not really wishing him not to hear.

"That," so it went, "is Gregorius the scholar, the Abbot's godson, a youngster really wonderful, although quite simply the son of Wiglaf and Mahaute, one wouldn't suspect it. Grammatica and Divinitas are to him clear as glass and he doesn't give himself the airs of it, on the contrary even with such a head he is as friendly as you please, an amazing chap. He'll get to be abbot himself, you may bet, and soon we'll all be kissing his hand. One would almost do it already for (whether he can hear my words or not) he has what makes curtsying easy for the likes of us and almost a pleasure—Lord knows where he got it! If I did not know he is a son of the hut I wouldn't believe it and in fact I'd rather not know it. What a pity it is that one cannot say he is of noble birth, for if he were, one might well say he

would be just right for the lord of some great country,"
and so on and so on.

With beating heart Grigorss listened to the talk. To
say that it was sweet to him would not be quite right,
it even hurt him, however thirstily he listened; it
sounded like a reproach, and as though things were not
quite right with him. It came like a confirmation of his
own fears, heightening the inward struggle he increasingly felt. When he stood as I have described him to
you, his head bent towards one shoulder, looking down
under his lashes into a dream, then understand that he
was dreaming of knighthood. That life of shield-bearing,
vassalage, and chivalrous courtesy he had read about in
books which, aside from the learned ones, the cloister
also had: books of tales and aventours, of Roland and
Arthur the Breton, a king who held festal court at Di-
anasdron. When he read them, his left breast, as the
poets use to say, swelled high. He dreamed of being
one of Arthur's parfit gentil knights; when he lay alone
on the strand in his choir-boy's cassock, his head on a
stone, he saw himself in far other wear, a scarlet mantle,
hauberk and harsenière—and so coming on a spring in
a thick wood where on a mighty tree hung a golden
basin. If one took this, dipped water out of the spring,
and poured it on the emerald platter beside the spring,
there arose in the wood a mighty tempest which must
undeniably have crushed foolhardy adventurers. But
lightning and falling trees left him unscathed; calmly
he awaited the coming of the armoured lord of the
spring, who, quite as expected, demanded an accounting

of him. The angry lord of the spring was twice as big
and tall as he, but Grigorss knew better how to con-
centrate and therefore he struck down the giant, and in
the sequel received the favours of the gracious widow
of the fallen one.

Of such kind was Grigorss's dream; but if the or-
deals which he underwent in his imagination excited
him, it was not they themselves which actually occupied him and weighed down his spirits. He was so made
that he not only dreamed but at the same time demanded accounting from himself for his dreams, as the
lord of the spring required reckoning of him for his
rashness. That he dreamed, that he coveted knighthood, that his thoughts ever and anon played on a
shield, that he so gladly would have raised his own
shield to his neck, thrust the shaft of his lance under his
arm, and spurred on his steed to bear him away in one
bound—he was conscious of all this, it made him muse
upon himself and on what was the matter with him.
We find it absurd when a person who cannot speak a
foreign tongue asserts that inwardly he knows it and
can speak it fluently with natural readiness. But about
riding it was so with Grigorss. Who ever in all the
world might sit a horse best, ride it with loose rein, or
make it caracol and gambol by pressure of the thighs—
he was inwardly convinced that he could do all that just
as well or even better. He told nobody, because he
could feel the other's mind and knew it would seem ri-
diculous. But in his own mind it was not, on the contrary it was the truth. And added to what he heard

said behind his back, namely that one could or would scarcely believe he was a son of the hut, it weighed on his mind and gave him doubts of his justification.

That might be the reason why sadness lay like a veil upon him; indeed, it became him and heightened rather than lessened the charm of his youth. Or shall I go further and venture the statement that deep in his soul, yes, truly, in his very flesh and blood he divined that if all was not well with his life it was quite distinctly not right with his own rightness. How could I bring evidence for such a bold statement? But the boy was overhung with melancholy as by a shadow, and the Brothers of the Agonia, as well as his fellow students, liked to call him the "mourner," the dreri moders sone—or if they were Normans from the continent they called him "Tristanz the full of care, qui onques ne rist." So he had another nickname besides Credemi, and truly he bore it without shame, for if he was named "the mourner" certainly nobody meant thereby that he was a weakling, slack-twisted, a shirker without virility. And how would that have suited with his secret dreams of knighthood? His body was slender rather than otherwise, not equipped with massive strength, with slight arms and slim legs. But at games with the scholars on the gravel-strewn playground of the cloister and on the common when the island youth sweated in disport—ball-throwing, wrestling, jumping, stick-fighting, spear-throwing, and distance-running—he came better off with his weakness than the others with their strength, in the same way, that is, by which in his mind he overcame the lord of the spring: namely because he understood better than they did how to pull himself together; not only, like them, to fight with physical strength, but with something else besides.

If Grigorss the mourner was always agreeable to look at, in combat for the reason stated above he was simply beautiful; nobody could help admitting it. His brown hair, softer than the others', fell upon a forehead tense with purpose. In the narrow face—with the all too arched upper lip, which lay firmly on the lower, and the thin, quivering nostrils—in this face, which did not, like his companions', swell all red like a turkey-cock with effort but rather went even paler, the blue-shadowed eyes turned with strange compellingness and were everywhere at once. They saw each motion and feint of the opponent and in a trice, pointed lightly on his toes, he met each move, warded it off, struck it down, and wrung advantage and the upper hand. There was no denying that in disport he was the best of the island youth, all save Flann, his milk-brother—he alone could face him.

Flann was, as I have said, a bull-necked fellow, very sturdy, broad-chested, with power in every ounce of his body. He had long been active helping his father with fishing, farm-work, field labour, and in stable and sty, and had his time taken up as much as had Grigorss with his studies. But whenever the latter took part in the games, Flann was always there, with his strength contesting the first place, so that no one could have told which was the better. Grigorss threw the spear extraor-

dinarily far, much farther than one could have expected
from his slender arms; but Flann's shaft would strike
quivering close beside it, not farther and not a finger-
breadth less far, so that no umpire could have measured
any advantage. It was the same in a race, when they
came in not a finger's breadth apart, with their last
breath, the one on legs fat with muscle and the other
on slim ones: together they breasted the tape and two
names had to be called out, for the victor had two. All
the boys loved it when Flann and Grigorss were both
present; the game was exciting because two combatants
were there who strained to the uttermost, and that put
them all on the qui vive. Never in the ball-game would
Flann play on Grigorss's side, he was always hand and
foot on the other; and everybody was pleased, since
each team wanted one of the brothers as leader, knowing they would be that much better than they were, at
storming, running, shovel-board, and keeping the gate;
each eleven seemed to melt into one, each giving the
other the leather like clock-work so that it went as
often between one set of goal-posts as the other.

One day they incited the so diverse and yet on the
playing-field so equal brothers to a wrestling-match—
with strange results. Flann, stronger but not better, soon
threw Grigorss; but the latter, bracing with his leg and
mainly by using the top of his head, held himself off the
ground with his hands so that his brother did not succeed in turning him over and forcing his shoulder to
the ground. Indeed, as the onlookers saw, the half-
conquered fighter would have let his skull be crushed in

rather than be forced out of his braced posture. It lasted
for minutes, many of these as it seemed to the onlookers,
and all that time the muscles of Flann's arms stood out
with his effort. Then two things happened at once—or
so swiftly one after the other that they as good as came
together: in the moment, that is, when Flann's effort
relaxed in the very smallest degree and he drew back
a little to renew his grip, Grigorss shoved himself from
the ground with his head and the braced leg, and flung
them both, Flann still holding him, sideways and down,
with Flann underneath, Flann's shoulder touching the
grass. But then, so swiftly that the peering umpire had
no time to shout Grigorss's name, Flann, still clinging,
wrestled the victor round again and thrust his shoulder
to the grass. So in the end he had won, though Grigorss
had won first; and again the victor was not easy to
name, unless one called both names.

I am not in the least interested in wrestling, nor in
sport in general. Moreover it seems to me somewhat beneath my dignity as well as that of the place where, and
the desk at which, I write, that I should be telling about
the games of such island youngsters in the far-away
Channel. And yet I grow warm as I write and seem in
my mind to share in their sports. Actually it was more
remarkable that Flann stood out so in the game than
that Grigorss was so good; for the latter was of different clay from the rest, while Flann was of common
earth, and such physical strength as he had, many others had too. Yet between you and me be it said that
Flann no more than Grigorss fought with physical

strength alone, but with something else as well. And if you ask what this additional and animating strength was, I answer: it was hatred. It was hatred of Grigorss, his brother, that animated him and made him equal in the fight. Yes, this hatred did still more: it made Flann rage within him, because between him and Grigorss the game was only a game and not bitter earnest.

The Knock-out

So it fell out at last in this wise: when the two foster-brothers were already seventeen, at about the same time one day they were both on the beach, and at nearly the same spot where once Wiglaf and Ethelwulf's bark had come safely in. It was summer and early afternoon. The sun was slowly declining over the sea; it did not yet redden nor kindle the water, which broke behind the sand-banks in low, long lines, not quite lifeless, yet peaceful, stretching into space, and strewing the blueness with silver sparkles. It was good to be here at this hour. Gregorius came first as his lessons were over. He sat in the sand, his back against a large stone, his feet in the broad straps of his sandals stretched out before him, and read a book, but sometimes raised his head and looked at the cruising, crossing gulls or let his eyes rove over the sea to where the waters darkened shadowy in front of the clearly defined horizon, that shut away the view of all the other lands of the world. On the fore-finger of his right hand, we may say here in passing, the lad wore a seal ring which his father in God, the Abbot, had lately given to him; a deep-green stone with Lamb and Cross incised.

Somewhat later came Flann. Thirty paces or so from
Grigorss's place he set to work on his father's boat
drawn up on the sand, no longer the same one as the
one Abbot Gregorius had searched for with such concern. This one was larger and more powerful, built
with swelling sides, bowsprit and lowered mast and
main yard; outside painted a dark red and even adorned
with a name on the bow. Whereas the old one had had
none at all, this one was called *Reine Inguse*, the Queen
of the Catch. It stood there on the bow for all to read
who could. Flann could not, he knew it only from
hearsay.

When he came he had cast a dark look at Gregor out
of his round eyes, then begun to busy himself with the
nets; hammered at an oar, at length threw it with a dull
thud into the boat and moved away. Whistling, idly
displaying his strength, he strolled along the sand towards where his brother sat. He wore only brief drawers
and a loose linen jerkin open over the breast, with
sleeves covering half the upper arm. As he passed he
brushed roughly against the other's outstretched legs,
regardless whether it hurt or not, rather as though they
were some nuisance lying about, and went on.

Grigorss looked at him with lifted brows. "Excuse
me, Flann," he called after him, "if my legs were in
your way." Flann paid no heed. When he had gone on
a piece further he turned round. When Grigorss saw
this, he drew in his legs and put up his knees so that
there was free space for Flann even if he passed very
close.

But this time Flann stopped in front of Grigorss, so
that the other let his book drop and looked up inquir-
ingly.

"Doing some reading?" Flann asked.

"Yes, reading," answered Grigorss with a smile,
shrugging his shoulders as though reading were just a
whimsy of his, and added: "And you, as I saw, have
been looking after *Reine Inguse*."

"That's no business of yours," said Flann, thrusting
out his short neck a little. "What are you reading?"

"One might say, in one's turn," continued Grigorss,
flushing slightly, "that has nothing to do with you. But
it is a book *De laudibus sanctæ crucis* I am reading."

"Is that Kriek?" asked Flann, again thrusting his head
forward a little.

"It is Latin," answered Grigorss, "and it means *In
praise of the Holy Cross*. That is what I ought to have
said at first. Brother Peter-and-Paul gave it to me to
read in my free time. It is verse, you see, and has good
prose explanations."

"Don't be boasting and swaggerin' to me," the other
attacked him, "with your learned jabber about prosy
expalations. You want to set me down a purpose with
your gibberish; you go on about it to make me feel how
much cleverer and finer you are than me."

"Oh, no, Flann," Grigorss answered. "I swear to you
you are mistaken. When you asked me about my reading I felt my face get warm, as was doubtless plain
from outside too. That could not have missed you. I got
red like a girl, because you forced me to talk to you

about reading and Latin verses. I did not like to do it,
I was ashamed and felt sorry you asked, because I am
far from wanting to challenge you."

"Oho, so you were ashamed! You were ashamed for
me, ashamed on my account! Don't you know that is
the cheekiest kind of dare? I asked you, to show you
that you can't open your mug, yes, you cannot even
be, at all, without daring me. But you say you don't
want to. I suppose you don't want me to challenge
you?"

"You won't do that."

"I did it. But you pulled your legs up. Why did you
do that when I was walking back?"

"Because I did not want you to tread on my feet
again."

"No, because then you would have had to get up and
demand a reckoning and satisfaction from me like a man
and a stout fellow of his hands. But you draw up your
legs, like a coart, you cowering, lowering monkey-
monk!"

"You shouldn't have said that," said Grigorss, and
got slowly up.

"I do say it," shouted Flann. "I say it because you
won't understand and won't see, you sneak around, like
a sneak-priest, and won't see that it has to be settled
between us, once for all, from the bottom up, however
it comes out that's all the same, you understand? For it
can't go on like this. You are a son of the hut just like
me and you came of Wiglaf's loins and Mahaute's
womb just like me and the rest of us; and still you aren't,

it's as though you crawled out of a cuckoo's egg and
you're something differnt to us, body and soul, differnt
so we can't stand it; the devil knows how he's let you
get differnt from the breed and into something finer
and higher, as though you didn't know it! But you are
so cheeky as to know it and even to be friendly with us!
If you were cheeky to us, that would be a lot less
cheeky! You're the Abbot's godchild, a bastard, and he
took you out of cheek and out of the hut at six into the
cloister and hast learnt the letters and science and mealy-
mouthed priest-gabble but you sit with us now and
again and let us see that you won't let us see it, you talk
our vulgar gabble the way our mouths do, which we
can't stand, because one can only talk common out of
a common mouth and if you do it out of a fine one it
is just mocking us. You are a mockery through and
through because you turn the world upso down and
confuse the distinctions. If you were a slack-twisted
fellow, a priest-half-a-man without guts or pep an honest chap might say: 'Good, you are fine and I am strong,
that is in order. I don't lay hand on you, sacred be to
me your weakness!' But you steal yourself guts from
somewhere or other and are good at disport, just as
good as me, who am good out of strength, but you are
good out of fineness—an honest fellow can't stick that
and so I say: it must be settled between us, once for all,
not in sport, but in dead earnest here on the spot, with
bare fists and right to the end. I challenged you when I
kicked you, you can't crawl out of it!"

"No, that I cannot, of course," said Grigorss and now

his face wore its beautiful look, dark-pale, grave, with the upper lip somewhat closed over the other. "So you want us here, by ourselves, without witnesses or judge, to fight with our fists, and to the uttermost, until one of us can't fight any more?"

"Yes, that is what I want," shrieked Flann and tore off his jacket. "Get ready, get ready, get ready, so that I don't go at it before you begin, for I cannot wait, I want to get rid of all the duty of sparing your damned fineness, you thief of my strength. I will cut you to ribbons, I will smash your mug, I will bash in your stomach, I'll crush your kidneys, so get ready for me to polish you off!"

"Take care of your own kidneys," said Grigorss and as he took off his habit and slipped down his shirt, knotting the sleeves about his waist, he directed his eyes to the spot in Flann's body where the kidneys lie. "Here I am," he said and stood there, a slight youth, with slender arms, opposing the other's power-charged physique. Flann flung himself on Grigorss head down like a bull and drove hard with his fist at his brother's arm as it protected face and breast by turns, striking out with the other, but not very hard; what he took on his neck, his temples, and his ribs was harder, though the flailing arm, which by dint of Grigorss's quick turns and swervings often missed its goal, drove into space and took the whole man with it so that in missing he had to take something from the other as well. It was a welter of pounding fists, jerking heads, braced legs, tripping, stamping feet, of running in and engaging of bodies, only to get free again for fresh pummelling. Once even it came to a pause when they only moved round each other, dancing, aiming, protecting themselves, finally to fall to again at each other giving and taking, missing and hitting; but not for very long either.

The truth is that Flann had, I think, a little over-extended himself in the challenge, he was a bit beside himself with rage. The words of the hated one rang in his ears, the warning that he should himself take care of his own kidneys; it seemed to Flann that Grigorss, with his never upset, uncannily collected bearing, his deep burning eyes, always aimed at that particular spot. He was doing so at a certain very brief and perfectly decisive moment when, moving his right arm only to guard himself, he drove with his left, which he used very well, at the above-mentioned spot, on which his eyes were directed. But just as Flann in a flash guarded himself by entirely correct measures against the blow, Grigorss's right, which had seemed to move without especial aim, came down like lightning on his antagonist's nose, with such violence as he had never used or tried to apply during the whole round, and the nose went to pieces, its bridge broke, the force of the lightning stroke being increased by the seal ring on Grigorss's finger, with the Lamb and the Cross. Flann's nose went flat, the blood gushed out and ran down his chin, his face was not his any more; he opened his eyes wide above the swelling, dripping shapelessness and raised it in the air, while his outstretched fists moved in space before him.

Grigorss, shocked at his own brutality, had drawn

far back. Flann rushed after him. "Come on," he bawled. "On your guard, cowart!" And he spat blood, it spattered Grigorss on the body. But Grigorss again avoided, did not defend himself, only held the red, foaming, unrecognizable, half-blind Flann away from his own body.

"Nay, Flann," he said, out of breath himself, one eye blue and not a few bruises on his body. "Not on any account; call me a coward, but I won't fight any more this time, we must put off the decision. You've broken your nose fighting and that's an end of it, no more sparring, just cold-water compresses and something done for the blood, that you have in the hut. Let me, I'll tear a piece off my shirt and dip it in the sea."

And lo, since Grigorss would not fight, Flann unwillingly desisted too. For it is certainly true that breaking a bone does shake a man's whole system quite extraordinarily. Flann might well have fainted, the blackness of a swoon did flash for a moment across his eyes, but he was much too strong to fall victim to it. He turned aside to where Grigorss had been sitting, took his jacket, sat down again with it, and held it up to his face.

When Grigorss came back with his wet piece of shirt he motioned him furiously away with his shoulder. Yes, he even tried to thrust at him with one foot as he sat there, but the movement so increased the agony of his crushed nose that he yelled out: "Ouch, Ouch!" quite involuntarily. "You see, you see," said Grigorss pity-

ingly, but did not dare go near him again with the rag.
Flann sat so a little while; then he got up and walked,
with the blood-dripping jacket in front of his face,
slowly through wild oats and dune grass toward the
parental cabin.

The Discovery

"BAD," thought Gregorius as he stood there and looked after his brother, "that turned out badly for me as well as for him, and for me probably worse. For I am now the guilty one even though it was his mania for fighting that began it. The hut will curse me, and the Abbot punish me with fasting and prayers, because I have dealt my own brother something which I am afraid can never be quite made good. And yet what could I do? He wanted us to fight to the finish in dead earnest and so it's bound to be bad with me either way, body or soul, and perhaps I might better have given in with the body than to have made myself eternally guilty by smashing his nose. But how can I help it if in a fight my vital powers gather themselves together so extraordinarily? Brother Clamadex in the cloister, who has experimented much with nature and privately gets pretty close to magic, has a lens so ground that it collects the sun's rays by the way it is cut, so that if you hold it over your hand the hand jerks away because it feels the burning and if you hold it over paper or dry grass it gets brown and smokes and flames up—only because of the concentration. It is like that with my spirits in a fight and so unfortunately Flann's nose got broken—I knew it beforehand, yes, as soon as he forced me to the round, I knew it quite definitely and ought, it may well be, to have warned him, but possessed as he was, that wouldn't have helped either. What shall I do now? Confess first to the Abbot? No, I will rather follow him at once and excuse myself to our parents as well as I can."

So after he had put on his clothes he went at some distance behind the battle-scarred Flann up towards the hut and only at the last hastened his steps when the other had already passed through the vegetable-beds in front of the house, and set foot on the sill. Mahaute was within, you could hear that Flann met her. Of course she saw the blood, of course she attacked him with senseless questions as she drew the jerkin from his face, saw the catastrophe, the nose, which meanwhile had certainly got still more swollen and looked perfectly impossible, and burst out in loud outcry and hullabaloo.

"So it had to be," thought Grigorss, "of course she had to break out when he ran straight into her arms. It would be better if Wiglaf were there too. He would look at the thing more reasonably. But he is probably in the turnip-field or at the market. I will just let her roar herself out a bit and wait till Flann has explained before I show myself." And he stepped behind the open door. Inside it was:

"Yes, for heaven's sake, almighty God! Flann, Flann, my child, all bleeding, soaked with blood? What is the matter, what is it, how is it, how is it you look like that? Let me see! Oh, just let me see—your nose? Oh, deary me, alack, alack! What the good day! Oh, it is all true, your nose is gone, it is broken, there is no nose any more. Flann, darling child, speak, what have you been doing? Fighting, a row, a set-to? Who with? Who did it to you? I've got to know!"

"That is not so important just now, who did it," Flann could be heard to say sullenly through the wreck of his nose. "Give me some red cotton-wool and water instead of weeping and wailing."

"So I am not to weep and wail! The red cotton and a compress! Yes, here, straightaway! But not weep and wail! Your own mother is not to cry or to ask who disgraced you like that, and disfigured you for life? Oh, what a day, what a day! Alas! Who did it? Who is the murderer?"

"That damned Credemi," Flann came out with it, "he did it, if you must know. He aimed at my kidneys and hit my nose, the cheat and fraud! I wanted to go on but he backed out."

"Credemi? Grigorss? How dast he? What did you do to him?"

"I asked him what he was reading and he said he would smash my kidneys and when I guarded them he hit my nose. If it doesn't come up again and I have to go round looking like a goat all my life, it was your darling son, my brother the priest, he did it."

Now the dam broke, the defences were down, there was no holding back the flood-tide.

"Ha, ha, ha! My son, your brother! He isn't my son, I didn't wrastle him out of my womb, nor did your father make him, he is as little your brother as the pigs in the sty! Don't believe that old swindle, that hanky-panky! He's none of our get. Woe is me for a ruined woman! A vagabond, a tramper, sea-tramp, a cursed bone-breaker, gallows-man, a raper of wombs! Is that the thanks we get? Have I brought him up with my own, the good-for-nothing, the nobody, the flotsam from the sea, and goven him souke when it belonged to others, for him to tear my own children apart, make hash of them, my own children, regular people, at home here among their relations, of whom he has not a single one on the island, the cuckoo! For nobody knows who he is nor where he floated hither from! But, Christ help me, I'll tell the whole world, God give me aid. I will say that he is a findaling, however high he has crawled up; a foundling, a poor foundling and nothing else. He's forgotten that, nobody has tipped him off he was once found, all wretched, in a cag, fastened into a boat, out on the open sea. Let him touch my child, I tell you, and I come out with it! Woe, alas, what does the bastard think he is? The Devil brought him here, to my sorrow. Well do I know his start, out of barrel and billow! I suppose he hoped people would just keep quiet for ever about his shame. Ha, ha! That would be fine, and him living here all safe and cheeky, protected by the lie. Curse the fish that didn't snap him up when he was

thrown away! It was all a fluke, he had a bastard's luck.
A skipjack—he floated right into the Abbot's hands, if
he had not brought him to your father and been his
almoner, he would have had to knuckle under to us, by
Christ! The oxen and swine he would have had to drive
and clean out the stalls with his hands! What was your
father thinking of, who fished him with ice-cold hands
out of the ocean seas, that he gave him to the Abbot
and let him get fine and impudent instead of keeping
him as a foundling with us to shovel muck and vraic!"

Thus Mahaute. Her loud railing rang through the
hut. Behind the door stood Grigorss breathing fast, big-
eyed. Not a word had escaped him, every one bawled
in his ear and burnt in his brain. What was all that, what
was it? The crazy fury of a maddened mother? Senseless talk and irrational slander? No, mother-wit did not
think that out in its fury: out of the cask, out of the
ondes, an exposed one, come to shore, a stranger and
foundling. Not a lie. Too true! Stiff he stood there a
space, then started up and sped away, but not to the
cloister, the cloister no longer his home, he the unknown, unfriended foundling, free as a bird, for a roof
only the heavens, from which the evening now fell and
covered itself with stars. Through sand and moss Grigorss ran, through patches of pine tree bent by the
wind, down to the sea and again inland, round the
whole island he ran, avoiding the villages, the huts,
threw himself down at last by a tree, covering his alien
face in his hands. So nobody knew who he was.—Oh,
the shame of it! Everybody, even the meanest, might

fling it in his teeth: "You nobody, you unknown!"—
and would not know what joy he flung at him with
the bad word, the joy that shook Grigorss's breast at
the thought of his shame. That concentrated blow on
Flann's nose, which had opened the mouth of the
woman, his foster-mother, that had been a blow of lib-
eration, a thump against a door which now stood wide
open: the door of all possibilities. He was unknown,
but he was, and somebody must he be. He had come
in on a wave, but he was no vraic of the sea, from some
shore he must have come. Where was his country,
where were his parents, and who? Had they, or who
was it had made him, scarce born, over to the sea? And
why? Was it so wrong with his rightness? Must not all
his life from now on be devoted to the search, howso-
ever it might turn out? It was a mystery, himself a mystery, but mystery is the vessel of all wishes, hopes,
guesses, dreams, and possibilities. Exposed because of
some dark blot? But where there is blemish, there is nobility. Baseness shows no blemish. How ready he was to
give up a vulgar right to live for a noble unright!

He fell asleep over it and slept all night under the
tree. When day dawned he went to the sea, washed
himself, and got to the cloister at the hour when the
Abbot with the Brothers and scholars were coming out
of the church after matins. In the vaulted passage the
good man gazed at his god-child and his face grew
dark; though in sooth at this hour of the morning he always had a red nose, which looked naïve and little con-
formable with his severe expression.

"Gregorius," he said, "where have you been?"

With bent head even so the lad stood there and for all answer bent it lower.

"Must I," went on the Abbot, "now you are growing up, recognize you as a delinquent, and undisciplined? You were not at evening mass or meal, you were out all night and were absent from matins. What madness! What has come over you, otherwise a pious lad?"

"Father," said Grigorss humbly, "peccavi."

"Peccavisti?" The Abbot was now seriously alarmed. His round under lip moved a while, without words, and the blood left his little matutinal nose.

"Follow me," he ordered at length. "Follow me this instant to my room."

This was what Grigorss wanted. With him who had bought him from Wiglaf and given him his name, to speak with him alone was all his desire. Hands in his sleeves, head bowed, he obeyed. The Abbot's room received them. At the head of the bed's footstool towered a crucifix with bleeding martyr mien; the Abbot motioned to it with his hand.

The Disputation

"In sight of this," he commanded, "speak!"

Gregorius knelt down, with folded hands.

"That will I," said he, "however ill I may succeed in it. For never can my lips thank you fitly, Father and lord, for all you have done for me. Yet I swear to you faithfully that all the days of my life I will add my voice and importune Him who leaves no good deed unrewarded, that He may crown you with a heavenly crown for that you have brought me up, a strange boy, me, a poor foundling, so tenderly before all your people."

Again the Abbot started, but quite differently. The last remnant of the morning blush paled from his little nose.

"What are you saying?" said he, low and hurriedly, seizing Grigorss's clasped hands in his.

"I have been deceived," the other went on and bent deep as though he had a deceit of his own to confess. "In love and goodness have I been deceived. I am not what I have been taught to think myself. The door of truth, which one might also call the door of possibilities, has sprung open to me at one blow. I have beaten

Flann, whom I call my brother, in fight, thanks to a faculty otherwise not common hereabouts, of extraordinary concentration. In anger, because I injured him, my foster-mother, his mother yelled it all out in my ears, that I am a foundling, nothing else, a God-knows-who, as infant fished cold-handed out of the high seas. Shame will overpower me body and soul if ever I hear that again, and credemi, I will never hear it again."

With that he got up. From humble knees he raised himself, setting his feet firmly, and stood there, pale his lovely face, where the eyes blazed blue.

"You must dismiss me, dear lord, for I stay no longer here. I must take on me the hardships of a knight-errant and be roofless as last night I was. Surely I shall somewhere find the unknown land from which I came. I have strength and understanding, I will, credemi, not perish, unless it be expressly by God's will. He must be put to the test and rather will I die and perish in the desert than live longer on this island. Dishonour drives me. Too much I fear scorn. How garrulous is a woman! If she have only said it to one, soon three and four know it and after that everybody. Then bless me, lord, for my errantry."

How dejected was now my friend the Abbot, whom in telling my tale I have learned to esteem ever more highly. His little nose was now red again and tears stood in his eyes.

"My child," said he, "now hearken. Well and from my heart will I counsel you, as is incumbent upon me to do for a dear human being who has from early on been

my care. Credemi, God has dealt most graciously with
you, for He has opened your eyes, that you no longer
walk in darkness and live out your days in ignorance
but rather by free choice. This decision had I to leave
to Him but might not anticipate His wisdom. You have
seen me startled at your first words; but truly I am relieved by God's dealing and by His having given you
freedom to decide about your life in the light of reason
and to choose between Him and the world. This fight
must now be fought out in your own bosom and it
must be shown how you use your freedom, whether
for your salvation or destruction. Seventeen years has
God waited before He set you free, but even so you
are much too young for your freedom not to need
counsel. My heart's dear son, have good will towards
yourself and follow my guidance so that you may
choose the certain instead of the highly uncertain, that
your boyish anger not overreach itself in its haste and
afterwards come to rue. Say nothing yet! You have not
yet heard me. Hear this: you are a most excellent youth.
Your affairs are altogether after heart's desire, the people here bear a high mind to you, their eyes grow lov-
ing when they see you. Forsake them not. You have
the habit of the ecclesiastical life, do not withdraw
yourself from its mild bonds, linked with so many
amenities. You are pre-eminent in book-knowledge,
your way is cut out for you. I am in years an old man,
already sixty-seven, dear me, how much longer can I
live? I do not say that if I were to close my eyes tomorrow it is decided that you should take my place at once.

An abbot must have age, although age makes but few the wiser. But some day it is a certainty for you, and I have set it down in my will, you will be Abbot of Agonia Dei, lord over old and young and guardian of the faith on this île. Will you let that go because of the gabble of a goose? Once she might and must gabble, God willed it, that you might have freedom of choice. But you will believe me that I am the man to see to it that never again such stuff comes out of her mouth."

Grigorss answered to him:

"I have heard the truth behind the door of the hut. Every word of yours confirms it, most of all that you, my lord, called the woman a lying fool, for were she my mother you would see better after your words. Moreover she is my foster-mother after all, and you yourself once chose her to be so. If you had seen Flann's, my one-time brother's nose, which truly was so dealt with in honourable combat, you would understand that a mother does not control herself at such a sight. I do not rail at her and would defend her from hard words, since she was the means of enlightening me. To you, truly, I am eternally indebted. In me, poor wretch as I am, you have in a way honoured God and so increased your godliness, that love and reverence ought to compel me to agree with you. And yet they cannot, by which you may judge how over-strong my youthful scorn at the mere thought that contemptuous words behind my back should be my lot. It is inevitably so that since I know I am not son of fisherfolk I have become still more sensitive in the point of honour than

I already was in the first place. And why? Because foundling state bears within itself the utmost conceivable possibilities. No one knows my forebears. Suppose they came from such a stock that knighthood became me? Lord and dear Father, all my dreams tell me that it and nothing else is my lot. True, you have the best life. Comfort and godly approval mingle pricelessly therein and he who rightly chooses it is blest. But I can neither share nor inherit it. I must be gone, for since I know who I am not, only one thing avails: the journey after myself, the knowledge of who I am."

"My son, my son, not to everyone is it blessed to know so precisely who he is, even though knighthood were gained thereby. If you have ever believed me, believe me now: you are in your right place within these walls. God has taken you, through me, under His protection. Against what? Perhaps against yourself. Will you run from His sheltering care and feel no fear lest you ally yourself with hell? For the uncertainty who you are no solution could be more suitable and no better answer to your riddle can be than that you end your days as pious and beloved abbot in this peaceful, world-remote island. So be warned, implored, and admonished by one who loves you: O, remain!"

"No, lord, keep me in your love as I will everlastingly cherish and foster mine to you in my heart; but I must go. All my thoughts are on knighthood and better truly be a knight of God than a sham cloister-brother."

"Son, credemi, it is for the old man no slight thing,

and a hard test of sympathy and patience to hear so
young a blood with breaking boyish voice uttering his
folly abroad. Knighthood! You covet knighthood! And
you haven't the faintest idea about it nor are in the
smallest degree therefore prepared. Can you even ride?
Of course not. How should you know how to sit a
horse? But you have proposed to make yourself a
laughing-stock. Ask anybody who knows about chivalry: 'If a person goes to school,' he'll tell you, 'and
spends twelve years with his books without riding, he
remains a parson all his life, for knighthood he is lost.'
But what does that mean? I mean that such a rider, a
silly cockerel who has not learned to read, and do all
he can could not make out the most pressing matters,
his nearest concerns, written on purpose for his eye—
such a one is lost to the priesthood. Each honourable
state is lost for the other; but you, you are born to be
a child of God, and when you pass, it will be said:
Look how charmingly the surplice becomes him!"

"Lord, let a knight put on the cowl, of course he'll
look a clumsy owl. But give me knightly wear and see
if ever it became anyone better than me! If I look absurd—my oath I take, straight back into the cowl I
creep!"

"The monkey!" thought Abbot Gregorius tenderly
to himself. "Of course the knight's array would become him and material to cut up would there be as
well." But he said nothing, only shook his head with
concern.

"You know not, dear master," Grigorss went on with

his youthful harangue, "how well prepared inwardly I am for knighthood. Never have I confessed it to you as long as the door of possibility was closed. 'You cannot ride,' fatherly-wise you say to me. No, physically I have never done it, but in my mind many thousand times, and whatever knight out in Hainhault, in Hespaye, or in Brabant sat praiseworthily on a horse, in my dreams I could do better and that not just out of conceit but truly according to the simple fact. What I know of books I regret not, grammaticam, divinitatem, leges, all these I studied easily and with enjoyment. And yet though one saw me sit over my books, in secret my thoughts on armour and combat were bent, my truest longings unsatisfied went. A steed, a steed! It whinnied clear so quickly it knew its master dear. And then my thigh aloft I was flinging, with my leg so nimbly I was springing, that neither on shoulder or flank you'd say I spurred the steed that bore me away. No, further behind I used my wits, a finger's breadth where the surcingle sits. My legs then reached near to the mane, who then saw me in the saddle, indeed I mean like a tapestry figure or painting fine to him I verily must have been. Yet with steady seat all is not won, if with beautiful ease it is not done. And my body knew how itself to bear as sweetly as though mere pastime 'twere. My spurs well fixed, for the volt prepared I rammed my opponent from distant start and in this doing ne'er forbore to aim in his shield on the nailes four. Now aid me, Father, with wisest rede that the dream of chivalry grow to deed."

"Son, son," said the Abbot, shaken by these avowals, "you have an eloquence and command words—I am impressed, I deny it not. Surcingle? Credemi, I don't understand a word, I could just as well understand Greek. Brother Peter-Paul didn't give you all that. But wherever you got it, I see quite well you are at heart no cloister man. A pity, Gregorius, most regrettable, dear child. But let it be so, I will advise you, fatherly and reasonably, my son. Good, take off your habit, renounce the clerical. Put on worldly garb or in God's name even knightly, in honour of the certainly vague possibilities which issue from the fact that you are not the fisherman's son. But stay here, Gregor, stay with us! Don't go roving, don't go into the world! I beg you, you haven't a sou, not a penny, not a denier. Like a church-mouse you are, dear boy! How then will you meet the world without subsidia? Yes, if for instance you had a hundred and fifty gold marks, then you might take up with knighthood. But where would you get them? There is no thought of it. So let me do something. I'll arrange it so, depend upon it, you will make a rich marriage, the likes of which may not be found here on St. Dunstan, but perhaps on St. Aldhelm or one of the other islands. So far at least change your mind, that until I have got that fixed, you will stop with us."

But Grigorss's obstinacy was unshakable and not to be counselled.

"Father," he responded, "I thank you. I thank you ever more and ever out of more depths of my heart, as already for the past and now again for your offer to wangle a rich marriage for me. But with all gratitude must I reject it. No youth of honour marries before he knows who he is, for he must perish of shame when his children ask after their forebears. To stop on here married in good circumstances, that is not given me, but only to question my fate in arduous errantry, whether it will not reveal who I am. Fortune beckons me, that ne'er yet denied him who aright applied. Lord, your blessing, be so good. Be here an end to our dispute!"

Then the good Abbot sighed deeply and said:

"Well, then, so the hour has come. I would gladly still have put it off, but your fixed mind, which I honour and lament, forces it on. How things are with you, my child, you shall learn. You shall read in this hour for what it was I made you a cloister scholar, that you might one day be able to read. Yea, know this: that grammatica, leges, and even Divinitas, all that is mere accompaniment and extra, only that you should learn to read, according to the instructions and to your information."

Therewith he went to his desk, opened it, and reached far behind to a drawer at the back; this also he unlocked with a secret key and drew something out, richly besene, highly valuable, made of yvorie, framed in gold and splinters of precious stones, and closely bewritten.

"This is yours," said Abbot Gregorius, "your property, though in the form of a letter to your finder, whom God made me. It was given to your infancy in the little cask and seventeen years I have kept it for

you. Now sit down, my dear son, on this stool and
make use of your readiness given you solely to this end.
It is not good to read it standing. You must, poor child,
be prepared for strangely mixed feelings as you de-
cipher."

Bewildered, Grigorss took the tablet from his hand,
looked at the writing, at the Abbot, at the writing again,
sat down on the stool and read, sometimes lifting his
head and staring into space with open lips and fixed
eyes. At him the Abbot looked, his hands folded, his
little nose red and his eyes blinking with tears.

The youth read long. At last he let the tablet fall,
and motioned, his head back, with his whole arm at the
old man, tottered towards him as he approached, and
sank on his shoulder with the most violent sobs, while
the Abbot patted him soothingly on the back and even
rocked him a little. How often has that come about! It
happens over and over in this world. One person sobs
uncontrollably on another's breast and that other says:
"There, there. Never mind. It's all right. Just be calm.
Not your fault. You'll get over it. Just trust in God"—
and so on. Thus Abbot Gregorius, patting though tears
ran down his own face. And he said with a sigh:

"Who you are is not there written for you. But what
you are, poor child, that you now know."

"I am an outcast!" sobbed Grigorss. "I am the abominable fruit of sin. I belong not to humanity. I am a horror, a monster, a dragon, a basilisk!"

"But no, you exaggerate," the Abbot soothed and
rocked him. "You are a child of man, and a very dear

one, even although not in the regular order. God is full of wonders. Very well can love come out of evil, and out of disorder something ordered for the best."

"I knew it," Grigorss went on moaning. "I felt it in my blood that things were not in order with me. Not for nothing did my companions call me the mourner, the dreri herte. But that I am a dragon and a monster, with aunt and uncle for parents, that certainly I did not know."

"You forget the other side of the picture," said the Abbot, "which to some extent makes up for what you exaggeratedly call the monstrous, namely that you are of very high lineage."

"That too," said Grigorss, freed himself from the shoulder and stood up, "that too I knew and felt in my blood. Ah, Father, my sweet, sinful parents, who conceived me in sin, to be a sinner! I must see them! I must seek them through all the world, until I find them and tell them that I forgive them. Then will God forgive them, probably He is only waiting for that. But I, according to all that I know of divinity, I who am only a poor monster will through pardon win humanity."

"Son, son, bethink thee well! Granted your parents still live and you find them in the wide world, who tells you that you would be welcome to them? Since they once gave you to the sea, that is not at all too certain. You can pardon them here too and through that win humanity and blessedness. It is here that God made the abandoned infant come miraculously to land, and assigned to you who had no place in the world this little stronghold of His peace for your asylum. Will you flee from it and fling yourself into the world at all cost? In my heart I hoped that when you knew what your condition is, you would realize that you are in your right place."

"Ah, Father, no, on the contrary! Since I have knowledge my resolve stands firmer than ever. How often have you read my tablet? I read it with ardour and will read it again a thousand times to my chastisement. Here it is. What do my sweet parents tell me? All too much they loved each other, that was their sin and my begetting. But I am to make it good with God—not by stopping in the cloister and saving my own soul, but rather by turning through all my life to other blood and as knight striving for its need. So will I thrust my way through the world to my parents."

"Son, be it so, I see well I shall not keep you. Gladly had my old age renewed itself in your presence; yet will I pray for you and speak of you to God, my child, for that also is a way to keep you. Let me now reveal what remains."

With that the Abbot led the youth to a chest, opened it; pushing aside all sorts of ecclesiastical trappings, stoles, neckbands, and mass vessels, he drew from under them at the bottom several layers of the handsomest brocade and handed them over with the words: "These are yours, besides the tablet. They were spread beneath and over you in the little cask and I suppose will be enough for a knight's wear or even two. From Alisaundre in the East, my child, and the finest stuff.

Those who gave you that, their presses are well stocked. I see, you rejoice in the dowry. But it was and is not the only thing, which in your reading the tablet you may have less remarked. When I told you, child, you are without heller or sou, a church-mouse, that was only a feint, it is not the case. There were two loaves of bread, besides the silks, given to your infancy, therein gold was baked, twenty marks in payment for your upbringing. Only three of them I gave, assuming your consent, to the fishing-men. But the others I did not bury and let them be consumed by mould or rust, instead I entrusted them to an excellent usurer, the Jew Timon, who made them breed and in seventeen years made a hundred and fifty of them. Of that you are now master, a sum with which one may well meet the proud world as a knight."

Bewildered and happy Grigorss stood there. Of course it is monstrous and a sore weight of guilt to be born a brother-sister child. But as it does not hurt physically, the consciousness of it is easy to shove into the background by dint of gifts of fortune, which, at the discovery, fall into one's lap.

"You smile," said the Abbot, "you smile, though pale and tear-blubbered. I did tell you that it would be with mixed feelings you would make acquaintance with your origins."

Maître Poitevin

MIXED feelings! I, Clemens, sitting at Notker's desk as
guest of St. Gall, may I suppose in the course of my
narrative speak of such. I candidly confess that in the
argumentation between Grigorss and Gregorius I was
altogether on the side of my friend the Abbot and
found his reasons excellent, whereas in my opinion his
foster-child talked like a greenhorn. What he learned
about his sinful connections, instead of urging him out
into the world, should have been just what would make
him cling gratefully to the refuge open to him and remain faithful to the priestly order. Therein, by all human reckoning, his father in God was perfectly right
and only too well justified in his warning that upon the
youth's venturesome spirit and wandering into the
world nothing good, yes, perhaps something quite
frightful might ensue. But human reckoning does not
go far, except in the narrator's case, who knows the
whole story up to its wondrous ending and as it were
shares in the divine providence—a unique privilege and
one actually not proper to the human being. I am thus
also inclined to feel some shame, to give human reckon-

ing its due and at the present stage of our tale to censure
what afterwards, overwhelmed by the voice of divine
mercy, I shall be forced to praise.

Thus it is with a certain reluctance that I relate how
Grigorss, in possession of all his dowry, the tablet, the
gold and the priceless stuffs, pursued with zeal his parting from the island to travel into strange countries on
knighthood bent. He put off the clerical dress of his
pupillage and put on secular garb, in part that of a
knight or squire: a belted coat of mail with hood, legs
and feet also in light armour. The costume was unpre-
tentious. But privately he gave the tailor-brothers of
the cloister an order for a highly aristocratic garment,
to be cut out of the stuffs from the cask: a brocaded
gala surcoat or houppelande, of a clinging fabric in rich
dark colours, shot with gold and silver and with thin
flowing sleeves, the end of which one wears hanging
down over the hand; in addition close-fitting hose and
a cap. But the upper garment was actually cote armour,
for there was an oval piece let in over the breast, with
a fish embroidered on it. That, as the youth conceived,
should be his crest on his travels, and I must say it is
the only thing about his preparations which pleases me.
For while the fish indicated that the traveller came from
a fisherman's hut, it is also the symbol of the Christus
and evidence that the wearer had grown up within the
walls of the Church.

The secular garb, as well as all he needed for the
journey, provisions, fresh water, and gold, he stowed in
the already provided ship made of curved planks with

lofty bows, also bearing his device. He had hired a small
crew, with money and fair words. The fish was woven
into his striped sail as well. Grigorss asked little whether
his bark were seaworthy, or even safe for the confined
but fretful waters which in jest one calls the "canal" or
"the sleeve." In far more fragile vessel had he once arrived hither, and his resolution to fling himself into
peril and straits sprang from his longing to do penance
for the abomination of his birth, whose nobility was yet
so precious to him. That his crew, born and brought up
haphazard, had nothing for which it was incumbent on
them to atone, that he indifferently overlooked, seeing
in himself the hero of a saga, in them but unimportant
adjuncts thereto. Involuntarily I do so in my turn and
blame myself—myself but not him, for who shall quar-
rel with providence?

When now—the autumn had already set in—the day
of his journey was come, away from the island that had
brought him up and where for honour and shame he
could no longer bear to bide, certainly he shed regret-
ful tears of leave-taking on the Abbot's breast, who
with some of the Brothers accompanied him to the boat
and blessed him for his journey, over and over again.

"Whither now, my child?" he asked in his concern.

"I follow my tablet," answered Grigorss, pointing to
his left breast, "whither God's winds shall waft me. To
them we give our sail."

And so in mist they pushed off from the shore where
once the infant had arrived, and father and son sadly
prolonged the farewell by watching and waving till the

mist and the wideness of water shut them from each
other's sight. That happened only too soon. The bark
disappeared in the woolly waste directly they left the
strand, and the blinding brume lay over them throughout their voyage, wrapping them day and night in seldom distinguishable duration as though for hiding or
in not too canny security. But whoever would have
foreseen for the wanderers wild wave-driven storm
and ship wrack would have guessed awry; there was
smooth sea and wind almost none. A north-by-west
wind, very mild, stood to their sail, for days it would
flatten away so that they made no headway unless by
getting themselves forward with the oars, unknowing
whether they were doing any good, hardly seeing the
sun and not the stars and never a ship, to say nothing of
a shore. They would, believe me, have better liked a
heavy sea with high breakers, to this dead discomfort,
this groping in the thicket of fog, day in, day out. I
must reckon at seventeen days that visionless voyaging.
Their drinking-water was gone, their food at an end.
They suffered the lifeless calm of the sea. Sadly hung
the crew in the boat, some looking, the rest luddering,
for such weather and an empty stomach make one dull.
At the mast stood Grigorss the master mariner staring
into the unsightable, wherein all peering hung dead.

Still he was the first who was aware of the miracle
which, when seventeen days were gone by, came to
pass soon after midday. Oh joy, the fog lifted! A breeze,
first sighing, then soughing, tore it, drove it into shreds,
a sheaf of sunlight fell direct and broad upon a scene

—was it a dazzling of the eyes, a deceiving Fata Morgana? No, for there were revealed port, landscape, towered city with battlements and gates, to all which they had been so near in the fog. Who shall describe the joy of the dejected ones at this revelation? Up then, with rudder and all sails set towards the city in the rays of the sun, castle-crowned, lying on the deep bay where now they rocked on unquiet waters. This new wind was contrary. Not without pains did they make head against it to their goal.

And were but wind and wave all that opposed their coming! Alas, the city did too, for the cleared-off fog had revealed to her their approach, as it had to them her lofty landscape. The burghers, it seemed, assumed the defensive against the approach of the stranger ship. Stones flew, and iron balls flung from mangonels. Greek fire fell before them and made a barrage on the sea. Only after they had given many signs of modest, peaceful, and friendly temper was the defence abandoned and landing allowed. Their boat was singed and two of the crew had bloody heads from the stones. But of course these were but underlings.

There approached Grigorss on the quay, where porters were emptying goods out of the bowels of some ship, surrounded by armed men with pikes and in striped costumes a personable man, of troubled rather than severe mien, a hat on his head, from the brim of which a cloth hung down over his ears to his chest, yet he had his arms and legs protected. His questions as to the person and origin of the stranger began gruffly and quickly softened in tone on a closer view. Yes, when he had done his questioning he did not even wait for the answers, but introduced himself first by way of excuse, in these words:

"Learn that I am one of the worthiest in this quemune, speaking precisely the worthiest, for I am its magistrate and Maire. I was given notice of your coming, which was regarded as hostile. So I came to see if it was, and when I saw it was not, I ordered the cessation of the defence. You must not be surprised at the surly reception. This once joyous city is full of distress, and if its postern were not open, I mean to the sea, where for prices not dictated by modesty she can get some supplies, it would long since be all up with her. As for you, we did not know what to think of you. Pirates make the sea unsafe and appear here and there on the coast with thievish intent. Before we saw you face to face we suspected you of being such a one. How far from our fears I will now hear from you."

"Very far, Sir Mayor," answered the youth. "And from afar I came hither in a long voyage in the fog, from Oultresea. I call myself the Knight of the Fish, but my name is Gregorius."

"Mine is M. Poitevin," the Mayor threw in.

"Thank you," responded Grigorss. "Shield-service is my manner of life and I travel on knighthood bent in foreign lands, at my own cost and not in the least tempted to robbery as I have gold in sufficiency."

"Very pleasant," said Poitevin, bowing.

"But on the tables of my life," added Gregorius,

"stands written, I shall offer all I am to stranger blood, and as knight fight for it at need. To this end I go my errant way."

"That is highly commendable, beau Sire, Sir Knight of the Fish," replied the burgher. "Surely a chaste woman gave you to the world, for your features are well marked and lovely and your bearing elegant. Are you Norman?"

"You scarcely err," answered Grigorss.

"My eye has some judgement," said the Maire with satisfaction. "May it please you, so follow me into my widowed house to a collacie with good drink afterwards, of which the cellar has surely still a remnant. No one shall say that this city, full of woes as it is, does not know how to practise hospitality."

"The grace with which through you the city knows how to receive the traveller," answered Grigorss, "speaks very much in its favour. I gladly go with you. But why," he asked, when the official had got them both mounted on mules and they were riding across a bridge of tree-trunks and through a gate into the streets, "why do you keep on saying that your city is full of distress, which indeed can be seen on the faces of the few burghers we meet? And why does it seem that most of them, oldfolk and children excepted, go armed and man the walls and lofty battlements?"

"Far," answered Poitevin, "must you come indeed from Oultreland and Oultresea that you clearly have never heard of the troubles of our land and this its chief city of Bruges, which once was called la vive and now might almost be named with the dead. But what wonder? Separated from each other men dwell, their hearing is limited in space, and even of the wildest events the news sticks in the near air, late or never does it reach the further off. I myself know little, not to say nothing at all, of what does and gets done among foreign folk, like Aquitanians, Gascons, Englanders, Lotharingians, Turks, and Scots. And just so you have heard naught of the wooing war, as our troubles will doubtless one day be called by the singers, since even so the word is already on every lip. Five years now it rages. Roger the Goat-beard, King of Arelat and Upper Burgundy has ravaged our land and castles, all Artoys and Flaundres lies broken in his hands, and to our lady, Duchess of the country, whom may God send His angels, there remains naught but this capital city, on whose walls the storm breaks very now—how long, the Merciful knows, may He be mindful of His mercy ere it be too late. But I fear me He suppresses it of set intent, because He is angry and our lady, despite her most holy life, is not on the best of footing with Him. For she is over-chaste, denies, to grieve Him, her womanhood, and has always refused to give the land a lord and duke—for this we pay in the so-called wooing war, the meaning of which you so justly inquired. For Roger of the pointed beard, he wooes our lady and covets her, avid of her beauty, for his wife, these twelve years long, seven of which he spent in peaceful suing if also the longer the more with menace than minne. Warriors called he then up for he has sworn, the hairy Hotspur, to snatch at all costs the

proud body of our lady into his bed. How we have re-
pulsed his attack once and again and victoriously driven
out the Burgundians, whereby fell many of our best,
for instance the Sieur Eisengrein, the faithful one—to
you, a stranger, the name means naught but moves us
even to weeping. Ah, all in vain! Possessed by the obstinacy of their leader, they ever renewed their cam-
paigns, three years they occupied and burned, drove off
our herds, laid waste our flax-fields, overpowered the
land, and in the fourth pressed as far as to this fortified
city, the last that resists them, and to which they now
for long have laid siege, ramming our walls with every
sort of machine such as 'high-as-the-walls,' hedgehogs,
cats, storming-ladders, and abominable stone-throwers.
But above in the castle, her last refuge, there she hides,
who is the prize of this campaign and to all our harms
says always only 'Jamais.' Do you wonder that voices
here and there, what though low-toned, ask the not very
remote question whether our lady, who has guarded
herself so long, would not do better at last to give him
of the beard her hand and thus make an end of this ac-
cursed war for love? Up at the castle, at the court itself, there is a coterie by no means small in numbers and
rank who openly favour this proposal. But the woman,
what says she? 'Niemalen de la vie!'"

It was in M. Poitevin's house and room, while they
refreshed themselves with a welcome meal of smoked
meat and warm beer with cloves, set out by the house-
keeper and chatelaine, a woman by nature easy-going,
though she too wore a worried face, that Grigorss re-

ceived these informations and showed himself extraordinarily moved thereby.

"Good my host and worthy burgess," he gave answer, "at your words a mist as it were falls from my eyes and there is revealed the reason why after long and fog-bound voyage the picture of this city was disclosed. I am at my goal. Hither has God addressed my helm and clear as in a sunbeam I recognize that I have come aright. For this I ever besought Him that He bring me where there was something for me to do, that my youth lie not idle, rather in justified battle throw itself before innocence oppressed. If it please my gracious lady, I will be her knight and pawn, and as the sore oppressed in words her will expressed, such shall my motto be: 'Niemalen de la vie!' For this Duke, whom you call Goat-beard, presumably because he wears a pointed beard and is altogether hairy, which for aught I know may indicate particular virility—for him, I say, is all my abhorrence, and the same goes for that coterie who loud or low advise surrender, and who would persuade the chaste one that she should give the bold wooer and hated thief of her land her hand in marriage. Fervently I hope that these contemptible people are in the minority at court and knights of loftier mind flock round the sacred person."

"Alas," replied the official, "precisely by reason of their loyalty their members shrink. For the why, let me tell you that too, in short and fateful words. Duke Roger de coutume rides up to the gate and challenges our bravest to single combat, in which till now no one has withstood him. For his prowess in a brawl is great and world-famous in all lands. Urged on by honour, ours take up his cartel in turn, but till now he has laid them all low and whoever offered fealty was dragged off before our eyes or else slain. So the noble entourage of our mistress is already shamefully thinned."

"This man," speculated Grigorss, "must have the gift of pulling himself together in a fight, beyond the ordinary measure, and collecting his vital spirit in one burning point?"

"I don't quite grasp," responded his host, "the meaning of your words. My own contention is that our campions fall to the fable of the Duke's invincibility. Honour brings them forth, not belief in victory, of which they, consciously or not, despair beforehand."

"You are very shrewd, mine host," remarked Grigorss with respect.

"So am I," answered the other. "Would I otherwise have become Mayor of Bruges? Besides, my shrewdness takes the form of complete clarity and general intelligence."

"And when," was Grigorss's question, "is the next self-assured challenge of this Duke to be expected?"

"He is not before the city," answered the official. "His tent is down. Come autumn, he returns home through our plundered cities till the next spring to his kingdom, which also must be governed. Our poor town, of course, remains under siege. But few engagements and skirmishes take place during the winter."

"And in may-time," Grigorss supplied, "he comes

back, to rob our liege lady of her protectors by his prowess at a brawl and force her to yield, which in this case means giving herself. She is young and beautiful, I suppose?"

"She might," answered his host, "be now perhaps twice as old as you, whom I guess to be seventeen or eighteen; but despite all the night masses and flagellations she is very well preserved—in God's despite, I suppose, for she refuses her beautiful body to all and every man."

"That she should yield it up to that goat-beard," replied Grigorss, "is certainly not His will. So far I trust myself to guess His thoughts, for at one time I occupied myself with Divinitas."

"What, you have knowledge of the books too?"

"A little. And little it helps me under these circumstances. What does help me, and whereto I implore your help, shrewd and worthy host, is simply that I may be set before the eyes of your lady, that I may offer myself as her knight and she should grant me for her freedom to put my life at the hazard and defend the refuge of her chastity against hairy sneaks."

"Your zeal does you honour," said the burgher after some consideration, "and altogether I do not conceal the pleasure your words give me. I have small doubts that you will hold your own, despite your youth, before the eyes of our mistress in upbringing and Norman tournure. Still, it is not easy, for she is sternly sparing of her countenance and vouchsafes it to few, in any case only in the cathedral when she prostrates herself before God,

then may one see of her so much as is to be seen of one
sunk in prayer.—I will gladly try to be of service to
you. M. Feirefitz of Bealzenan, the princess's major-
domo, is my friend and patron—a man of polish, a man
of the finest courtly school; picture him fat above and
very thin in the legs, clad in light flowered silk and
with a parted beard, also silky. This only a quick sketch
of his outer man. To him will I speak of you, report
your will and desires, and determine him, I think, with
the insinuating ways native to him to direct the eyes of
our liege lady upon you. Until then remain my guest!
I mean, lodge with me as boarder and table-mate. With
interest I heard that you are supplied with gold. That is
a refreshing exception. Knights-errant are usually high-
minded but pover, a mixture to which I was always inclined with only half a heart. But you pay fairly for
roof and subsistence from your gold. Your nourishment
shall be ample and still so reasonable that it will not de-
tract from your slenderness and your valour not sleep-
ily fatten away. Shall it be so?"

"So be it," said Grigorss, and they pledged each other
in their spiced beer, a very good drink, with cloves,
which I have never tasted but let glide with pleasure
down their gullets. Very oft is the telling only a sub-
stitute for enjoyment which we, or the heavens, deny
ourselves.

The Meeting

I WELL knew that M. Poitevin would keep his promise and at the first opportunity would speak about Grigorss and his desires to the major-domo, whose person he so capitally described. I never doubted it. Much too well had his young guest pleased the magistrate, his firm and refined mien, his tactfulness, and his generous pay for bed and board, for M. Poitevin to be likely to forget his words. He put them into action only two weeks after the youth's arrival in his mairie, where he from Bealze-nan, ridden down from the burg, was visiting him to discuss the state of the winter truce in the wooing war, at this time carried on half in jest. Likewise to be discussed was the provisioning of the court with certain necessities and commodities; it being Poitevin's task to preserve as far as possible the distinction between the two, not without, in respect of mere commodities, pointing as a model to the austere practices of the mistress herself, full of fasting and watching.

In his response M. Feirefitz mentioned that in city and country distress over the said way of life held equal

with popular admiration. At this interview he was not
clad in flowered silk; in so far his appearance differed
from the portrait which the magistrate had sketched.
Rather was his expansive upper torso covered in harness
against flying stones, with which he wore a starched
ruff; a helmet ringed with studs protected his head. On
the other hand his excessively lean legs were covered
only with close-fitting silken stuff in two colours ending in pointed shoes whose points in the saddle rose high
above his stirrups. But the courtier even half-armed lost
nothing of his affability, and in bargaining succeeded in
transferring the rank of several commodities into the
class of necessities. Afterwards the official said:

"Au reste, major-domo, incidemment et à propos,
a well-provided knight-errant, still young, has lately
landed here and has taken bed and board with me: Gregorius from Oultreland, a worthy knight. He bears the
fish in his arms and swears by heaven and earth that
God has brought him in view of this distressful city expressly in order that he should bear himself knightlike
towards her and her sufferings. Above all is he gire to
approach our liege lady, the hard-pressed one, and offer
himself as her liegeman. Would you, skilful as you are,
arrange it?"

"It would be a small thing for me," replied M. Feirefitz. "But are you quite sure of the purity of his rank?
To lead astray the attention of our lady would be a
culpable faux pas on my part. Oultreland, I must confess, is a somewhat vague designation, for from over
land and sea anybody can come. The presentation of

somewhat more precise evidence of his knighthood would oblige me."

Poitevin's embarrassment was plain, for the speech made him somewhat tardily sensible that he himself had not troubled at all about details of the youth's origins (he would wonder at that, yet to his surprise wondered not at all) and the little he knew—and that, looked at in a clear light, was almost nothing—had amply satisfied him. Thus he spoke, as much to himself as to the questioner, when he replied:

"I do not know whether I can count on your having given such close attention to my words and so kept them in your memory that you recall my telling you that this young blade carries the fish in his coat of arms. To say nothing of the Holy Name (and yet not quite nothing, for I learn that my guest lived for a time within pious walls and studied Divinitatem), this sign as you know has more than one meaning. It is the symbol for water—as in fact the youth came to us on the water, with the fish woven into his topsail. It is further the sign of manliness and of an especial quality and virtue included in it, called reserve. It is scarcely to be called striking, if the bearer of the sign practised himself in manly reserve. If knighthood is a refinement of manhood, then at one glance your eyes tell you more than your tongue would ever ask, so that you are more inclined to hold it. In addition I will only tell you in confidence that the stranger has displayed his valorous courage even prematurely, not yet at all as our lady's vassal, but to the higher heart-beat of us all. He straight-

way climbed up to the battlements, to the sentinels
there, for he wanted to have a good view of the Burgundian camp and the untoward encirclement of the
city. With drawn brows and compressed lips he looked
at it: tents, storming apparatus, land, and folk. What he
then said to the warder of the east gate about what he
had in mind and how he won over the soldier for his
audacious project, I do not know. That he persuaded
him I ascribe more to his tenue and his eye than to his
words. In short you may hear tell of marvels and miracles the very top: the third day betimes the mercenary
lets him draw the bolts, the drawbridge falls, and all
stark living alone steps out he from Oultreland—surely
we all believed that Death stood at his hand. The fish
upon his armour, so bare and bright he swung the two-
edged sword he carried, his sole companion. So then
they came a-running, the men of Roger's train, for they
the open gateway and flashing sword had seen. They
meant to take advantage the single man to slay, but how
he made them rue it I am now about to say. Whatever
ails me? I do not want to rhyme, but curse it, I keep
on making jingles all the time. Knight Gregory of the
Fish from them he did not stay, of Roger's doughty
warriors three he struck down straightway. He thrust
them through the helmet with swiftly swinging sword,
two rolled into the moat, the third lay on the sward.
By all the devils, major-domo, I must be able to tell you
sensibly, without jingles, how thoroughly he polished
them off. They thought it would be a joke, but the
blue fire in his pale face made them laugh out of the

other side of their mouths, I tell you: him with their swords they could no longer withstand, so they shot so many spears into his shield that the rim turned round and on account of the weight it fell from his hand. They, when they saw it, rushed upon him, but he, as the boar in the wood before the pack, was too quick to give them their blows back, with which he pierced the armour of one, so that his harness with the sparks was coloured fiery red. The tale is not a lying one, he sank down and was dead.—Major-domo, I will pull myself together and stop singing! We all saw: he seized up a dart aimed at him, and with it shot one of the Burgundians in the head—the end stuck out of the helmet and so he dragged himself from the bridge, he has belike no longer any thought of life. I swear to you, another one he even cut slantwise through and due to the blade's swift keenness the blow he never knew. Only when he bent down his sword to lift, then he fell off as being cleft.—In short, major-domo, doing this pace by pace the doughty blade avoids backward before them, towards the gate, that he alone had held, and with a rattle behind him the doors fall and right before the noses of them all! Think then of the jubilation and mockery from the wall. They took him on their shoulders, I ran up in haste. With blood his garment ran and so did the sharp weapon gripped so tight in his hand. 'Now tell me, dearest degen, how are you so red? I fear indeed you suffer much and sore have bled.' 'Have on that score no sorrow,' said he with courage good; 'you see me here unwounded, it is the others' blood.' "

"Very remarkable," replied M. Feirefitz. "Under these circumstances, officer, your proneness to song is most comprehensible."

"If I could but ill struggle against it," answered Gregor's host, "that has mostly to do with the blue blaze of the eyes in the pale face. Anyhow I have let myself be carried away, I confess it. That he split one crosswise so that he did not mark it and only afterwards fell in half, that I made up in song, it really did not happen."

"Even so," responded the major-domo, "the sally remains impressive without this detail. Of the knightliness of your juvenile, and that he can be useful to us, of that there remains hardly a doubt."

"I will confide a theory to you," went on the magistrate, "from which the extraordinary proof our guest gave us of his prowess might at need be explained. There must be vouchsafed to him in battle every minute to pull himself together beyond all the otherwise usual measure and as it were his vital spirits to assemble in one burning point. I usually give my thoughts a clearer form, but in this case I am forced to express myself in a rather involved way."

"Let that be as it may," answered the major-domo, "I hesitate no longer about directing the eye of the mistress upon your guest and presenting him to her, that he may offer himself as vassal. Scant are the opportunities; but the feast of our faith, the Conception of Mary, is not far away. On that day, as you know, she shows herself and rides down with all the court from the cita-

del to the cathedral to comfort herself with the mass.
There your young warrior might appease his desire to
see her, and in the right moment to point him out, let
that be my affair."

Thus it fell out. On the day when the most glorious,
rose without a thorn, in the flesh, yet at the same time
through infusion of the spirit, sinless, was conceived
(such our well-tried faith), the princess on an Asturian
palfrey led by two pages at the bridle, with noble
retinue from the castle, rode down the winding way
into her last town and before the chiming minster;
there she dismounted among the bare-headed, kneeling
folk, who looked at her red-eyed and pressed towards
her as she paced with her lords and ladies through the
wide-open portal, rich with carvings, and with downcast eyes, her left hand at the broche of her mantle lined
with the white belly-fur of the squirrel, somewhat lifting it with two fingers of the right, and took her way
through God's holy temple to her stool and the gold-
embroidered tasselled cushion ready for her knees. So
Grigorss saw her from his place across the nave at the
Maire's side, mid song and sparkle and scent saw as
much of her as can be seen of one sunk in prayer. Her
side-face he saw, under the diadem and in the region
of the cheeks it gleamed like yvorie in the rainbow twilight, when she once lifted it and cast her eyes painfully
upwards; and as she raised it, so the young heart of the
watcher lifted with a thrill. "She it is," it spoke within
himself, "my lady, the sore oppressed, whom to free,
to free out of her extremity whereinto a hairy coxcomb

drove her, I have been led hither." And clenching his
fist he swore an oath which should be a battle-cry for
all—or so thought he—those hotly engaged in battle for
her sake: "Niemalen de la vie!"

Behind the princess knelt her major-domo, who today had on his silk waist-coat with a fine flowered pattern, and thus looked precisely as Grigorss's friend had
described him. He bent, as the sacred pageant drew to
an end, his silky beard to the ear of the mistress and
spoke a few words into it—what might they be? Did he
say: "Noble lady, greet that man there! Good service
can he render to you"? Strongly to be feared it was that
he did not say "man" but "youth," and possibly even
worse, as "lad" or "boy." But no, he most likely said
"man," since he wanted to recommend him to her. And
still she hardly bent her head to him, not in the least
turning it towards the spot his words indicated; after
the "Ite, missa est," she made once more the sign of the
cross and went down the nave, her ladies before, her
cavaliers behind. But the major-domo took Grigorss by
the hand and led him after her into the stone-pillared
vault of the vestibule. There he spoke well-chosen
words:

"This, my lady, is M. Gregorius, a knight from Oul-
tremer. He craves honour and above all that of bowing
the knee before you."

Thus Grigorss did, cap in hand; he let himself down
on one knee, with bent head. The princess stood surrounded by her state in half-circle and looked down
upon his crown.

"Rise, Sir Knight," he heard her voice above him, that had a deep, mature, and lovely sound and was not like a maiden's cooing. "Before God alone and the Queen of the Rose-garland may one kneel here."

But when he now stood up before her there happened what he had feared: her red mouth had to smile, because she found him so young. That was like a considerately soft smile, almost pitying, with mischievously lifted brows, but faded quickly again from her lips; not because he flushed and tossed up his head; that she did not see, for her eyes went down his figure, measuring it, and paused peering at his garb. For Grigorss had put on today his cote armour, the splendid garment made from the stuff of his dowry; phelle it was from the Orient, darkly bright, inwoven with gold threads, and the brocade arrested her gaze, in such a way that her lips opened and her brows drew together as she looked. But even as she peered her glance faltered in anguish.

"O Sword, how once again grimly thou piercest my heart! Taken, taken, have they him from me, my little babe, pledge of my beloved, his body's sweet gift, and brought it in the cask the prey of the wild wave! God forgive them, whom in my deepest soul I not forgive! Such stuff, the same, have I laid over and under the poor little mariner with tears; in truth this is just like the other in quality and colour, for that I could vouch, it could, my God, be worked by the same hand and possibly was. Terror and torment and a thousand sinfully blissful memories pierce me at sight of this exactly similar weave and at once I cannot help guessing it must be

a noble house with rarely furnished chests that willed to
the boy here this brocade."

Her bosom rose in anguish, it filled the tightness of
her bodice which below the girdle fell in wide folds of
snowy velvet to her feet, embraced in purpel by her
mantle. Its hem she lifted with a beautiful thin hand to
her girdle. Her blue-dark eyes with the bluish shadows
of night-watching under them looked into his. Lovely
seemed to her this earnest face in his youth resolved to
manhood, it appealed to her in her deepest soul; but to
him it was not otherwise than as though he saw the
earthly image of the Queen of Heaven.

She said mildly:

"You have a plea to me?"

"Only one, yes," he answered zealously, "to serve
you, lady, to be zealous in your service have I most
willing mind. Take me in vassalage, and grant me with
all I am and can to fling myself before you against the
brigand and to stand for you until my death!"

She said:

"I have heard of you, knight, and of certain honourable rashness, blameworthy as well. They say you were
bolder than one ought to be. You know to what mad
and rash diversion I refer. Have you still a mother?"

"I never knew her."

"So let me in her place admonish you. You have
tempted God. Were you in your right mind, you
would not have adventured the prank."

"Noble lady, they have exaggerated the details of the
sortie into the fabulous. The winter pause and drowsi-

ness of the wooing war put me past my patience. Within me I said to myself, one must lighten it and make the foe learn in fear that in this city lives a spirit which in your honour does not shrink from undertakings such as is not given every day to see."

"So I thank you, without taking back my warning. That loyalty for my threatened state emboldens itself to rashness, that is bitter for me, poor woman, to need. Still I do not like noble youth to waste itself heedlessly on my account. Promise me not to do such a thing again and for the future avoid frivolous rashness."

That she called herself a poor woman rent his heart, and he sank again to his knees straightway, his glowing face turned up to her.

"To obey you, my mistress, I promise, so far as zeal to serve you allows me."

She took from one of her gentlemen a naked sword and with it touched his shoulder.

"Be my vassal! In battle for this city, for the down-trodden land, take special honour. Major-domo, I commend this knight to your charge."

As he rose blissfully, she looked once more at his dress, in his face, and turned away as her court closed quickly round her. But Grigorss stood self-forgotten on the spot, quite lost in looking, until his host, the official, twitched his sleeve. Such a woman he had never known, never the sweet ripeness her voice had in his ear when she expressed her royal concern for his youth. Wonder-strange to his experience was her image and nature, yet wonder-near to his.

The Duel

I AM glad, in all the inward horror which on account of the course of this history dwells in my heart, that M. Feirefitz, in that interview with M. Poitevin, had asked for certainty about the genuineness of Grigorss's knighthood, whereby he loosened the magistrate's tongue and made him give the details of his guest's daring single-handed sally on the bridge. We should probably never otherwise have heard of this adventure. Lyrical exaggerations willingly discounted, which in the heat of the narration escaped the teller and which at need are pardonable in one unpractised in factual narration—still enough remains to assure us that the knightly dreams of the cloister scholar from the fisherman's hut were no empty vaporing, but rather that the language of knighthood, of which he asserted that he spoke it inwardly with ease, was genuinely fluent in his mouth in word and gesture; if also it was needful for him to perfect it in the best and most actual conditions before he could venture what since his first conversation with Master Poitevin, but especially since he had seen his mistress with his own eyes, sat as fixed design in his heart.

If anyone in all simplicity and a little slow in the up-

take should at this point ask what sort of design that
would be, he might hear broken fragments which Grigorss when he was alone sometimes muttered fitfully to
himself. They sounded like:

"And be he ever so frightful, yet I will face him
down."

Or: "And were he very Valande, I still would face
him down."

To ask whom he meant by that probably no one is
slow enough. But hearing him thus mutter, I am truly
glad of the dispensation of God, that Grigorss came to
the city in the winter and at the time of a general slow-
ing down in the war. That gave him time to practise
himself diligently in speaking (and not only inwardly)
the language of chivalry, whereto the winter war almost
from day to day gave him occasion. For all sorts of
knightly skirmishing, slight sallies, rivalry half serious,
half only for the sake of passing the time, came about
almost daily before the city, on foot and horseback,
and he did not remain idle; so little, my faith, that soon
with sturdy burghers, with knights and serjents the
saying went: Attacking a head and retreating a tail. I
give the talk of men as I learnt it. To me that sounds
clumsy, and also when they said he was "the hail of the
foe." That too is for my ear an awkward figure; still
his tenue gave them the pictures.

On horseback he was at his best, for he had practised
too often and thoroughly in dreams the thigh grip, am-
bling and circling, for the actuality not to seem long
familiar and second nature. The art was to him as we

say inborn, he had hit on it himself and could practise
it at once, so that nobody dreamed he had never sat a
horse before. In Master Poitevin's stable stood a good
animal, bought with his gold, a dappled stallion, of
Brabant stock, a blaze on its forehead, with eyes beautiful as the unicorn's and full of fiery friendship for his
master. When Grigorss neared him he turned his shining neck and whinnied clear for joy and willingness,
piercing as cock's morning crow. Sturmi his name. I
love him myself and to sing his praise, in his stockiness,
with whitish tail and name and forelock the same—the
fine powerful fetlocks and little hoofs. Like satin was
his well-groomed skin, beneath it full of power the
muscles played and twitched. How the chain-mail cover
suited Sturmi, out of fine close steel rings with which
the page armed him, over it the couvertiure of green
Arab achmardi! That hung down to his hooves, and was
embroidered on both sides with the fish. Thus Grigorss
rode his beloved steed—and it was all from dreams and
thanks to innate knowledge familiar to him—himself
well protected as to head, body, and leg, the sword at
hip-girdle, arm and hand in the strap of the shield—
thus, I say, he often rode Sturmi, together with other
blades, liegemen of the mistress, out of the city, accompanied by a carrier full of jousting-lances without
points. For, believe me, the lightness and half-friendli-
ness with which in winter the minnewar was carried
on, went so far that townsmen and besiegers offered
each other friendly jousts and the Lady Sibylla's knights
as well as the Burgundians, each side before the eyes of

the other, held mock tourney with blunt shafts, partly
for their own diversion and partly to give the other side
to think, at sight of their riding and thrusting skill. Thus
Grigorss won some early dreamed-of honour and the
applause of the foe.

Yes, it must rejoice me that such space and chance
were granted him to practise himself in actuality; for
I must wish that the purpose which sat so fixed and
mute in his heart might find success—since after all as
narrator I see all and know beforehand how horrible
things, hardly to be told or thought, grew out of his
success. If I did not see, in my unsuitable omniscience,
also beyond this horror and to the end, I should have
to wish that the lad, however sorry I would feel on his
account, had found security in death while carrying out
his programme—and to wish this I am tempted despite
all foreknowledge, because of the unspeakableness of
what is to come—though again I am aware that my
wishes would have no sense, since I know the story and
must tell how God to His greater glory let it fall out.
I would like only in all humility to indicate the conflicts
to which the soul of the teller of such a tale is prey.

Lo, through great sin, namely of his birth, and
through the hot striving to wash it away was my young
man driven into still more frightfulness. Much he read
in his tablet and indeed with tears—yes, it was with him
just as once on the island, if he showed himself stout and
of burning presence of mind in knightly sport, was yet
at the same time a careful and a dreri herte, Tristan le
preux, lequel fut ne en tristess, as Master Poitevin said,

shaking his head, when he saw him coming with wet eyes out of his chamber. For it was Grigorss's habit to shut himself up with his tablet, which he kept there, in order to read for the hundredth and thousandth time the circumstances of his birth: that he had his mother for his aunt and his father for his uncle and so to speak was brother to his parents, whom they bore in sin and to his inborn sin. His body was quite like the flesh of other human beings, was straight and well built, and yet from head to foot was a work of sin and shame. The offence of his birth forced from him bitter tears when it stood written again before his eyes, and greatly strengthed him in his silent purpose. He wanted to cast into the scale this young body composed all of sin, to wager it away in rash cast of the dice, and either die (which would, he felt, be quite right) or justify his perverse existence by freeing the land from the dragon. Yet that was not quite all.

For in his heart he wore, sanctifying even this heart likewise so formed of sin, the image of the woman whose voice rang so pure and ripe to him, so kindly reproached him for his rashness, so motherly had pleaded with him for himself. How did one obey such a command and give thanks for such a request? By sacrificing oneself for the mistress, or else conquering for her and freeing her from the dragon! The dragon was a man she abhorred, and a man, if also ridiculously younger than she, he also was. To fight with that other man against man meant hotly to fight not only for her but also over

her, and whether one thereby lost the body or conquered, through either one must win her favour in
measure as she felt repulsion from the other. Yes, I will
simply say all and here write down that Grigorss
thought: If he triumphed whom he hated, because he
coveted the woman, and if the hated one carried her
away, then in his forced embrace she would think of
him and call on him who had fought over her and for
her and so it would be victory in defeat. The cast of the
dice, he thought, would be a lucky throw in any case,
and more than his body of sin he could not lose.

But not that he therefore thought to grant his defeat.
Not at all, he thought to win the duel for his lady, and
when spring came, the lark mounted, the wild geese returned, and the white stork from the land of the Moors,
and when the news went round that Roger the Goat-
beard had got back to his besieging troops before half-
dead Bruges, the guest confided to his host his long-
cherished resolve to oppose the hairy one, cost what it
might, so soon as confident of victory he gave his challenge.

"That I would like to discourage," answered the
magistrate. "Believe me, I trust your courage as does
everybody else here now and confide in your honour.
But if you did cut them off splendidly that time on the
bridge and many times outside have proved yourself
the hail of the foe, yet I do not see how this undertak-
ing of yours is to prosper. True, you have courage,
skill, and a good seat and Sturmi is steady and supple

under you. But after all you are still slender and immature, and your experience in fighting is not equal to the Duke's, who at a tourney is as victorious a cockerel as in ladies' beds. Put the whim out of your head! Shall we look down from the walls in sorrow and shame when he drags you away as conqueror and you live henceforward as he wills?"

"That will never happen," Grigorss quickly broke in. "For never will I give him fyanze, rather win or die. But all else you say, about the tilt-yard and the bed, is more likely to confirm me in my purpose than to put me off it. It is now in the long run ennuyant for me, to fight for our lady as one among many. On a duel for her my mind runs, and there shall prove itself whether he does not fight better who stands for her freedom than he who in the battle thinks of her shame and violation."

"Ah, friend," sighed the Mayor, "the uttermost of shame it is not, to be the spouse of the King of Arelat and Upper Burgundy, and in some hearts there sticks the doubt whether the Duchess's affair is so without blame, when she absolutely will not give the land a duke and therefore keeps it under ban of this miserable minnekrieg."

"In my heart," answered Grigorss and put on his beautiful face, "her cause is sacred."

Then the Maire looked a while at the youth and if his eyes got blurred it was because in his thoughts the words "for" and "over" mingled strangely.

"I wish for you," he said at last, "this highflyer goat-beard may not resume his practice and not again issue his cartel."

"Your wish I ban," cried Grigorss, still with his beautiful face. And according to his ban so did it go.

For—how soon it was!—there came two horsemen under the walls, one with a trumpet he bellowed into, the other with the lion standard of Arelat and Burgundy, who shouted up that if the Duchess had still a knight bold enough to measure himself in single combat and tourney under the city walls against Roger her unconquered master, the next day, for all the burghers to look on and learn, he might come out and show himself; safe entry among the besiegers granted him and fair conditions of combat. To them, to their surprise it was vouchsafed that the knight would appear and hope with God's help to withstand the Duke.

The next morning before daybreak Grigorss heard early mass and then made ready like one going to the field: armour laid he on, and Master Poitevin, although with much head-shaking, himself assisted him to gird himself with harness, jamber, hood, helmet and harsenière, shield, sword, and tall lance, whose little pennant, like his cote armour, carried the fish, and his right hand in fingered steel gauntlet grasped the shaft, testing many times the firmness of his grip. During the arming Grigorss spoke thus to his aide:

"Be of good cheer and shake not your head all too much! The thing is, on the table of my life it stands written that I must confront the man, whether I conquer or fall. If I fall, what is that? Not so much de-

pends on me. This stronghold may go on holding out
against the Spitzbart as well as before I came. But if I
fall him, then is the land freed from the dragon and delivered from the wooing war. That is to be thought of.
The duke has the disadvantage of risking more than I,
but yet just on that account he is advantaged, for he
fights better who ventures more than the other. But
again he is less advantaged because he fights to snatch
and enforce our liege lady, but I for her honour. All in
all more advantage lies on my side than on his. Therefore
I hope with God's help to upset him, but have not, so
far as in me lies, aimed at his life. The greedy violence
of this turkey-cock's wooing is indeed repulsive and
makes him my deadly foe; but that he has considered
the possession of her the highest of all goods and worth
a war for so many years, for that I have again an understanding mind and cannot quite hate him to the
death."

"Ah, younker," answered his host, "rather hate him
with perfect fury, for that you need, to withstand his
mature and experienced skill in a brawl."

"I am conscious of my youthful instability in comparison with him," answered Grigorss, "and even think
it possible that the temptation to avoid and save my own
young life will overcome me when with terror I realize
his superiority. Yes, it might prove that I have rated my
manhood too high, that at his attack all my courage
might sink away, and out of sheer youngness I might
take to Sturmi's heels, in order at least to win a little
applause for my agility in running away."

"That would not look much like you," M. Poitevin opined.

"Like or no, one may in youthful panic do what is not like one. So I beg you, give heed to the gate, when I am on the field, place men behind it and keep it watchfully ready for my re-entry, whether I near it at the victor's pace or in the full flight of the fugitive."

"For that," promised the good host, "I will take care." And he did not cease to shake his head as the younker's horse was led before the door, this beloved little animal—I actually rejoice to see it again in battle array, well bridled, with chain mail and couvertiure, and how it proudly tossed its head and defiantly snorted. M. Poitevin folded his guest in his arms at farewell and said:

"God be with you, friend, all knightly hail, bonne chance! And as you said, that do: if you see you are not equal to him, avoid and show your skill in flight. The gate shall be ready and from laughing you will have a good share on your side."

"Very good, farewell, think kindly of me, in case I remain on the field," responded Grigorss. "There is no great danger, since I have two chances of return, either I strike him down or timely escape him."

With that he swung his armoured leg over Sturmi's back, flung his shield aloft, took the reins in his armoured hand, and rode out to the city and upon the trodden mead before it, under the eyes of innumerable citizens, men and women, crowding walls and battlements in their eagerness to see—rode calmly among the

Burgundians, who also came running en masse to see
how once more a vassal of the Duchess would come to
disgrace before their lord.

"Cock sparrow!" they called to him as they recognized the Knight of the Fish, "feeling your oats, young
colt! Wants to measure himself with Roger the Invin-
cible! What impudence! Can't you wait to find your
master? Better offer surety at once, the better for you!"

That Grigorss harkened to and rode on into the field,
directly towards the Duke's tent, until he saw him
coming, most knightly to behold. On a high-legged
black destrier armoured to the heels Sibylla's hardy
wooer rode, and over the steed's armour hung a couvertiure of red velvet. Upon it he sat, inured to victory,
he too all in iron, and flashes shot from his shield rim,
that was adorned with gems around the red-gold boss,
all bathed in flame. From it came the flashes. The helmet went over the redoubtable one's whole head, and
came out in front over his face, with eye-holes. (Grigorss's face however was free in his hauberk.) The
spear-shaft the fearsome one carried was a young tree
with the bark on, quite particularly grim to behold.

And then it was as though the foolhardy youth on
Sturmi could not bear the sight of his enemy, for as the
Spitzbart approached, he threw his animal around and
sprang back nearly the whole distance he had come, almost under the gate, while behind him came his glittering foe swinging his bark-covered lance and shout-
ing through his helmet: "Stand, milky-mouth, coward,

misfortunate worm! If you were rash enough to come out, then stop and take your punishment."

That caused a great laugh among the Burgundian knights and men. But Grigorss, turning back again, shouted:

"You are laughing, I suppose, at your Duke, who, it seems, does not know that one must take care in the mêlée for a long puneis? Blow the signal now that we may carry it out according to his will, without conditions and à outrance, until one of us can no longer fight!"

So then the trumpet sounded and the duel began.

My monkish heart has no part in such violent doings and knightly brawls, I do not like them at all, and were not the issue very strange and for the moment so happy but in the sequel so frightful, I would not even tell of it. Also I would definitely not fall into rhyme and rhythm, as did M. Poitevin in relating Grigorss's exploits. For that the set-to leaves my priestly feeling too cold. Anyhow everyone knows how it is held and what they do. They thrust the lance under their arms, flung their shields aloft, and in full career with great rattling and clanging ran at each other to a crashing encounter, that one might reach the other with the lance and knock him out of the saddle. Both failed. The lances splintered on shield and buckler, their pieces flew high in the air, among them the bark from Roger's tree, and nothing was achieved. Still sat Grigorss unshaken on Sturmi, just as firm on his black armoured steed the Duke! Little, a poet would say, were they unmindful of their swords! And how should they be, now their spears were gone? For the swords the moment was now come. Out of the broad sheaths they drew them and with them cut at each other, so that the blows rang out over the field and to the ears of the gapers on the walls, with a glowing and a spark-flying at the meeting of steel and iron. Truly, they were good alike, and several times was each half deafened from the ringing of his helmet whereon the other's sword had struck, the steeds danced and pranced round each other as their riders fought and sought to win from each other the advantage of the blows, now they stood sidewise, now forehead to forehead. But the Duke's onslaught seemed, just as his campions confidently trusted and the townsfolk feared, more powerful than that of his youthful opponent: slowly Grigorss avoided before his master-blows, always nearer the gate, and a moment came, frightful for those whose hopes were with the youth—he was disarmed! Yes, now was displayed the Duke's superior maturity; suddenly he struck the other's sword out of his hand, so that it flew away from him on a curve, and sheer exultation and yells of triumph burst from the Burgundians and loud wails from the townsfolk. But while the sword was still flying, something else happened, lightning-swift, which in all my aversion from man's pugnacity delights my soul, and which no one at once understood: Grigorss with his sword-free right hand in the iron glove seized the Spitzbart's steed by the bridle and in the same unconditional grip also seized his sword, which was still down from the victorious blow. He now held them both firmly, bridle and sword, and in the same trice Sturmi began with all the power of his dear, short, well-knit body to go backwards and to drag before him to the bridge and before the gate the lofty steed together with the Duke, who for all the world could not succeed in freeing his weapon from that absolute grip.

God, He may know whether the priceless animal had practised this manœuvre beforehand or whether in a moment it understood the guidance of its master's thighs, enough, it pulled, and Duke Roger, cursing through his helmet, might tug at the rein and at the same time spur his mare; thus she made only one pace forward, so that Sturmi also had to take one backwards—not further undesired by the animal. As for Grigorss, I still have in my mind how in the wrestling with his equally matched brother he would rather let his cranium be pressed in than be pushed out of his stance. So here, only much more unconditionally, and rather he would then have let Flann press his shoulder to the ground than that now he would have loosened his grip on sword and rein. The sword cut through the inner armour of the hand and into the blood, but not on that account did he let go; fending off with his good shield the blows which Roger with his own sought furiously to direct on his head and arm. And Sturmi tugged.

Brief was the general daze at this sight. Then the Duke's men with cries of fury dashed to his aid, and against them the manhood of the city flung itself through the gaping door so that on the bridge ensued one of the hardest grapples ever seen. A flung spear pierced through Grigorss's harsenière into the neck by his collar-bone so that sore wounded he was scarcely able to shake off the shot, and Sturmi too was bleeding in many places on his body. But now they were so near the gate that one wanted to shout to the Duke: "Dismount, man! Bid valet to thy captured sword that is in such an absolute grip and let yourself fall from your horse into the arms of your defenders!" But that the hero would not and could not do. Let go his sword, with which he had disarmed the popinjay? Sink from his steed like one defeated? No, never, never! And besides, he probably had not a clear look round on account of his helmeted visage and did not quite know what was happening to him. Ringing blows he dealt with his shield on the shield of his bleeding abductor. But soon there was quite another sort of noise: the creaking wings of the heavily armed gates, which fell behind horse and man and man and horse, and in their grooves the bolts ground home.

Not a few fighters from the city were shut out; they were likely slain. But of course they were only the lower ranks, and Roger of the pointed beard was taken.

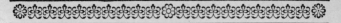

The Hand-kissing

IF only I could without reservation and heavy foreknowledge share the citizens' delirious joy, the air-filling
jubilation, the delight and thankfulness, when through
Grigorss's absoluteness the country was freed from the
dragon, the ravager was disarmed and lay bound in the
dungeon of the gate-tower! I would embrace the so
youthful victor and kiss stout Sturmi on the nose, but
in the first place the thought of all the horrors to come
keeps me back and in the second one might not embrace
Grigorss at all, for he was wounded by spear and sword,
his garb ran this time with his own blood, and he sank,
when the folk brought him home in triumph to his
lodge in the Mayor's house, unconscious from his
horse's back. Balsam and tendence did steed and rider
need, and they were given. But the citizens had much
else to do that day besides rejoicing and clapping their
thighs; for the outraged foe did not fail an assault in
force to recover their royal Duke, and up till evening
the furious attacks went on: with thundering beams
they rammed the gate; towers high as the walls, equipped
with fighters, they rolled across the filled-in moats up to

the walls, set up storming-ladders and hurled masses of stone and iron into the fortress. Many a burgher and many a Burgundian lost his life. At evening the storm died down, and as the citizens let the besiegers know that if they raised hand again against the town the life of their Lord Duke would at once be forfeit, the attack was not renewed.

Negotiations were going on, it was said, between Flaundres-Artoys and Arelat-Burgundy on the subject of abjuring the ancient feud and ending the wooing war; and for so long those outside might well keep quiet. Very accurate was the news, for Roger the Goat-beard found himself faced with the choice of being shortened by a head or voiding the land and its strong-holds, drawing back within his borders and paying to boot penalties and ransom-money for ten years a shrewdly reckoned sum in payment of all the damage his minne-obstinacy had made him guilty of. He gave proud answer, if only after inward struggle. He had, he said, wooed knightly for the lady's favour many a year and made every effort to win her heart. When however she shut herself in against his offer, whose good faith he had proved in every way, and at the end sent into the field against him a young trickster, whom he had eas-ily defeated but who then in defiance of all the rules had dragged him into this trap, so now he was insulted, withdrew his offer and rejected her hand, without leav-ing her hope that he would ever trouble himself about her more. He was quite ready to take abjuration oath and void the country, and he was rich enough to pay

damages for his wooing without having to abate anything on that score. But the woman, so he scornfully
subjoined, instead of his own noble person might take
the young trickster into her marriage bed instead,
whom she had sent out against him to shame by low
cunning the sacred custom of single combat.

He knew not what monstrous thing he was suggest-
ing in his scorn and calling down as it were from heaven
—or rather up from hell. If he had known may be it
would have cooled his heart. But I believe even he as a
Christian would have been horrified to make such a
suggestion however mockingly. One did not need to
worry about the flourishes with which he tried to make
his submission more tolerable. It was the submission
which counted; and on the cathedral square, in solemn conclave, by Burgundian worthies who had been
admitted within, with the blessing of the clergy and the
"Yea, yea, so be it!" of all the folk, the oath of peace
was signed, in presence of the Duchess and in presence
also of Grigorss the deliverer, who, with his neck still
bandaged and hand still plastered, in this hour saw again
for the first time her of whose sacred ripeness and goodness he carried the sound and image always in his heart.
And she saw him again too and rejoiced in his honour,
for be it only said that before her too had agreeably
hovered his young image the whole of the time; further, that tender concern, such as life had never yet
taught her till now, visited her for his wounds and pallor and at the same time swelling pride that he had so
unconditionally served for her. Scarcely, I say, did she

heed the ceremony, for she knew that after it the youth
would be set before her up at the castle for her to thank
him; and the woman, I confess, rejoiced at the thought.

I confess: she stood in the half-circle of her ladies
and looked at him down the length of the carpeted
hall, whose beams were supported by pillars with coats
of arms on them, as he approached her with graceful
gait, on slim legs in clinging silk; and of his graceful gait
too, I confess, she was proud. Good God, he looked like
her as he stepped before her, for he looked like his father, Wiligis, and so why should he not have looked
like her? But this likeness appealed to her quite differently, namely only as charm, which pleased her and if
she thought of likeness at all, it was only with reference
to the lost one and not to herself. Could not a young
man remind her of the brother-beloved and so move her
soul without her being obliged to fall into extravagant
speculations? But that she was so proud of him, even of
his walk, that ought in my view have given the woman
to think.

He knelt and she spoke:

"Knight, I bade you rise when you knelt before me
at the sacred place, because all honour there was due to
the exalted Mother of All. Today and here all honour
is yours and again I bid you rise. Were I not a woman,
and were you not so young—so young the blood you
poured out for us—truly, it were fitting I knelt before
you, for miracles have you performed for the land of
Duke Grimald and his daughter. Where is the hand

that unflinching and firm held fast bridle and sharp
sword till the malefactor lay in bonds? Give it to me
that my lips may thank it!"

And she took his right hand, the one still poorly
healed, which he had hid in his girdle, and carried it to
her lips.

That was not good at all. The ladies-in-waiting found
it extravagant and I am still sharper in my judgement.
For why was she drawn to kiss his hand? Because he
had done deliverance with it, or was it because he reminded her of Wiligis, who had arch-sinfully caressed
her body with his? I say to you that the woman did not
prove herself enough, and between gratitude and tenderness did not distinguish with due care. For the former she had just ground—so just that because of it she
found examination superfluous whether the gratitude
might not be but a pretext for the tenderness. She was
a pious princess and kept many night-watches; but in
spiritual discrimination she was to seek. To kiss a
wounded member is for the sake of Christ's martyr-
wounds worthy of praise; but to be on one's guard
whether it happens out of humility and love for the ailing or out of pleasure in kissing, that is but Christian
fine feeling and therein the woman lacked.

Grigorss stood, the pallor from his wounds over-
redded with his blood.

"Lady, what do you? This touch will burn on my
hand and constrain it to noble deed, that I swear, all my
life long! But wherein have I deserved this homage? Of

sin is our flesh compact. For what then is it good, save
to fling it in the scale and give it for innocence oppressed?"

She cast down her eyes, so beautifully belashed, nor
did she raise them again to him as in a half-whisper,
shaping the words only with her outer lips, she said:

"Children of sin are we all. But to me it often seems
as though a contradiction were in the world between
sinfulness and high courage, between the wretchedness
of the flesh and its pride. If it be corrupt, how then can
it gaze free and bold and brace itself to such a noble
gait that it fills with pride even the beholder? The
spirit is ware of our unworth, yet unconcerned with
its knowledge Nature considers herself worthy. Your
words were those of a Christian knight. But even between word and deed to me there seems to yawn a
contradiction. Wherein does the humility and abasement of the Christian draw the courage, nobility, and
presumption of the knight?"

"Lady, all bravery and every daring emprise to which
we dedicate ourselves, and on which we set our all and
uttermost, springs only from the knowledge of our
guilt, springs from the fervid yearning to justify our
lives and accordingly before God to redeem a little of
our debt of sin."

"So then you fought for God's and your justification?"

"I fought, lady, for you and your honour. Unjustly
do you distinguish one from the other."

"You fought miraculously. Will you say true and

tell me whether it was the Duke's skill that struck the sword from your hand?"

"Not quite. I tell you true. It had to happen, with the help of his skill, that I might be able to do what I had set myself."

"You would well show by your audacity how one wins the match after sacrificing the Queen?"

"No, lady, but I had thought that the prisoner would be worth more to you than the dead."

"So young and already so statesmanly! You did not hate him at all then?"

"With my whole soul I hated him. But I would not pander to my hate. I know not whether I could have killed the robber. It might be, in a moment so all-collected as that when I seized sword and bridle. Still I was drawn into this fight not for my hatred but for you."

"Wrongly, it seems to me, do you separate the one from the other. The man whom you spared had marked me down for violence and shame."

"To possess you, madame, was this man's goal. He fought for you, and did the same in the duel with me your knight, whom no duel might make to forget he fought only for you."

"Wisely this time do you distinguish and yield fairly to your antagonist the right to the higher goals. As shrewdly as heroically have you fought and taken the dragon who fought over me. Drawing its free breath the land thanks you, to which through you new life is given, and kisses the hand of the extraordinarily firm grip. It will, I think, be eager for new holding so soon as healed. This fine adventure is to you, I would guess, one among many. You wander onward on your knightly service?"

"Should I, lady, forfeit your homage if it seemed to me as though this state were the foreordained goal of my errantry; if it were about my heart as though I should remain and dedicate my whole life to your service?"

"How could I, knight, refuse you anything? I am altogether favourably touched by your wish. So stay. Indeed you must no longer dwell in the mairie. Your place is at my court. I raise you to be my seneschal, confident that none will chide me because I clothe your youth in this office. Your service dignifies your youth and strikes down all objection. There is no elevation which your merit would not justify. Kneel not, I wish it not. Take now your leave. In my train I will see you again."

And she passed, among her women, who followed her.

This conversation one must imagine as very swiftly carried on, that was peculiar to it. In but few minutes, half-whispered, without pause for thought, it ran off. Before witnesses it was held and yet was like a hasty appointment in private, at which the eyes oftener avoided than sought and there was no break between sentence and answer nor between two sentences, rather the words fell swift, clear and low, until the "Take now your leave. In my train I will see you again."

Sibylla's Prayer

THE LAND breathed free, new life was given to it by Grigorss's firm unflinching hand. On the part called Rousselaere and Thorhout, towards the sea, once more flourished the useful flax, it was green upon peacefully tilled fields, and again the peasants in their rude joy danced in the taverns. New flocks fed on the slopes of Artoys rich in pasturage and gave wool for good cloths. Free were towns and castles, cleansed from the filthy foe, the damages repaired, and Sibylla, Grimald's child, held court at Beaurepaire, where she had spent her childhood and her sinful youth. Hither, whence the sweet brother had to go in crusade and she herself, the blest-unblest, depart to hide herself in Sieur Eisengrein's water-castle; hither irresistibly she had come; for in all of us is the wish to return to the has-been and to repeat it, that if it were once unblest it may now be blessed.

Grigorss the knight was her seneschal. No grumbling was there in her retinue against his elevation, and when he, of equal rank with Sieur Feirefitz the major-domo, at her side paced to table, everyone was pleased. For now the princess seemed more animated, not so aus-

terely confined to watching and praying, no longer so
averse and strange to the joys of the court, song and
lute-playing and light conversation in hall and lawny
courtelage. That certainly came from the happy end to
the minnewar, and the easing of her spirits after such
long distress. But whether it was thence or whencever
else, a hope came to court and country, which for long
had not stirred because of the harsh disinclination of the
Duchess, and became the subject of discussion. For now
the land's wisest and best came together and consulted
on what was to be wished or at all events to be hoped:
to each was the word in turn and each with emphasis
said the same as the one before him.

At Arras it was, in the lofty hall, there consulted and
resolved, as I say, the counts of castles, gentlemen of
rank, and heads of cities. For now the word went round,
this country late so full of need had mastered its mis-
fortune and once more flourished in peace; yet to the
careful remained the care, and doubt gave them distress
lest there might be the same again and some other impudent enforcer come coveting their dear region and
bring it to shame. So great a land was ill guarded from
criminal aggression by a woman, be she the worthiest of
all devotion and homage, and if it had a master and
duke, long wanting, yes, if the lady had a lord, whose
mere existence would nip in the bud another minnekrieg, who with drawn brows would lay hand on sword
at threat of the slightest abuse, how different, in faith,
would be the state of things! True, one knew, and took
it reverently to heart, that their liege lady for God's

love was minded never to have a man. But they, the
land's best subjects, granting all respectful understanding were yet unanimously of opinion that she did wrong
therein and wrongly interpreted God's will. Ill would
befall them if she left so rich a land to perish without
heirs to the kingdom. Besides, marriage and wedded
state made the best life that God has given man; but
how much more in a case like this! To bring this before their mistress as decision and as fervent plea of the
whole country and the best subjects in it, and to sup-
plicate permission for the proposal, was without contradiction or abstention adopted by acclamation, with
the addition that it should be left solely and freely to
their lady, and without conditions, whom she should
take for her lord and duke.

Thus ran the will of them all, and if I study it, especially this last addition, which might make one suppose
it was the custom for a princess not to let herself be
wooed but herself woo and contrary to chaste feminine
habit point out whom she would have, I cannot avoid
the supposition that the thoughts of the best in the land
went a definite route in their proposal, that they wanted
to build their princess a golden bridge, and also that
Sibylla could not fail to recognize it. According to state
practice she was acquainted beforehand with the contents of what they wished in all frankness to present to
her and it rested with her to refuse the offer. She granted
it however, in her better state, of course reserving her
opinion. But how much the granting was calculated to
strengthen the hope!

Before the stool of the mistress stood the best of the land, and one of them read the accord almost literally as I gave it above. Then he let the parchment fall and looked on the ground, Sibylla too and in the stillness my sharp ear heard her heart beat—the best of the land heard it too, I think; they all raised their eyes a little, slanting, corner-wise, and listened to the beat. Then came the voice of the woman in ripe and ringing cadence, as they were used to hear it. She did not fail to realize, she said, the seriousness and importance of the proposal and still less their loyal concern for the welfare of the land and the destiny of her house, from which it proceeded. Thoughtfully and compliantly she accepted the advice, in so far as that she found it worthy of consideration. Still, it ran too contrary to the picture of her life and her intent to spend it as God's maid, without a husband; it passed too idly over the inherent difficulties it made her, of finding in the Christian world a consort actually of equal birth with herself, for her to give a decision at once. She must ask from the land a period of consideration, seven weeks she would say, had not the appeal borne so strong a stamp of urgency. So she would content herself with seven days. On the eighth the noble and reverend gentlemen might appear before her to hear what she had decided and as well prepared to hear a nay as a yea. For she was showing great graciousness even to consider it.

Thus dismissed, the petitioners took leave of their lady. But even after they went her heart throbbed high with anxious bliss. She smiled, shrank from her smile,

expunged it sternly out of her face; tears came in her
eyes and when one ran down her cheek she had to smile
again. Such confusion the proposal she received had
caused her. Into the castle chapel she hastened, there
no one saw her and there her heart could flow out in
prayer; not to the masculine Essences of the Godhead
but to the Mother, the august Bride of Heaven; thither
flowed all her trust, as with God Himself she stood not
very well, on account of her sin and afterwards of her
defiance.

In front of the stool where she knelt hung a beautiful
picture of the Blessed Virgin from a good school; it
showed how she heard and in sweet humility received
from the winged messenger the miraculous message. In
a wooden chamber she sat, in flowing robe, behind her
little head a gloria and between the lifted little hands a
book, wherein in all artlessness she was reading, half re-
luctantly turning her head as though she would rather
go back to her quiet occupation than pay heed to the
curly-haired angel who swayed half-kneeling in the
doorway in full-draped white robe and blue mantle,
pointing upwards with a finger of his left hand, while
in the right hand had it in writing: a rolled-up sheet
whereon stood written that which his little red mouth
revealed to the maid. But she looked with drooping lids
down to the floor between him and the book in demure
piety, as though she would say: "I? How so? That cannot be. True, you have indeed wings and have it written down, and you came without opening the door, but
I was sitting here at my book without the faintest am-

bitious thought and in not the slightest degree prepared
for such a visitation."

At this sweet picture Sibylla looked up from her stool
and prayed:

"Maria, mild Queen, now help me, holy Mægden,
sweet one, Bride of God, counsel and aid the sinner, of
thy frail sex a member who quite bemused is by the
suggestion they made her a weak woman, so flees and
prays to thee for thy great favour that thou wilt save
her and bear with her in all her weakness and unknow-
ingness; of Christendom thou the trust, chosen vessel of
Holy Ghost, which He so strangely did elect for won-
der-honour to select out of thy womb to manifest the
man of all on earth the best, namely God's self, who
thee for His Mother planned, that is full hard to understand!

"Sancta Maria, gratia plena, the heavenly host sing all
thy praise, praises thee the cherubin, lauds thee the ser-
aphin, all the host of holy angels standing before God's
countenance, from first beginning, apostles, prophets,
all God's holy saints, who praise thee without stint, O
purest Mægden, who bore to God the Son, who was
Himself and in Thy womb went in, oh dreadest wonder!

"Mild Mary, gracious Maria, sweetest Maria, benedictus fructus ventris tui! Stella maris art thou called
from the star that guides from far the weary bark to
land, thus likewise hadst thou planned the way to me
of the so lovely boy in whom I have such joy by day
and night since he me healing brought with his firm-

holding hand and saved the land. Hardly can I say how sweet he is to me. Gladly, Lady, that is sooth, would I kiss him on the brow, and if he joy did show, then on the mouth!

"Gracious Maria, loveliest Maria, holiest of women, on whom such strange lot fell that out of all womenkind to thee He had a mind; now poor I thy counsel seek, oh understand how 'twas with me when they the offer made wherefor my heart does laugh, for now so glad I'd be to raise the boy to me, lord of his lady to be, for him 'twould well become. Alas, 'twixt him and me there lies the sin I gave me to with him whom God hath snatched away. Then would I in God's sight no woman be, no more, no more at all, and that I now so deep withinne do rue by power or minne I bear unto the boy. But sweet Ste Mary, say, oh, is it now vouchsafed to me once more on earth in bliss to be, in womanhood my joy to find, if I my sin to his immaculateness bind? And yet my heart of doubt is full and fearful if I dare; now to my spirit lend thy light, thou knowst in anguish sore, and me despite my guilt unto God's grace restore. For thou art of the Highest child, as are we creatures all, and yet art thou His mother mild and thus He all must do that she doth say, and her obey. Somewhat thou ow'st to me, with woman's guile I said, that thou with God shouldst aid since He for sinner's need in thy pure womb came in and thee His mother made. Had never no one sin committed, ne'er had been what God with thee hath done, nor hadst thou everlasting praises won. Lady, forgive that I jest in my agony. And also when

I see the boy so young, for him my heart is wrung, I
being of riper years, in love and suffering deeply versed,
yet praises be to God I still am able, and rule besides
with master hand o'er all the land. Surely it flattereth
him that I him favour show, for that he doth not know
my sinne, yet can he minne, me with heart and senses
woo, I ask, and how distressful is my heart because I
know full well how hot the blood of youth doth lust
for virgin woman's flesh. Would he so hotly lust after
my still unwearied breast, for only him I find of my
bed worth, or grant of equal birth! Of his skin I'd fain
be glad, yet hear no owlets' screams about my bed, nor
Hanegiff up to the beams howl fearsomely and loud.

"To my help be invoked, Maria, thou truest maid,
come to my aid and with God intercede for me and
the so loved lad, thou of the highest Child, mother and
bride!"

Thus Sibylla's prayer to the image above her. I think
that at the end it seemed to her as though the pious
downward look of the Chosen One was visited by a
quite tiny fine benign smile on the little mouth. For
when after seven days the highest in the land stood
again before her stool, to arrive at a decision on their
offer, she said that she had made the wish and will of
the land her own, and she recognized it must have a
protector, master, and duke. Therefore she had acqui-
esced, resolving to say valet to her god-maidenhead and
become the wedded maid of a husband. Such was her
decision. The consequences, immediate and remote, followed of themselves and were no matter of her finding

or of any choice. For if the land was to have a duke, it could only be he who with his unflinching firm grasp had freed it from the dragon and fought for her in a duel, for the sake of her honour. That was Grigorss, at present her seneschal, the knight from afar, brought here to land by favour of God and His mother. To him she gave her hand, in order that he, if it please him, should by it mount the steps to her, to her side as goodman of her house and princely consort, in fulfilment of the ferventest wish of the redeemed land.

Thus she spoke to the messengers, surrounded by her whole court, and by her lovely hand Grigorss mounted to her under the canopy and turned his grave young face next hers to the hall and to all Christendom. That should he not have done, much, much better in mild penance have remained in the abbey with the Father who found him, my friend the Abbot. For deeper was he to plunge than the few carpeted steps were high. But now before him the swords sprang out of their sheaths, the knees were bent, and the rafters rang with the shout:

"Long live Gregor, victor in the minnewar, protector of the land, our lord and Duke!"

The Wedding

THE SPIRIT of story-telling is a communicative spirit, gratified to lead his readers and listeners everywhere, even into the solitude of the characters spun out of his words and into their prayers. Still he knows how to be silent too, and sparingly to leave out what to make present seems all too mistaken to him, and whatever he may keep in the shadow of wordlessness, events leave no doubt that in the time between there were word, presentness, and scene. State matters like these which ended with the homage to Duke Gregor are not events which could run off otherwise than in the way they in fact did; they are not entered upon at random or without due preparation. That worldly wisdom knows. Instead everything is discussed and arranged beforehand, and Sibylla could not have offered in public hand and crown to her deliverer, lest he scorn them both. Between her prayer to the Virgin and her public decision in answer to the country's request a private conversation must have taken place between the two, which youth and maturity carried on with each other in brief words and at the end, God help them, no longer only in words;

in which the grammatical question of "for" or "over" once more played its role, wherein the "for" came into its own by mutual, hot confession.

There may be some to chide me that I banish this scene into the darkness and do not grant it presentness, for much dangerous sweetness and subtle heart-searching might doubtless be wrung from it. But in the first place the portrayal of love-scenes is not suitable to my station or my habit, and in the second I like better to see Gregor's eyes in the austere young face watching with that unusual calmness of his the movements of an adversary than clouded by sweet unmanning love. And in the third place everything that was said there, sighed, confessed, and tenderly performed, rested on such a frightful, diabolically conceived misunderstanding and false interpretation of that which drew the one to the other that I will not be present; and in consequence you too will see only unclearly through a veil of tears of shame and anguish how she held his head between her two hands, and he, his mouth close to hers, for the first time confessing breathed her name, and she breathed his into his breath, in mutual ravishment, saying: "So lovest thou me, my darling from afar, thou precious, dearest one, so close to me since first I saw thee." And their lips sank into each other, in a long, long silence, a delusion blissful as contrary to all sense.

So I leave it out, leave it unuttered, in darkness; to deal with it I should be unskilled. Such was their betrothal—heyday, the wedding followed hard upon. Hey nonny, hey bonny! Trumpets announced the joyous

tidings through the whole land, that Flaundres-Artoys
had once more a lord and duke; mirth and jollity out
of all bounds, dancing in the streets, fireworks, feasting
and drunkenness, of all that enough, in town and village, and the fountains ran wine by the hour. On
Chastel Beaurepaire the marriage took place in great
splendour: guests, more than five hundred, who in part
camped in tents at the foot of the lofty citadel, were
invited from near and far, they did themselves well at
fifty tables, constantly laden by squires and pages with
platters of beef and venison and fat pork, also sausages
and geese, fowl, pike, barbel, trout, burbots, and crabs.
Blithe with much wine they held the bridal procession,
torches before, through all the halls: then Grigorss
sought Sibylla home, and crackling brands lighted them
into their chamber and they became man and wife.

Why not? I desperately ask. He was a man and she
a woman and so they could become man and wife, for
that is all that Nature cares about. My spirit cannot find
itself in Nature; it rebels. She is of the Devil, for her
indifference is bottomless. I would like to challenge her
and ask her how she manages, how she can be capable
of wreaking and working on a decent youth just as
usual, in a case like this, making him revel like a mad-
man at the breasts where he had fed and distent with
pride revisit the womb that bore him. To such an objection Nature, whom some call mother and goddess, may
reply, it is his ignorance, not she, lets the young man so
behave. But there the lady goddess lies, for it is precisely
she who is at work, under cover and shelter of igno-

rance, and if she had but one living spark of decency
would she not feel outraged at the ignorance and hold
her hand, instead of making common cause with it and
by dint of it to license the youth? This she does out of
an indifference so bottomless that it is deeper than ignorance for it is her very self. Yes, Nature is all one,
even to herself; how otherwise could she consent to see
her own direction, her own time and procreation turn
the wrong way, making a man born of a woman beget
not forwards in time but backwards into the mother-
womb, rousing up to himself descendants whose faces,
so to speak, are turned the wrong way?

Fie upon Nature and her indifference! Of course one
may say that without it, and supposing that Nature had
set her face against such ignorance, Grigorss would
have found himself in an awkward and unknightly situation; and this, again, I cannot wish for him. I do not
and will not know why Sibylla in her private prayer
had been concerned about his feelings. They were certainly highly exultant and he rejoiced in the ripeness
of his mate as much and heartily as she revelled in his
youth. In short they were very happy, not otherwise
can one express or report it, utterly and entirely happy,
with body and soul, on the night and many nights and
days, a blissful ducal pair they were, one might well call
them Joidelacourt, the joy of the court as once Grimald's
and Baduhenna's lovely children. For their joy—I speak
but according to the truth—lighted up everything
around them, its reflection lay smiling upon every face,
like sunshine it lay upon all the land, while as for that

which one calls, speaking generally and in regular and
proper connections, blessing of children and descendants, for that too Nature, working with entire indifference, took care: the Lady Sibylla was promptly in good
hope, her body, that had lain fallow as many years as
her consort was old, rose high and higher; and a scant
nine months after they had been lighted into the bride-
chamber she came down, in quite natural and moderate
pains, of a maid, whom they named Herrad. The babe
departed somewhat from the immediate pattern, being
not of foreign ivory pallor but white and apple-red,
like her forebear from the mother's side, the departed
Lady Baduhenna, and in her way very nice. That she
had her head on the wrong way, nobody saw.

Certainly the rejoicing would have been still greater
if a male heir and future protector had at once been
vouchsafed to the land. But on the other hand the be-
getter himself was still so future-young that in a manner
of speaking he himself substituted for the descendant
still owed by fate; and if Sibylla, more advanced in
years, showed herself a proper breeder and fount of
life, her consort was a Duke whom all Christendom
might envy. Often he sat as judge in settling disputes
and domestic feuds, and since in the cloister he had
studied de legibus, about which never a lord before had
troubled himself, he was a better judge than ever sat in
judgement and held Thing, bosom friend of the right,
therewith mild and mindful of wise satisfaction for all
and sundry. His arm, that had conquered the savage
wooer, was feared round about, none made war on a

land that stood under the protection of a lord of such absolutely firm-holding hand; while to break the peace which they perforce granted him came not in Duke Grigorss's thoughts. He might probably, counting on the gift native to him of pulling himself together beyond the usual bourne, have been inclined to conquest and tempted to make subject more land than belonged to him. In God's name, however, he forbore, kept measure, and asked no more than that what was his own should serve him.

So passed three years. In the third, in sign of the happiness she enjoyed at the side of her young consort, the Mistress Sibylla was again in good hope.

Jeschute

I THINK I have, though privately in despair, sufficiently praised the well-being and bliss of the young pair. The moment has come to tell the whole truth by setting bounds to the praise-singing. A shadow fell across their joy, it came from both sides, his and hers, unseen by men, kept and known only to the two, each for himself, for each believed the shadow came from him. They shared a secret of sin and guilt which each in all sweet intimacy kept from the other. That was the shadow and the darkening.

Sibylla in silent anguish kept from her beloved that she had once shared unsanctioned love with her dearest brother and that to the departed one she had borne a child for whom there had been no place on earth. A body of sin she offered to the pure one in each embrace, with bliss indeed and yet in torment, with shame and anguished conscience. Her bliss, that was sin's hope of bathing itself white in purity, her craving for purification through the pure. The agony and shame, that was the poor sin's fear of God, lest it merely sully the pure and bring it to shame through contact with her. Often

Sibylla wept alone in her shame in face of the pure one whom she had bound to her sin; yet she carefully concealed her tears from everyone and in especial from the beloved, the only one whom she could love since the loss of her sweet brother. So he saw not the marks of her tears, nor the affliction which but made her passion the more ardent.

He had his own cross, if even so it was the same as hers, and Tristan the dreri herte he remained in all the good fortune of his lot and his wedded bliss. Had he not set forth on his quest to find his sinful parents, to fall at their feet and pardon them his existence, that God might pardon them all three? Instead of which he had become Duke in the first spot he came to, whither his voyage in the fog had brought him, and had indeed won a wife of sweet maturity, whom he had at once felt so near to his own nature, Sibylla, image of heaven's Queen, yet made for earthly joy, so that childlike reverence mingled strangely with male ecstasy in her arms. In her arms, on her gentle breast he enjoyed perfect blessedness, the sweet security of the nursing babe, and no less mighty male delight.

Thus from the horrible may perfection flower, as in the seclusion of the cloister I reflect. Truly in Grigorss's married joys my monkish state enters only by dint of spiritual courage and on account of the misery which dwelt with it, with him as with her, like the worm in the rose. For alas, he deceived her, the pure and exalted one to whom he had been lifted up, he hid from her who he was, who had fought for and won her, to whom

she had given her faith, namely a goodly-shapen monster. A cheater was he, who hid from her that he was a
foundling, swum hither on the billows and bred up out
of Christian piety, a son of sin, whose seemingly sound
body she should never have caressed since in truth it
consisted wholly of sin. True, he had cast it in the balance, this body of sin, in the fight with the dragon, but
he had known beforehand that he would triumph,
thanks to his gift of concentrating his power, and in the
duel had won the woman who now bore him little
Herrads, never dreaming that they were the fruit of sin
on the father's side, seed of inherited guilt, grandchil-
dren of evil. How could he dare to beget little Herrads
with his body and smuggle them into a princely house
whose head he now was—poor little bastard born of
innocence and vice! Thus he was careworn even unto
tears.

All this he concealed from everyone, in especial from
his wife, who thought him happier than herself; he concealed his care as he hid his tablet, which he kept ever
by him and read again and again. I have already said
that never a tablet was so read as this. In his own chamber, where he was alone, there was its secret place, high
up in a nook in the wall, where one could shove aside
the wooden panelling: he could just reach it with outstretched arm if he stood on tiptoe to open the almost
invisible slide and take out his tragic treasure, the
dowry that went with him in the cask, this jewelled
object whereon stood written all his unallowable connections. With it he sat or knelt on the little bench and

held his being up before his eyes: how he was indeed of high but horrible birth, his father his uncle, his mother his aunt. Read it over and over, beat his breast and bewailed the lamentable origin of his flesh. For his parents he prayed, whom he pictured as touchingly and uniquely lovely, since they had so sinned with each other, and whom he had not sought out but used his gifts to free this land and win it for himself along with the sweetest wife—or rather the wife along with the land. For himself he prayed too, with many a contrite heavenward look, begged God for pardon for his life and that he hid his secret, lay with the pure one and was Duke of the land—a very good one indeed, as all said, but certainly so good a one only because he so urgently needed to be. For little Herrad he prayed too, whom he scarcely dared to kiss because he had given her his sinful blood, and not less contritely for the new little fruit in Sibylla's receptive womb.

Almost every morning, quite early, when he left his wife's side and was safe from disturbance he did this reading and performed this penance in his room. He entered forthrightly as the proud upstanding youth that he was, and like the penitent from the whipping-chamber, in such figure went he ever out of it. That did not remain unseen.

Hearken now: among the base retinue at the castle was a maid, Jeschute by name, good for naught save bed-making, sweeping up, and strewing sand; but a creature quick of eye and tongue, more than inquisitive, better said, avid, and by Nature formed to get to the

bottom of anything strange that others do not see, to
which, however, when one saw it one would say "Well,
well!" and "How so?" and "One must look into that
privily, the little heart might discover something tick-
lish and exciting and revel in bringing it to light." That
sort of thing she spied out with sparkling eyes, running
her tongue round the parted lips. With the mistress she
might sometimes chatter when she shook up the marriage bed or made the fire, rolled on her tongue the
stupidest and basest twaddle about everyday life, earn-
ing a laugh; she might very likely prattle what she
should not, matter she had come on by devious ways;
without getting much thanks for it, more to amuse her
lady and perhaps also out of pleasure in initiating high-
born innocence into the under sides of things and soil-
ing it a bit thereby.

The head-shaking and blushes of her lady, half-
laughing but with frowning brow, that tickled her to
the core; for since the sovereign did not forbid her jab-
bering she must have only pretended disgust and had
nothing against letting herself be thus a little soiled.

Jeschute's burning curiosity would of course have
had ground to spy on the mistress herself and her more
private life, the trace of tears which she sometimes surprised. But the wanton did not pay them heed, or at
most only in connection with similar spyings which
concerned the sweet master Grigorss, the young lord;
about him her inquisitive and lustful looks after the
striking thing to be ferreted out were quite otherwise
occupied. With him in mind she stole cat-footed, in

wide circles, feather duster in hand, and gogled after
him out of the corner of her eye, or leered with drooping head; so lost in greedy spying that her tongue no
longer ran round outside her lips but stayed motion-
less, fixed and stiff, in one corner. When she saw him
but not he her, that was a joy. Remote from her wish
or hope was to draw his eye on a slattern like her,
rather ugly than agreeable, her unattractiveness at most
enlivened by prickling curiosity and urge to pry—and
he a blissful lord, provided at night with the loveliest of
wives. And still it sat sweetly round her heart like
minne dream when unseen she prowled after him; for
it looked to her as though not everything went well,
in order, cleanly and regularly in the soul of the good
young man with the manly, youthful mien, as though
there were a secret shame and sore, of which it must be
simply lovely to air the cover and pull it away.

Why waste words? Jeschute got behind his prayers
and penances. She saw, at first prowling by chance,
then by lurking again and yet again, how in the morning he went into his room like a lord and after an hour
came out red-eyed and looking like one who has
scourged himself. She sprang noiseless to the door
when he next went in, and eagerly put her eye to a
crack in the panel, long since noted by her and secretly
somewhat enlarged; much view it did not afford, still
a little, she could see how he took a thing out of the
wall and did penance before it and beat his breast, reading secrets from the secret thing, in the delusion that
no one saw.

Was not that a spying sweet as love? Away she sprang, ran through halls and passages, forced herself to slacken her pace, so as not to be out of breath, and entered into the most noble bride-chamber; there sat the mistress, plaiting her hair and singing a song the while, to the maid giving no heed. And Jeschute went to her bed-making, industriously beat up the pillows, and spoke to them:

"Yes, yes, little pillows, you silken cuissins, you lordly soft ones! I shake you and plump you up after your pressure, but you betray to Jeschute naught of all you have to tell: of secret tears that trickle into you, of sighs from high-born breast, which you nightly smother lest the dear one hear. . . ."

Then she gogled sidelong at her mistress, to see whether she had understood. But she had not, she combed and sleeked her hair and paid no heed. So the wench began again and talked sotto voce to the pillows:

"Oh, yes, ah, no! Naught you confide to the maid, noble head-cuissins, which I beat and plump, nothing of your secrets, of bitter salt wætnesse which you, I must suspect, have drunk in the silent night, of the sighs from deepest breast, which a blissful young mouth secretly breathed into you when the beloved slept, hidden, unbidden. . . ."

Now Sibylla did listen and asked:

"What fablest thou, slut, at thy work?"

But Jeschute twitched her shoulders as though starting violently for fear and answered stammering:

"Naught, naught, sweet mistress! For God's love, naught did I say! To the cushions I spoke, the lordly soft ones, here under my hands; I swear not to you, how would I come to be so bold? I am horrified that you should have listened and it made me jump. You have listened to me unaware where I was alone with my make-believe. One should never listen to people when they think they are alone, one reaps only sorrow. But truly when God purposes it so and makes us to be listeners of their privacy, then He must of course mean that we should learn the grief."

"But of what grief then pratest thou, thou thing?"

"Of a secret one, lady, hidden from all the world, and truly from the common world so it should be. But hidden also from you? That is not just to you, and surely God wills it not."

"Listen, Jeschute, as prattler I know thee well, but now I believe thy mind has somewhat gone astray."

"That may well be, sweet one, august one. I am but a poor, weak thing, and to get to the bottom of a grief, by God's doing, that may well take the senses of such a poor thing."

"Who then bears the grief?"

"Ah, God, you ask that, blessed lady, because you heeded me all unsuspecting. What would the maid not give that you had not heeded! And still it urges upwards out of my breast like a cry to you: take care!"

"Of what?"

"Of what? Ask rather of whom? Nay, ask not!"

"Of whom then, fool!"

"Now you ask truly, of whom, and I am to tell. Never will I say it, never! And yet must out with it, for the sake of your happiness. Of the sweet lord Duke, your spouse."

"Of Duke Gregor! So forsooth I do not give him care and wedded tendance enough? In thy opinion I do not read his wishes from his eyes?"

"Oh, lady mistress, rightly mock you at the poor stupid maid. Mock me, slap my face, till my cheek burn, if I dared to venture such an idea. And so it is clear: you share his secret, you know his sadness, for which he so sorrows and does penance when no one sees him, you know all and only seem not to know."

Sibylla's lips were somewhat wry, and a pallor came upon her face as she cried:

"Of what secret dost thou fable, wretch, of what unhappiness and what should I know? You talk nonsense."

"That not, alas, dear lady. With these eyes I saw him but now wrapped in such affliction that truly it went to my heart."

"How could that be?" asked Sibylla and her cheek throbbed strangely. "What sorrow can have come upon my lord since he left me? Only one hour ago he went from me like a hero rejoicing."

"That is it, sweetest. Like a hero he goes into his own chamber, and like a sinner, broken with remorse, he comes forth."

"Hark now, Jeschute, it is enough, be quiet. I know thee, girl, this is thy way and ever was, to pollute me with filth from thy mouth and hast before now made

me angry, even though I laughed. Never dost thou
bring good news, thou croaking raven, only trouble-
some and vexing, that gives thee joy. Better be silent
rather than tell me such lies in which harm lurks. So be
silent, I command it."

"Yes, noblest," said Jeschute. "Quite so. I am silent."

A little time passed. Sibylla sleeked her hair though
it was already done, and the maid finished her cham-
ber-work. Then the other said: "Jeschute, thou hast an
ill-bred way of being silent. I told thee to keep quiet
and thou hast obeyed. But thy way of obeying is rude.
When thou beginnest to speak, so speak to the end.
What hast thou seen or listened at?"

"Most blessed one, by my faith, a long time I have
known the master is sad. Mistress, I implore you, what
can that be, that he even keeps from you, in otherwise
so close a fellowship? Golden one, in whatever it con-
sists, it must be a great heaviness. More than once have
I perceived it, and have come to the conclusion that he
bears a cross so great that till now he has confessed it
to no one. Today by God's will I was still in his room
to brush up and dust when he came in, as blind for my
existence as for chair or press. That is a dispensation
from heaven, said I to myself, hid and crouched and
saw all his doing. A thing he took to him and fell on
his knees before it; from it he seemed to read his anguish, striking himself on the breast, looking up by
whiles, mid praying and bitter weeping. Never saw I
a human being so weep. So I in hiding realized beyond
all doubt that his heart is full of secret woe. For, I said

to myself, if a man of such courage is driven to such
weeping, then a great heart-grief must be at the bottom
of it."

"Alas!" said the princess with trembling lips. "Art
thou telling truth? Yes, yes, it seems so. Oh woe, alas,
for my dear lord! What then may ail him? For I confess, Jeschute, I know it not. His sorrow is to me unknown and not understood. He is young, healthy,
and rich, as it should be, what can lack him? For that I
see that it shall lack in nothing and am in all things as
he will, that the Eternal seeth."

And she wept.

"I am a little older than he," she sobbed, "a little too
old for him. Still he wooed me stormily, for that I have
a thousand proofs and bear his pledge for the second
time. But he lives with a secret apart from me and shuts
me from his pain. Alas, alas, poor woman that I am!
Never in my life were things so well with me nor ever
will be, and all through his youth and his troth. I tell
thee no better man was ever born! But what ever may
have happened in his youth, that in secret he must so
do penance and weep as I hear you tell? Advise me, for
I have no one to counsel me how to come behind his
trouble and pain, without peril of destroying our joy."

"If you were to ask him?"

"No, no," cried Sibylla in horror. "Not ask! In asking, that I feel, lieth danger and death. His suffering—
this much I see—is unspeakable, for were it not, why
had he not told me it long since? Clearly it is of such
kind that we may not both of us consciously know it,

and however much I long to share it with him—he must
not know that I share it. We must bear it together, yet
each for himself. Perhaps then my knowing love can
stand by him and be his good angel in this anguish."

"That might be arranged," Jeschute replied. "I saw
clearly the hiding-place wherefrom came the thing
wherein he conned his misery, before which he so
scourged himself. In the wall it was, above his head.
There he hides it again after penance done. Precisely
did I mark me the place. If you so will, I would lead
you to the spot when he is away, ridden to give judgement or to the chace, and show you slide and hole, that
you may see instead of ask and know without his
knowing."

Sibylla mused.

"Jeschute, girl," she said then, "I shudder at the
thing in the wall—it is unspeakable how I shudder. And
yet thou sayest aright: if I would share his suffering
with him without his knowledge, in order perhaps to
be his good angel, then I must see what he grieves at,
wherein, as it seems, his grief is written down. He has
ordered a shoot in the wet wood with falcons, five days
from now. When they are gone and remain some time
at the lodge, then you may lead me and show me the
hole. Do you perhaps think impatience devours me?
It does devour me. And yet what is the human heart?
I thank God that there are still five days before they
ride."

The Parting

But the days and nights went by and the morning came
when the knightly train agog for the hunt rode from
the burg with gear for falconing, by the pond in the
wood and in swampy ground round about, to hold a
shoot for heron and cranes, partridges, quail, and bus-
tard—Duke Grigorss in the lead, a very good falcon,
trained by Sibylla herself, in its hood on his fist. He
had wondered why at parting his wife so anxiously
clung to him and pressed him to put off the ride, or at
least very soon, ah, soon! to be back, before mischance
befell him or her.

"What mischance, love?" he had smiling asked and
promised her to be back not later than on the third day.
That seemed to her love too long.

Scarce was the train ridden down to the valley when
Jeschute slipped to the mistress and said:

"An it please you, exalted one, the coast is clear, so
I will conduct you."

"Whither, thou raven?"

"To the hole in the wall and the thing within."

"Fie, still thinking on it and will not let the foul thing drop? There is not time. Any hour the Duke may be back."

"But no, surely not till the day after tomorrow. Twice will they bide the night in the lodge at the wood's edge. You are quite safe."

"Safe from my husband? How dar'st thou, creature? Shall I take ways with thee behind his back?"

"But you said you had to know without his knowing, that you might be his good angel."

"Yes, that I said," admitted Sibylla. "And if it is to be, then go ahead, far ahead, that it need not look as though I followed."

So then they came into the Duke's cabinet and private chamber, and Jeschute pointed out with her finger the place to the mistress.

"There it is," said she. "Up there. One hardly sees the crack in the panelling, where it opens. You cannot reach. Shall I mount on the chair and get it?"

"How dar'st thou!" rebuked Sibylla. "Push up the chair, I will get it myself."

And supported by the maid she climbed up, shoved back the slide, saw the hiding-place, took the hidden thing, 'twas wrapped in a silken cloth, which she took off, so that it dropped on the chair, and held the tablet, of yvory framed in gold, set with gems, written like a letter by her hand.

It was only a little cry sprang from her lips—not more than would express emotions of astonishment, remembrance of old grief. With anguish she looked down at

it. All at once a coldness came in her hair and trickled
down her back. Her lips, from which every drop of
blood had fled, murmured low: "But how?" repeated
aloud, menacingly, as enraged at her own bewilderment: "But how?" Thereafter she was silent, looked at
the thing, read, lifted her eyes from it and stared into
space.

In her head thoughts went round and round. Where
did he get it? It is here and he has it. So it lies not at the
bottom of the sea, it got to land. Little cask and bark
got to land. The child got to land. It lives. It has grown
big and beautiful, like Grigorss. He gave Grigorss the
tablet, the one to the other. Why? Probably he did not
get it from the child, his friend and mate, but rather
from people who found the child, found it dead or
slew it and plundered the cask. The child, though
landed with the tablet, is dead, and Grigorss lives, that
is the difference between them. It is a vast difference,
and Grigorss has the tablet, the child has it not. Only he
does penance before it and beats his breast, as though it
were his own sinful state written on it, not that of another man, but of the child. That narrows sickeningly
the difference between the two, the one and the other.
With the tablet here were stuffs. They too lie not at the
bottom of the sea. I hardly mind me, it is too long since,
it is impossible for me to remember and with all conviction I deny that Grigorss wore before my eyes a
garment out of such, out of just those stuffs and still
has it. Sickening, sickening, in blazing laughing brain-
sickness, that too lessens the reasonable difference be-

tween Grigorss and the child. Where is my common
sense? The child was not named Grigorss—that is, it
was not named at all. Is it now called Grigorss? *Is Grigorss the child?* Have I my child of sin for a mate?
Madness, blazing, laughing, shrieking—and blackness,
blackness.

She fell in a faint from her chair, snatched up just in
the nick by Jeschute, so that she should not fall too
hard. Jeschute ran: "Help, help! The mistress lies like
death!" They came, they bore her to her chamber.
They gave her to breathe pungent restoratives. A mes-
sager went riding like mad to the wood, to the Duke.
She asked urgently for him so soon as she opened her
eyes, and heard he was on his way. The tablet she held,
they could not take it from her, not even in her
swound.

To the lodge came the messenger. The hunters were
sullen. Lost their best falcon: crammed, he had flown
away, without scenting the bait, to the wood, where he
stayed. Now they must hear worse news: "Lord Duke,
would you find the mistress yet alive, so haste or you
come too late. She is ill unto death."—"Fellow, how
can that be? She was in health when we rode off."—
"My lord, I must confirm my words."

No lingering was there. They mounted and rode
homewards. Believe me, there was no rest till they
reached home and word went to the mistress, her consort was at hand. In green hunting-dress he came to her
—what had he there to see? Tottering, wan, quite limp,
eyes unnaturally large and flickering with horror in the

wailing face. "Grigorss!" she cried, and sank into his
arms, hid her face on his breast, and groaned again:
"Grigorss! So I call thee, whoever thou art, for, God
in heaven, by name one may call this one and that one,
there is nothing wicked in it. My Grigorss—for mine
thou art in any case—speak, since when art thou so
called? Who gave thee the name? Grigorss, my darling
—for that art thou, so or so—Grigorss, who art thou?
Heaven and hell hang on thy lips—who gave you
birth?"

He bent over her. "For God's sweet sake, lady, how
is it with thee? Dearest wife, my chaste lady, what have
they done to thee? I guess, I know it. Thy question re-
veals it to me. Has an enemy, a creeping coward, told
you I am a low-born man from a peasant's hut? Now
what croaking raven has betrayed it and made you suffer anguish? He lies. Let him hide himself from me, for
if I know him he is fordone. I say to you, the wretch
lies in his throat. Not deceitfully did I lift my eyes to
you and fought for you. High am I of birth, I have it
signed and sealed, equal to thee in birth, dearest, quite,
be fully assured: I too a Duke's child."

"Equal in birth," said she shuddering and looked at
him wild-eyed. Then she lifted the tablet: "Who gave
thee this?"

He looked and went so pale that he looked like her.
His eyes were hollows. Deep drooped his head.

"Well, then," said he at last, "you know it. The tablet given me as my dower when they left me to wind
and wave, it came into thy hands. Farewell, our joy!

'Twas built on a lie. For I hid from you that I was the child of sin in all my members. And even now I lied to you when I said that not deceitfully had I lifted up my eyes to you, the chaste one. Yes, I deceived you. I have brought impurity to you with my love, impure the fruit of your body through mine. I have so oft prayed God He might not look upon my sin. It was a false prayer. He has brought it to the light and now I go. You must thrust me out did I not do it myself. You will see the castaway no more. I go to seek my parents."

"Grigorss," she besought him, "so I name you at least, but thou—name me not. Grigorss, beloved, speak, tell me that you are two and not the same, the man of the tablet and thou. Another gave thee the tablet, not of thee was it written. And be it a lie—yet tell it me."

"No, lady, enough of lies. Mine was the legacy. A godly man who brought me up preserved it for me, till I should be grown. The child it lay with, that was I."

"Grigorss, then are we lost. Then is our place the uttermost hell. Grigorss, if you speak truth instead of mercifully lying, then is there no difference between my wedded spouse and the child, except the child is now a man. Grigorss, 'twas I wrote the child's tablet."

Each looked narrowly at the other, hollow-eyed. To think this out together took time. Then they went apart, each to the opposite wall, pressed their foreheads against it, and waves of heat, one after the other, flushed their pallid cheeks, ebbed back to their hearts, and again mounted glowing to their cheeks. For long only moans were heard in the room.

Then they left their walls, the youth first. He sank down before her, bowed over her feet.

"Mother," said he, "forgive the sinner."

She would have stroked his hair but drew back her hand as from hot iron.

"Son and my lord," said she, "forgive me. I saw thy garments of the same stuff."

He asked: "Where is my father?"

"He died on pilgrimage," she answered with lifeless lips, "thy sweet father. In thee I found him again."

"I look like him?"

She nodded. Then they started to move apart again but bethought themselves and stopped as they were. She spoke:

"Why ever came I into the world? Accurst through God's mouth the hour when I was born. Heaven help me, I dreamed I bore a dragon who flew away but came back again and thrust himself back into my torn womb. Grigorss, it was thou! A curse has sworn upon me and kept its oath, for a thousand times has heart's anguish come to me after joy. I longed for happiness in innocence. So then hell brought to me the child of my sin that I sleep with him, as wife with man."

He shuddered and put up his hand.

"Mother, desecrated one, speak not so plainly. But yet do so. I understand why thou dost. We shall speak expressly and name things by name to our chastisement. For to tell truth, that itself is chastisement. Hearest Thou, God, how we chastise ourselves and put it in crass words? This is it, then, for which I had prayed,

that thou wouldst bring me to the state where it would
be well with me and with joy I should look upon my
dear mother. Otherwise hast Thou vouchsafed it to me,
Thou rich, Thou very good God, than I had begged it
from Thee. Lend me strength, great strength, that I
suppress the anger that will lift itself to Thee. Better,
meseems, what dost Thou think, I had never seen her
than that I had ever lived with her as husband, three
years long, my father's successor, and got children
lying with her for whom there is no place on earth even
much less than for me, and who even by much thought
are not to be provided for, no man knows what he is
to think of them. This is the defeat of thought, the
downfall of the world! Lady, thou mayst call me Grigorss, but I may call thee neither by name nor mother,
both are madness, and how it hurts me especially
about the word 'mother'—that I have gambled away by
befouling it. Fitter and more kindly might I call thee
dear cousin, for to fondle with such is less shocking.
But how I am related to my children, with Herrad and
the expected one, I know not yet, I have not yet fath-
omed it. If I do not like Judas, who hanged himself out
of remorse and disgust at his own act, I shall have time
to think it over."

"Grigorss, my child and my lord, I must regret that
I gave you an example by speaking things out in penance, for you make it still crasser. My horror grows
every minute and with it amazement that long before
now flaming anger has not crashed down upon the ac-
cursed, that earth still dares to bear me, after what my

flesh committed. I, I am the chief criminal, I know too
well, and unspeakable dread mounts in me of the hell-
fire that threatens me, that is as good as certain for extreme misdeed. Lord and beloved child, could you tell
me—for you have read many books—whether a penance is thinkable for such heaped-up vice and sacri-
lege? Is there here no counsel—no, certainly none—that
if I, poor woman, must dwell in hell, it might be after
all a little milder than to other damned?"

She, she had not dared to touch his hair, but he, because hers was covered with cloth and bands, stroked
gently her head as she lay so mournfully on his arm.

"Lady," said he, "speak not thus, neither give way
to despair, it is against the command. For of himself
may man despair but not of God and His fullness of
grace. We are both thrust into the marsh of sin up to
our necks, and if you think you are deeper in, that is
pridefulness. Add not this sin to the rest or the pool
will go over mouth and nose. God's hand is stretched
out that that may not happen; this consolation I gathered from my books. Not for naught have I seriously
studied Divinitatem in the cloister of God's Passion. I
learned that He takes true contrition as atonement for
all sins. Be your soul never so sick, if your eye be wet
only an hour from heartfelt rue, believe thy child, thy
spouse and sin, then you are saved.

"I know," he went on, "what must happen, and I decree. For see, the child grew to a man, while you remained a woman. I am the man here, and your wedded
spouse, even though in the maddest way, and so I must

decree. The larger share of the penance is mine, not on account of pride, but because I am the man. And besides a good share of your penance falls away if I go. If I go, then it is impossible you should continue to govern the land as duchess. Call your orders together and have a new duke chosen, Wittich, your uncle, or Werimbald, your distant cousin, that is all one. Then descend from your seat and practise humility, more than ever you did when you mourned your brother, my dear father. As from the ducal seat so from the castle. At the foot have an asylum built from your jointure, on the high road, for the homeless, the old, the sickly, the halt and crippled. There shall you preside, in the grey robe, lave the sick, wash their wounds, bathe and cover them, and give to wandering beggars, washing their feet. I have naught against it if you take in lepers, I even consider it right. Herrad, our child, about whom I have not yet thought out how she is related to us, except that she would be your granddaughter, I being your son—she might help you to drink the water of humility as she grows. In error was she baptized. The one to come, whom you bear, my love, shall not be baptized, so I must decree. Call it by some humble name, like Stultitia or Humilitas or little Miserabilis, that I leave to you. So live, till God thee call.

"But I go and offer myself for repentance, and indeed no ordinary one. For a man so plunged in sin there never was on earth, or at least exceeding seldom —I say it not out of arrogance. I go the way my poor father went. Not on knightly pilgrimage I go, as I, poor fool that once I was had thought, when I learned of my birth, to go; but penitential-wise, as beggar, like to those whose feet you will wash. So shall I find my place, as in the fog I found this, the place which corresponds to this, and shall aby it. These are the last words here on earth I shall speak to you. Farewell!"

"Grigorss," said she with faltering gaze, and her lips sought to find a sweet smile, which, alas, turned out a frightful one, "Grigorss, beloved child, could we not then before the world leave it as it is, without ever nearing each other, and bear in common our secret? My love to you is now all motherly, all man-woman love fell away as from thine. And yet perhaps deeper is the penance if we, mindful of our sin, are together than far apart in the world. The asylum I could still build and bathe the plague-stricken."

"Womanlike you speak," he answered, "for woman you remained while I became a man. To your undoing I became one. Now I will be one to your salvation. As the husband decreed, so shall it be. Again, farewell. No, no kiss at parting. Not even on the brow—nor yet the hand. With the hand it began. God be with you!"

And he went. She stretched out her arms to him in her agony.

"Wiligis!" she cried from her heart's depths and then bethought herself.

"Be merciful, child, to thyself," she called after him, "be mindful, and overdo it not with the penance."

But he no longer heard.

The Stone

HE put on beggar's garb, a hair shirt with a rope girdle, and took nothing with him but a gnarled stick, no bag for bread, not even a begging-bowl. The tablet, however, written by his and his children's mother, that he took, and wore it next his bare body. So he went down in the twilight from the citadel of his unhappy joy, down and away, resolved to grant himself no grace but this, of bearing his distresses with willing heart. What he wished was that God would send him into a desert, where he might do penance unto death.

That night he slept under a tree, which let the first leaves fall upon the pilgrim, slept there as once on the island when he had learned of his birth, so that neither hut nor cloister could longer shelter him and only heaven be his roof-tree. Men and the highway of men he avoided as he went onwards under the new sun. The red heath, wood, and pathless wilderness, through them he set his staff, waded the water near the bridge, and trod barefoot the stubble of the fields. The first day he ate nothing, the second some charcoal-burners in the forest gave him the left-overs of their meal. On the third, towards evening, he was far away and knew not where; a shower of rain darkened the sky and in the fallow light there led from among the hills through which he had come a hill path, winding, grass-grown, and no broader than a spear laid slantwise, to the valley, into the region of a large lake. This path the penitent followed and saw below him, not far from the reedy shore, a little house in the waste, that infinitely drew him towards it, for his soul was full of yearning after rest and shelter, and he drew near.

Nets, spread out for mending before the house, showed him that it was a fisher who lived there. The man stood at the door with his wife and looked mistrustfully at the wayless one, whose beard had long since darkened brow and chin, and his body hair grown matted. Gregorius humbly gave him evening greeting; with clasped hands begged, for God's love, shelter for the night, but in his heart hoped that his plea would be scorned and the man refuse him shelter, roughly and if possible with reviling. For that had not yet happened to him, and stronger than longing for rest was his longing for penance and deep debasement.

Such was his portion. The fisherman began to rail and railed for minutes long although behind him his wife tried in low whispers to hush him.

"Yes, you vagabond, you chete, you loafer!" he berated him. "So you came here to my house, you rascal, you big trickster, you lazy-bones, you tramper, and want to eat off honest folk, who earn their bare bread with God's help and their own sweat. Woman, stop whispering behind me to be kind, my words are decent and just. How did you grow up, you saucy beggar, what kind of arms hang down from your shoulders, that you don't use them for honest work? You need a broad field and a hoe; an ox-goad would do well in your hands instead of your loafing round like this. Ow, a bad world is this, that it lets such a worthless fellow as you, and many another like you, live on it, for whom God gets no honour and who just sponges on people! Woman, leave off your silly whispering. Who says this rogue here if I keep him and when we are asleep won't do away with us and make off with our goods? Take shame to yourself, you lout, for your strength which you want to have papped up by others and at most use it for villaining. Scramble now, get out, away from here or I'll find your legs for you!"

"Just so, friend," answered him Gregorius mildly, "just so had I wished you should speak to me. So must I hear it and so has God whispered it to you. If you had given me a box on the ear as well, that would have been more useful yet, to ease a little the burden of my sins. You are right, I may not beg for shelter, the sky is my refuge. Farewell." And he turned away in the rain which began to fall.

But inside, whither they had gone from the rain, the fisherman's wife said in the flickering light:

"Husband, husband, I don't feel right, I am not a bit comfortable about the way you acted to the wanderer! You spoke so foully against him and rated at him so that it might cost you your soul. Shall one treat a beggar like that, let him be Christian, Turk, or heathen? That was

certainly a good trustworthy man, I saw that by his
eyes, but you had nothing but cruel contempt and
spurning for him, now just you wait how God will pay
you out! When a man just keeps himself from day to
day with the fishing, as you must if you are lucky, he
should keep God before his eyes and not risk much by
failing of mercifulness, for He can easily take away the
fish from you so that you have nothing to bring to the
village market. We should do better to call the poor
man back."

"Rubbish!" said the fisherman. "Hast thou indeed
swallowed down a fool for his handsome legs, sweet and
young, in his beggar smock, and would like to sport
with him, you adulterous, likerous creature?"

"No, husband," returned the wife. "Truly it was a
strange feeling I had at sight of him but I believe not it
was lewitness made my eyes water. His beggar smock,
true, was something like a disguise, and it does not seem
right to me that we thrust him away. In the poor, they
say, the Lord Christ is fed, and with reverence, it is said,
shall one encounter Him, the less one knows whom one
has before him, hiding in rags to try us. When he spoke
of the blows, it all seemed to me completely different.
Truly you should let me call him back!"

"Oh well, then, run and fetch him to stop the night
with us," said the man, now a little perturbed himself.
"That he should be eaten in the forest by wolves I
would wish as little as you."

So she ran, her skirt over her head, through the rain,
overtook the stranger, curtsied, and said:

"Beggar, my husband the fisherman has bethought himself and regrets his unfriendly words. He finds the weather too bad for you and also thinks there are wolves and wants you to take shelter for the night in our house."

"As it shall be, so be it," answered Gregorius. "I follow you not to make it softer for myself but because your husband may give me counsel."

When they re-entered the hut, the fisherman sullenly turned his back, for the impression of his wife's warning had meanwhile worn off in his mind. But the woman made up a wood fire that the rain-sodden man might dry his clothes, and said she would bake a pancake big enough for all three of them to enjoy with milk. Gregor stopped her.

"This body," said he, "is scarce worth a meal. I think not to feed it from the pan, rather a crust of oaten bread and a drink from the spring be all my cheer."

It remained at that, though the good wife pressed him to let himself take a little more ease. And when they sat down to eat, the dwellers in the waste with their pancake and the stranger with hard crust and water, the fisherman was sore angered so that he could not keep back his angry words and said:

"Fie upon thee, that I have to see thee make a show before us, beggar, by starving thyself, and it is all a hoax. I do not hold with chetes and yarn-spinners. Up to now thou hast not fed on such diet, I'll take my oath. It makes me laugh: neither man nor wife has ever seen a better-formed body, so thriving and shapely, from

bread and water you did not get it. Straight thighs,
arched insteps I have seen, toes even and shapely.
Splayed and crusted should thy feet be like a proper
tramper's, but the dirt is just surface dirt. Thy arms and
legs, they have not long been bare, don't tell me, they
were well covered from wind and weather, and thy
skin—I will tell you what kind of skin that is: it is the
skin of a well-fattened feeder. Look what a lighter
streak runs round thy finger: there was a ring there
once. I have eyes in my head, and I know rather than
just suspect that thou usest them otherwise, thy dainty
hands, when thou art far from here, than thou makest
out. Thou canst find a better place to stay and I care
very little that thou wilt make sport tomorrow of the
crust of bread, the spring water, and us poor folk."

"Better I should go now," said the beggar to the
woman, "into the night."

"No, better wouldst thou do," cried the fisherman,
"to answer and tell thy kind-hearted host what sort of
man thou art!"

"That will I," answered Gregor, "and remark in passing that I like it and it is fit and good that you thuten
me while I say you to you. I am a man sinful not only
as all the world is but whose flesh and bones consist entirely in sin and besides that plunged in such sin that it
is like the end of thinking and the end of the world.
What I seek after in my wandering is the hardest spot
I can find, where until my death I can pay with the
agony of my flesh for the greater exaltation of God.
Today is the third since I renounced the world and

went on pilgrimage. In the woods besides swineherds and charcoal-burners were hermits as well, but they had it far too easy for me. Since today my way has led me to you, lord, so let me ask you for grace and counsel. Do you know anywhere a place which would be right for me, a wild rock or remote cavern of the extremest discomfort, I heartily beg you to show it to me. You would do well to do so."

Then the fisherman pondered grimly and laughed within himself at his idea. "I'll give it to him," he thought, "I'll bluff him so that sheer shivers take him at my proposals and he nips off. Then the swindle will be shown up." And he said:

"If that is what thou'rt after, friend, then rejoice. Thou canst be helped and it will be me that helps thee. Out there in the lake I know a reef of rock, quite alone in the wave, that will be a fine home for thee, rugged enough, there canst squat and wail thy woes to heart's content. If it like thee I'll take thee across and help thee up. Up, that is, one can get if one must, but down again, that's the rub, for so is the shape of the rock. But we must make quite sure thy mind to punishment doesn't change even if thou'lt have it so. For ages I have had an iron leg-fetter, a stout one, with a lock. We'll take it with us and I'll put it on thee. If afterwards the joke pall on thee and thou wouldst try to get down, thou must stick it, willy-nilly, and spend thy life up there as long as it holds out. How dost thou like my proposal?"

"It is very good," Gregorius answered. "God gave it

to you. I thank Him and you and beg you to help me to
the stone."

At which the fisherman roared with laughter and
cried:

"Well, beggar, that is shrewdly said. If thou meanst
it, go to sleep now for before dawn I go out to the fishing and if thou wilt go along, be early up. Only to please
thee, in spite of time lost, will I take thee to the islet,
help thee up, and settle thee snugly in the iron fixture—
here it is in the chest. Then canst thou nest up there
like a falcon on its cliff, get as old there as thou canst
hold out and never again be a trouble to anyone on
earth. Till tomorrow!"

"Where would you have me to sleep?" asked Gregorius.

"Not here," said the fisherman. "I trust thee not in
the smallest. Thou canst bed in the lean-to. It's not in
the best of state, but compared with thy stone 'tis fit for
a king."

The outhouse was half-fallen and foul, and if the
fisher-wife had not been pious and thoughtful enough
to lay a few rushes for the guest, he who had been Duke
Grigorss must have lain in the dirt. His meanest sweeper
at home had it better. But he thought: "It is very good
so, only it is still much too fine. The rock tomorrow
will be the right thing." He stretched out on the rushes
and laid his tablet beside him. Long he lay awake in
prayer. But then his youth would have it that he fell
asleep, very soundly, and when shortly before daybreak
the fisherman was up and starting to go earn his bread,

Grigorss lay still in deep sleep and heard not that his host called: "Hey, beggar!" Twice he called, but not a third time, only said:

"I'll just make a fool of myself shrieking my throat out after the swindler. I knew he didn't mean it and that he would make himself scarce about the place I suggested. I'll go my way."

And started down as every morning he did, to the water. When the woman saw, she hurried with good intent to the shed, shook the sleeper, and told him:

"Good man, if you want to go along, then make haste, the fisherman is already on his way to the lake."

Then Gregorius started up, looked dazed, and scarcely came to himself, so deep had been his sleep.

"I don't like to wake thee, thou gently bred soul," said she, "tired as thou seemest and with several days' beard, or to send thee up to the stone. And still something told me I should do it that thou mayst not lose thy place. For it seems to me thou hast a real yearning for it and who knows whether thou art not perhaps a saint."

At the word Gregorius shuddered. Starting up, he cried: "Wretch that I am, how could I sleep? For God's sake away and after him!" And rushed out of the hut.

"Forget not your leg-iron!" cried the woman and pressed it into his hands. "Perhaps it is needful for salvation, or it may be the fisherman only thought of it in his anger. And take the ladder here, you need it as well, and my man took nothing with him. Carry it as the Lord Christ His Cross—farewell!" she called after him.

"I stop here, but my mind misgives me for thee." Then she turned away and wept.

But Gregorius, weighed down with leg-iron and ladder, ran sweating after his host and kept crying: "Friend, fisherman, my good angel, wait for me and forsake me not, I am coming, I am coming!" But in his haste he had left his tablet behind him among the rushes, which pained him sore.

Only on the crumbling causeway below, where the boat was, and quite out of breath did he reach the man, who shrugged his shoulders. And when the boat had taken them both in, with the gear, the fisherman without a word ferried him through the shallow waves to the open water, perhaps an hour or two, then the rough stone reared up out of the flood, red-gray and skittle-shaped, godforsaken, out of sight of land. They came up to it and the fisherman hooked the ladder on a nose of rock, saying:

"Go on ahead! I don't want thee at my back."

So they climbed up one behind the other, first up the ladder, then laboriously a piece over the bare rock with the help of cracks and notches, and when they had reached the little flat space at the top the fisherman, laughing grimly as he did so, fastened the leg-iron on, locked it, and said:

"Now thou art fast to the rock. Here must thou grow old, for even the Devil with all his wiles cannot carry thee away, never and nevermore shalt thou get down. Sit there, for thou hast caught thyself in thine own trap."

So then he threw the key of the fetter in a wide curve out into the water and added:

"If I ever get it again out of the deep and see it again, then will I cry thee mercy, holy one. Good howling and teeth-chattering to thee!"

That was his farewell salute. He climbed down again to the boat, drew in the ladder, and went hence.

The Penance

CHRISTIAN reader, hearken and believe! Great and
strange things have I to report to you, things it takes
courage to tell. But if I find courage to utter, then shall
you blush not to find courage to believe. Not hastily
will I chide you for a doubter, rather I count on your
belief, just as far as I count on my ability to tell in a
credible manner what has been told me. Upon this ability I firmly confide, and so also on your belief.

My truthful tale is this: on the narrow square at
the top of this wild rock in the lake Gregorius, son of
Wiligis and Sibylla and husband of the latter, all stark
living alone and wanting all mercy, spent as many years
as he had numbered when he so culpably left his island
far away in the sea and the cloister of God's Passion—
full seventeen years he spent there without other comfort than the roof of heaven over him, without shelter,
not from frost nor snow, rain nor wind, nor sun-burn-
ing, covered only—but how long did it last out?—with
his hair shirt, his arms and legs bare.

You believe it not? I will assure you of it, and indeed

not by taking refuge in my trump card, that to God nothing is impossible and no miracle too great. That would indeed be crushing, but too cheap. Outwardly must your doubt be silent before it but inwardly it might go on gnawing. That may not be, and therefore I will not invoke God's omnipotence. Without preaching, reasonably, calmly, if also deeply moved by my knowledge, I will answer the questions which with wringing of hands, with many a "Yes, tell us for God's sake," and "Monk, consider then, how—" you would like to put, the first of which of course is how the penitent fed himself on the naked rock, even a short time, not to speak of seventeen years. Did ravens come flying to feed him? Did manna fall from heaven for his sake? No, it was quite otherwise.

The first day after the fisherman had left him with mocking words, and Gregor remained behind quite solitary, he stopped where he was, sat with his arms round his knees or knelt with clasped hands before God and prayed for his poor lovely parents, for the vanished Wiligis, for Sibylla his wife, who even now very likely was already bathing the arthritic or making arrangements to, and also for himself, in that he gave himself over utterly and unconditionally to the will of God, as he was in simple fact actually given over. But the second day was only a few hours old when hunger and thirst let him no longer rest and almost without knowing or willing it, on all fours, because he could not take a step with his feet in irons, he began to creep and seek round his little platform.

In the middle, almost exactly, there was a little trough
in the stone, and a whitish cloudy wetness filled it up
to the margin, probably yesterday's rain, he thought,
only quite strikingly cloudy and milky—welcome to
him in any case as a drink, however and whencever unclean it might be, he was the last to make conditions.
So he bent over the little basin and sucked up with lips
and tongue its contents, lapped it all out, little as it was,
only a few spoonfuls, and even licked the bottom of
the little hollow when it was empty. The drink tasted
sugary and sticky, a little like starch, a little pungent
like fennel and also metallic like iron. Gregorius had at
once the feeling that not only his thirst but also his
hunger had been satisfied by it, with surprising thoroughness. He was filled. He belched a bit and a little
of what he had drunk ran out of his mouth again as
though the little had already been too much. His face
felt a little puffy, warmth rose in his cheeks and red-
dened them, and when he had got back by creeping to
his first place at the edge of the stone, he fell asleep like
a child, with his head resting on a small ledge of the
rock.

After a few hours he was awakened by slight colic,
enough to make him stir his fettered legs in annoyance
and at which he might well have cried out. But it soon
passed and of hunger he felt none. Only out of curiosity
did he betake himself towards evening to the hollow in
the middle of the level place. At the bottom of it some
fluid had already collected, not more than thinly coated
the bottom. Still one could calculate that if the trickling

went on at the same pace, during the night the trough
would have filled up again.

So it came about, and on the next day Gregor
strengthened himself anew with the sap, lapped it all
up, warmed to the point of sleepiness; for during the
night he had suffered much from cold and not known
how to pull his scanty shirt to find cover in it, so the
juice from the stone helped for several hours, simply
because it filled him, wherefore the solitary in the evening, when there was again some liquid fed on it again
in order not to be so cold.

I am able to tell you the meaning of all this, for I have
read the ancients, among whom and quite rightly the
earth got the name of great mother and magna parens,
out of which every living thing sprouts and springs, as
it were reaches up to God, or in short has been born of
the mother-womb. So likewise man, who not for nothing is called homo and humanus, in token, that is, that
he comes to the light out of the mother-matrix of the
humus. But all that gives birth has also the necessary
nourishment for its children, and thereby one can tell
whether a woman really gave birth and was not produc-
ing a strange child as hers, by whether she does or does
not command the sources of nourishment for the new-
born. Therefore these authors, for whom I feel respect,
assert that in the beginning the earth nourished her children with her own milk after birth. For her uberi had
reached down deep like sluices with their roots, and
thither nature of herself guided the channels of the
earth and made milklike juice flow from the mouth of

the veins as even now all women after child-bearing
have sweetish milk flowing into the breast because
thither the whole stream of juice of the maternal body,
or rather a nourishing extract of it, is sent.

Small, unfinished, and immature, they say, not yet
called to the initiation of higher nourishment, the culture of the grain, man then hung on the breast of the
mother and enjoyed infant-food. But how right are my
authorities, the ancients, in this explanation, the history
of Gregor shows. In some few places of the earth, in
all only two or three and even so in remote and un-
inhabited spots, there survive such nourishing nature-
sources of primeval time, reaching deep down into the
maternal organism, as it were out of old habit, even
in reduced activity, and one of these, where the well-
ing early nourishment in four-and-twenty hours still
filled a little basin, had the penitent found on his
stone.

That was a great mercy, and I will leave open the
question whether a blessed chance obtained in this instance and the mother-source had been active all the
time; or whether the act of grace went so far that God
himself had caused it to flow anew for Gregorius the
sinner. In any case there came to him through this find,
in all his endless forsakenness, for the first time the
hopeful, yes, the blessed presage that God not only accepted his repentance but would not let him perish of
it; rather, when through harshest penance he had redeemed his parents and himself from sin, had something
of a blessing in mind for him.

This intimation benignly streaming through him he certainly needed as much as the warming mother-drink, and they had to work together to make him hold out in what he had taken on himself, and what, like everything hard, in the beginning, before nature, yielding but tough, has come to terms with it, was hardest of all to bear. For now imagine and picture vividly to yourself how winter came, with darkness, snow, rain, and gales, and how the man on the naked rock in mere hair shirt was pitilessly delivered over to his persecutions—if this word be entirely right, considering the existence of earth-milk and the warming intimations of mercy. Yet truly it is only too far-reachingly correct, especially when one thinks that snow and rain were very bad for the nourishing lymph, watering it down. And still in thinned condition it was strong enough to satisfy. Belching now and then, somewhat slobbering, the man lay drawn up into himself, knees at his mouth, under all kinds of weather, and his skin too was drawn together, always in the condition of pimply protection which we call gooseflesh, which produced changes in it. If the sun came out warm, he might steam and dry, and his hair shirt the same, but that soon rotted and in great part fell away like touchwood. Still what was left covered more of his body than one might think, for his constant posture of being curled in on himself made him grow visibly smaller.

Moreover one must or one may add that the winter went by strangely fast and seemed to him altogether short, on the simple ground that he slept much and jumped over and disregarded time. He took notice again only when the light grew, the breezes blew milder, and a spring, which indeed altered nothing of the treeless and grassless nakedness of his rocky seat, being able only mildly to warm the stone, passed over into long-dayed summer-time, where the sun described her highest arc in heaven above the lake and if storm-clouds did not shroud it, streamed down powerfully on man and rock, often making the latter so hot that the former could scarce have borne it if his defensive skin had not already turned very horny and granular. Also against the glowing beams his head was thatched in thick hair like felt and disguising beard, and so he took what came till the star-bestuck night with sickly waning moon, or sickle-shaped, or gleaming and full mirroring itself in the water, brought cooling to nature and to the shrunken little human being that grew more and more one with her.

And after that again the days grew shorter and shorter, the autumn mists brewed, till now a year had rounded out since the man had been exposed. One year, you say! But seventeen, you say, he lived through there. Yes, that I say. Yet so great as you think the difference is not, and let one be past, the others follow after without making any great difference in them or the man-creature living in them shelterless. In the first place one must take away a good quarter of their volume considered as experienced time, for the penitent spent the winters in timeless winter sleep as small creatures do and during it not even crept out for food, since his physical

life was reduced almost to a standstill before it stirred
again as the sun's arc increased. Secondly, time, if it be
nothing else but time, and has no objective content but
the change of seasons and the behaviour of the weather,
no content of events, through which alone she becomes
wholly time—time I say, will then not mean much, it
loses in dimension and shrinks together just as does the
earth-suckling creature crouching on his stone in the
sea, who in time became so dwarflike small as, according to authorities, was unfinished and unclean early
man, who did not yet enjoy food worthy of human
beings.

Finally, in fifteen years he was not much bigger than
a hedgehog, a prickly, bristly moss-grown nature-thing,
whom no weather could affect, and whose shrunken
members, the little arms and legs, even eye- and mouth-
openings were hard to recognize. It knew time no more.
The moon changed, the constellations revolved, they
vanished from the sky, they came again. The nights,
moonbright or gloomy and dripping, icy with storm
or sultry and close, shortened or lengthened. Dawn
came, early or late, greyer or redder, flamed up and
died down again in brilliant crimson that mirrored itself in the region of the east. Blue-black, sulphurous
storms came on with shuddering slowness; where it
lightened, came on, unloaded with crackling above the
sounding waters, which they sprinkled with hail. Their
lightnings plunged into the excited waves, that sprayed
and rammed the unshaken base of the stone. Afterwards all was good, peace, as high and incomprehensi-

ble as the previous rage, filled the world, and in the
sweet rain, shined on from above, there spanned from
one shorelessness to the other in moist beauty the seven-
coloured bow.

And amid all that the mossy creature, when it was not
asleep, went its creeping way to the mother-breast and
returned filled and a little slobbering to the verge where
the penitent had once been set down. If by chance a
boat in the lake had neared the remote rock, the boat-
men would have observed nothing striking up there: If
the fisherman down in the wasteland had taken a notion
to make the trip again and look round for the tiresome
fellow he had landed here—a moment would have convinced him that he was long since perished and decayed,
what remained of him dried, evaporated, and washed
away from the stone. He might have expected to see a
glimmer of bleached bone and been disappointed. But
he never came.

The Revelation

AFTER so and so many years, as I have read, there died
in the renowned and ruin-rife city of Rome he who
as successor of the Prince-Apostle and Vicar of Christ
had held sway there, worn the triple crown, and shep-
herded the folk with the shepherd's crook. But upon his
death and over the burning question who should receive after him the sacred seat and inherit the power
to loose and to bind, there ensued great and sanguinary
conflicts, which God seemed not inclined to compose.
For His spirit descended not in conciliation upon the
Curia of ecclesiastics, nobles, and citizens; instead a
schism cleft the people, and two hostile factions, each
acclaiming its own candidate as the only worthy pre-
tender to the throne of the world, opposed each other
in violent dissension. One of them wanted as pope a
certain presbyter of aristocratic origins named Symmachus, the other a very corpulent arch-deacon Eulalius, who equally with Symmachus fairly trembled with
eagerness for the honour.

The Holy Spirit had no share in either of these nomi-
nations. They were simply the work of man, and with

chagrin must I confess that bribery with gold played a
part and party struggle for power formed the moving
principle. Therefore the Divine did not descend with
light and leading upon the electors; the assemblage
broke up in angry discord, the parties took up arms,
and a savage war broke out in the city—in squares, in
streets, and, alas, in the churches as well. The gate-
towers of the bridges, the ancient monuments and their
heaped-up ruins served as strongholds and entrench-
ments. It was a shame and disgrace, I must say. Out of
the one conclave grew two, each chose its own man
and installed him as Pope and Bishop of Rome. Symmachus was ordained in the Lateran, Eulalius in St. Peter's, and thus they sat, one in the Lateran Palace, the
other in the Emperor Hadrian's round fortress mauso-
leum; sang mass, issued bulls and decretals, and cursed
each other while the weapons rang in the streets. The
names they conferred on each other were many, and
endlessly they excogitated new ones: "Spoiler of the
Church," "Root of all sin," "Devil's herald," "Assyrian
rod," "Filth of the century," "Writhing, repulsive
worm," thus one called the other, frothing at the mouth.
Eulalius, who as I said was very fat and full-blooded,
exceeded himself in curses, got a stroke and died. But
likewise fate overtook Symmachus, for the Eulalian
faction to avenge their Pope made a great attack upon
their enemies, defeated them, and stormed the Palace
of the Lateran, so that Symmachus was forced to escape by the back door. Being pursued, he plunged into
the Tiber and was drowned.

Thus instead of two Popes they had none at all, and this effected a mighty disillusionment among the Romans. They perceived that they had handled the affair badly and godlessly and a penitential mood spread abruptly among the citizens. Their resolve, taken in general assembly, was that now they would leave the choice wholly and utterly to God, and fasting weeks, days of alms-giving and extended prayers were ordered in all the churches, that He in His mercy might make known His choice for vicar and wearer of the world-crown.

Now there lived in Rome a pious man, of an old family which had received Christianity earlier than most: Sextus Anicius Probus, already on in years, past fifty, and as rich in goods as in public esteem. Together with his wife, Faltonia Proba, he occupied the palace of his forbears, who had all been consuls, prefects, and senators: a huge estate covering miles of ground in the fifth region, on the Via Lata, having three hundred and sixty rooms and halls, a race-track as well as marble baths, and set among spacious gardens. The baths no longer ran water, the hippodrome was long out of use, and most of the three hundred and sixty rooms were empty and dilapidated—not because means and labour were lacking the owner to keep them all up but because in his eyes decline, disorganization, the disintegration of the very great under the weight of its own greatness appeared the timely, inevitable, and God-ordained thing. Of course in the few rooms which he occupied with his wife there was no lack of beauty or amenities: in beds and couches covered with costly Oriental stuffs, carved and gilded furnishings, chairs of antique design, bronze candelabra, cabinets wherein were vases elegant in form, gold beakers, and rosy drinking-shells. But this group of rooms was a livable island surrounded by spreading desolation, courts with partly fallen rows of columns, fountains whose ornamental figures lay broken on the ground, and wrecked salons with damaged mosaic floors, where the gold hangings hung in tatters and the facings of fine silver plate were warped and stood away from the walls. Probus and Proba were used to it like this and found it fitting.

The gardens too, in which the palace lay embedded, were run wild and overgrown almost to impassable thickets; but so much the more were snug nooks to be found, attainable between riotous growths and trees half-choked by sinuous vines. The Anician especially loved a marble bench with Pan's heads, close-embraced by laurel bushes; seated there one could look past a statue of a charming Cupid with bow and arrow, headless, fallen and lying on the ground; and beyond that a little free space gay with coloured wild-flowers. There sat the worthy man on a fine summer-warm April day after dinner, troubled in his mind over the general helplessness and abandoned state of the Church. That morning he had shared with fervour in the general prayers in the Church of the Apostles Philip and James near his palace. Now he might have fallen asleep in the sweet air of the sun-warmed laurels, for he had a dream-vision which yet did not move him from his station, for where he sat there he saw and heard what stirred him to his depths, so that one is obliged to speak of a vision and a revelation rather than of a dream.

Before him in the meadow clover stood a bleeding lamb and spoke to him. It bled from its side, it opened its pathetic lamb's mouth and spoke in a trembling voice which yet went with surpassing sweetness to the heart:

"Probus, Probus, hear me! Great things will I announce unto you!"

Tears sprang to Probus's eyes at the lamb's voice and his heart filled to overflowing with love.

"Thou Lamb of God," said he, "certainly I hearken. With my whole soul I listen; but thou bleedest, thy blood makes red thy soft fleece and runs down into the clover. Can I do aught for thee, wash thy wound and tend it with balsam? For I fervently crave some such service of love."

"Leave we that," said the Lamb. "It is most requisite that I bleed. Hearken to that which I must announce to you. Habetis papam. A pope is chosen unto you."

"Dear Lamb," answered Probus in the dream or in the trance, "how so? Symmachus and Eulalius are both dead, the Church is without a head, mankind lacks a judge, the throne of the world is vacant. How am I to understand thy precious words?"

"As they are spoken," said the Lamb. "Your prayer is heard and the choice come to pass. But thou art chosen to be the first to hear it and to take measures

accordantly. Only believe! The Chosen One also must
believe, however hard he may find it. For all election
is hard to understand and not accessible to reason."

"I will pray," said Probus, sobbing at the moving
sweetness of the Lamb's voice, and sank on his knees
before the bench. "Let me learn: what is his name?"

"Gregorius," replied the Lamb.

"Gregorius," repeated the old man, overcome. "When
I hear it, it is as though he could not be named otherwise, dear Lamb. Wilt thou not then in thy loving-
kindness also make me to know where he is?"

"Far from here," responded the Lamb. "And thou
art picked out to fetch him thither. Up, Probus! Seek
him from land to land in Christendom and let no travail
of the journey rue thee, let it lead thee now high over
barren mountain heights, now across raging torrents.
On a savage rock sits the Chosen One quite alone for
full seventeen years. Seek and fetch him, for to him belongs the throne."

"I will seek with all my strength," Probus assured
him. "But, thou touching Lamb, Christendom is so
broad and big. Must I research it quite through till I
stumble on the stone where the Chosen One abides? In
my human weakness I tremble before the mission."

"Who seeks shall find," said the Lamb, in a particularly heart-searching voice, and all at once there mingled in the bitter fragrance of the laurel bushes wherein
the Roman sat a scent of roses so strong and delightful
that one perceived only it. For every drop of blood that
ran down to the ground out of the Lamb's wound and

its curling pelt turned there into a full-open red rose, of which there were soon very many.

"Surmount boldly the Alps," the Lamb standing in the roses went on to say. "Traverse the Alemannian country, not being lured to linger even by famous St. Gall, and address yourself further, to westward and northward toward the North Sea. Comest thou into a land bordering thereupon, which five years long was overrun with war, from which a firm-grasping hand delivered it, then art thou right. Turn towards its hills and mountains, woods, wildernesses, and wastes. In such a one enter in, in the house of a fisher, on the marge of a lake. From him shalt thou have guidance. Thou hast heard. Believe and obey!"

Therewith the Lamb vanished and the roses of its blood as well, but Probus found himself still kneeling, hands clasped, before the bench with the Pan's heads, his cheeks wet with tears which the sweet voice of the Lamb and the moving motions of its mouth in speech had lured from him. He tried his nose on the air after a breath of the fragrance of roses and truly there seemed to him for a short time a trace, outweighed and soon in any case quite overborne by the odour of the laurels.

"What has come over me?" he asked himself. "It was a vision, the first ever vouchsafed to me, for it is otherwise not at all in my line. Faltonia calls me a matter-of-fact man, and it is true: she is far more susceptible than I am and studies Origen with philosophic intrepidity, although his theories have been condemned. But anything of the sort as just now me has never befallen her.

The scent of roses is now quite gone but my heart still heaves with love to the Lamb and I cannot doubt that it has announced to me the truth and that actually a pope has been chosen for us, whom I am to seek. At once I must tell Faltonia all, first that she may see of what extraordinary experiences my soul is capable and second to hear her opinion about the practical conclusions I must draw from what I have heard."

Thereupon he got up from his knees and hastened as quickly as a man past fifty can still move to the palace, where in one of the ten or twelve habitable rooms he found his spouse as she applied herself to the highly intellectual occupation of excerpting Origen. With astonishment the matron saw his great emotion and listened attentively to his headlong account, which he accompanied with many a "Just think!" "Imagine!" and "Just listen to this!"

"Sextus," said she finally, "that seems indeed remarkable. You are a matter-of-fact man on the whole, and when suddenly such a vision confronts you it quite possibly has grave significance. The blood-roses are poetic, and of yourself you produce no poetry; it must have its origins outside your personality. On the other hand I should regard it as extravagant if you just so proceed to follow this prompting received in solitude and at your time of life plunge into the adventure of a journey into the Cimmerian regions where they grope perpetually in darkness and night. You have been adjured to believe, but it is risky to believe all by yourself, and acts which rest on a basis of a quite personal and single faith may easily become foolish. And besides, you could not without the agreement of the public set out on the search for the Chosen One and bring him here if you should find him. But would your fellow citizens ascribe enough significance to what they might call the vagaries of your afternoon nap to commission you with the expedition?"

"I doubt it myself, Faltonia. But I confess I had hoped for more from you than a critical analysis of my situation—in other words, some advice."

"You are wrong, Probus, to expect such a thing from me. This is an ecclesiastical matter, concerning the very highest things, and you know that in the Church the woman should be silent. Whether it would not better serve the Church if rational women had some voice in it, that we will not discuss."

"Your bitterness troubles me, Faltonia. But it is probably the case that your habit of confining yourself to the theoretic analysis of things does not permit you to come to a conclusion and so you take cover behind the ruling that the woman be silent in the Church."

"Very shrewd. It seems, dear Sextus, that today you are living the whole day above your resources. And therewith you neglect to think of the simplest and most immediate thing, to suggest which I have been long since about to do, wherein I couple with good advice the modesty suitable to the female. Talk over your experience with your friend Liberius. He, as an ecclesiastic of high station, whose character and intelligence I recognize although he rejects the doctrines of Origen

and considers that a Christian philosophy is not for
Christendom, is altogether the man to put himself in
your place and tell you how he would behave in it."

This proposal at once struck Probus as good and
right. The man of whom Faltonia spoke, Liberius, was
the Cardinal Presbyter of Ste Anastasia sub Palatio, a
highly respected prelate, even belonging to the gre-
mium charged with the administration of Church affairs during the vacancy of the Holy See, and actually
close to Probus in ancient friendship. The thought of
opening himself to Liberius was welcome and benefi-
cent to the troubled man.

"Faltonia," said he, "you have spoken capitally. Forgive me that I turned first to you and interrupted you
in your studies. In any case I cannot regret it, for if
you did withhold actual advice from me, yet you
showed me after all the best way to arrive at it. I will
at once have myself carried to Liberius."

After these words he struck with the drumstick at a
round bronze gong and gave the entering servants orders to make ready his litter with all speed. He mounted
it in one of the courts with the ruined colonnade, en-
joining the bearers to speed. In an easy weaving trot in
order to shake the litter as little as possible, they bore
him through the famous city of Rome, whose streets
wound among mammoth ruins of magnificent buildings
from earlier times, half-buried in rubble, and where
everywhere the marble statues of Cæsars, gods, and
famous citizens lay about mutilated, waiting to be
thrown into lime-pits and burnt for mortar. In front

of the covered litter and its four bearers ran another pair of servants whose task it was to clear by shouts and gestures a free passage through the crowds for the patrician's litter. They had been warned not to do it in a peremptory way, but more as pleading or invoking.

The house of Liberius was near the Church of Ste Anastasia below the Palatine Hill: a new building it was, decorated with ancient corbels and friezes and bay windows broken by small pillars. Steps led up to its vestibule, which was borne by columns taken from elsewhere, and at the foot of the steps there waited on the square the presbyter's own litter. Yes, as Probus got out of his he saw his friend himself, still occupied in putting on his mantle, coming out of the house and down the steps. Liberius stopped half-way, surprised as he saw Probus. He was a tall handsome man, grey-haired, with the arched upper lip of the Roman, contemplative dark eyes, and a mouth which got its dolorous, pious expression from the fact that—at only one corner—it drooped. Faltonia's husband was much shorter than his priestly friend, also rather thickset, as it strikes me on this occasion, with very round chestnut-coloured eyes and above them eyebrows of a blackness striking below the thick snow-white thatch of his hair.

"You here, Probus?" said the prelate in surprise as he came with outstretched hand to meet the other mounting the stairs. "Do you know, I was just on the way to you, and truly on important matters."

"That is a strange coincidence, my Liberius," answered the Anician. "You may be sure that the motives which urged me to you are at least as urgent as your own."

"I can scarcely believe it," replied the other, while his eyes darkened and the corner of his mouth drooped even more. "But come, let us go in, let us sit down in my zetas æstivalis, where the coolness and quiet will be favourable to our interview."

This airy and pleasant apartment was in the upper storey of the house, near the dining-room, and the friends entered it, not before the master of the house had impressed upon the servants under no circumstances to disturb the colloquy.

"Impatient as I am to open myself to you, my dear Probus," said he, when they had taken place near each other on a stone chest covered with cushions, which on a nearer view I take for a handsome sarcophagus from other times, "yet I would like to accord you as host to guest the first place and ask you to begin and tell me what you have on your mind."

"Thanks, my friend," responded Probus, "but in fairness I am compelled to call to your attention the fact that when I have made my communication, nothing else whatever can be the subject of our talk. So I beg you to speak first."

"I cannot in fairness do so," replied Liberius, "since for my part it is my conviction that when I have spoken it will never come to a discussion of your affair."

"No, you talk first," persisted the optimate, "so that we can discuss and get done with your business in short order."

"You deceive yourself as to its bearing," said Liberius, "when you talk about short order and getting done with. Still, very well, I yield to your importuning. Learn then, my dear old friend, that I have been vouchsafed a manifestation."

"A manifestation!" Probus said in a subdued voice, laying his hand on the other's as he spoke. "Hearken, Liberius, I take back my offer and would like above all for my own part to—"

"Too late," answered the presbyter. "My eagerness to confide in you can no longer be checked. The fullness of my heart overflows in such force that I am irresistibly urged to fill yours with it. Once more, then, as you see me sitting here, I have been not two hours since given a revelation."

"A manifestation and a revelation!" repeated Probus as he pressed his friend's hand. "I conjure you, how did it come to you?"

"In the following way," answered Liberius. "You are familiar with the little terrace in front of my dining-room with its balustrade overgrown with ivy, whence one has a view of the hill of the Foundation of the City and our most ancient shrines. After the meal I had had an easy chair put out there in which I was resting, given to careful thoughts on the fate of the Church, which in our impotence and bewilderment we have given over to God. You will say I had fallen asleep, for I had a dream-vision. But I would sooner speak of a waking vision, even conceding that the state in which one has visions is not the same as that of ordinary wakingness.

In front of me on the balustrade stood a most touching
lamb, which to my unspeakable awe and amaze was
bleeding from its side; it opened its mouth, and in a
voice most evocative of love spoke to me in the words—"

"Habetis papam!" shouted Probus.

"I admire," answered Liberius, "your divination. Yes,
that was what it said, 'A Pope,' it said, 'has been chosen
for you. Named Gregorius, he bides far away from
here, for seventeen years on a savage rock, and to him
belongs the papal seat. But you are selected to be the
first to hear this.'"

"It said that to you too?" asked the Anician, slightly
crestfallen. "I confess that I was of the opinion it said
it only to me."

"Sextus, you talk as though—"

"Yes, my dear Liberius, to me also the touching Lamb
appeared and made me its revelation, apparently at the
same hour as to you. And not enough with that, it also
announced to me that I was selected to seek out the
Chosen One, with however great difficulties, and bring
him to Rome."

"But just that I wanted to tell you," cried Liberius,
"that to me, to me too it imparted this sacred task."

"To you too, then," said Probus. "To both of us,
and at the same time. Friend, what a miracle! The Lamb
was on your terrace and it was in my garden and to
each of us it spoke as though only to him. 'Surmount
boldly the Alps,' it said—"

" '—And address yourself to the west and north,' "
broke in Liberius. And now they repeated in chorus

and by turns all that the Lamb had said to them and what instructed them in general on the place where the Chosen One abode. "Ah, the Lamb!" they both cried out repeatedly, singly and together. For they could not get out of their minds the so heart-piercing image of the Lamb, its infinitely mild, long-lashed eyes, the moving movements of its mouth in speech, the trembling sweetness of its voice, the blood that dripped from its curling fleece. They got up from the sarcophagus, fell into each other's arms, and despite the disparity in height kissed each other on the cheek, amid tears. Probus's head lay on Liberius's breast, the dalmatic was bedewed with his tears, and Liberius, his head bent on one side, looked out from above past the other's head, his mouth drooping with piety at the corner.

"Oh, and the roses," Probus recalled, his head on the other's breast, "into which his dear blood changed when I shrank from my mission!"

"Roses?" asked Liberius, relaxing his embrace. "I know nothing of such."

"Hosts of roses in mine," Probus assured him. "Their fragrance quite overpowered that of the laurels."

"I can only repeat," replied Liberius, and made an end of the embrace, "that no roses came into my vision. But let us not, my friend, do dishonour to so glorious an event by regarding each other with envy. I consider it possible that in view of my quality as Son and Prince of the Church, the Lamb did not consider it necessary to strengthen my faith by a rose-miracle."

"Certainly, my dear friend, it may be so," the Anician

agreed, "although you must not lay it up against me that I admire the poesy of this exclusive manifestation and invite you to do so with me. But what above all we want to admire is the wisdom of the Lamb in announcing not to just one of us, be it to you or to me, but to us both, that the election has been made and imposing upon us both the journey. With how much greater assurance shall we enter on it together than if only one of us had received the instruction! It is hard indeed without companionship to have faith, and undeniable that actions which proceed from an entirely private and single belief have easily something unbalanced about them. And our fellow citizens? Reflect, my friend, that we need their confidence in order to act. True, we are men whose word is to the Romans like an oath. And yet shall the individual be surprised if his revelation be interpreted as the little significant product of an afternoon nap? But just therein lies the wisdom of the Lamb, that it doubled the visitation and provided voice for two witnesses, whose unanimous declaration, unanimous with the single exception of the roses, must put an end to all doubts. What say you to my words?"

"They are capital, my friend," responded Liberius. "Every one of them shows that you owe your offices and dignities only in part to your ancient name. Yes, hand in hand shall we go before the speedily summoned assembly and with hearts full of remembrance of the Lamb with one voice give testimony on the miracle which befell us!"

The Second Visit

THE FISHER and his wife had in seventeen years no
more visitors to their solitude on the marge of the lake;
and probably for just as long a time before that. The
more lively, though they never spoke of it, was the
memory of the one they had once received, the husband with anger and bad words, the wife with pious
intuitions. I will add that the man did not in the least
want to remember the visit and shoved it out of his
mind as much as possible. For in retrospect it always
seemed to him, though actually he had at that time done
just what the strange man wanted, as though he had
committed something like a crime—in short, a murder.
And one would rather banish such ideas. He did not
succeed badly, indeed, so far as the upper layer of his
consciousness went, for after all he did see people when
he brought his roach and carp to market, and that diverted his mind. But his wife saw no one, she lived and
faded all alone in the desert spot beside her churlish
husband, and as she had no reason, as he had, to banish
the event of that time from her memory, she cherished
it silently in her heart through all the years, and thought
of the handsome, humble beggar whom she had fetched

in out of the rain, for whom she had strewn the reeds
for a bed; thought of him very often, yes, every day,
and tears would come in her eyes.

It does not mean much that her eyes got wet at the
thought, for anyhow she wept quite easily; that is, she
did not exactly weep, but without alteration of her face
and without occasion apparent even to herself, her eyes
would silently run over, and a few tears roll down the
weather-beaten cheeks, so that her husband always
called her a cry-baby. He, from contact with men and
trade with them, had continued hard, common, and
sure of himself, while the woman, entirely without re-
lief from monotony, was in her loneliness the fuller of
feeling and susceptible as a sensitive plant.

Now came for them both a day—it was in some re-
spects a day of miracles, that day and the day after.
Very favourably it had begun, for early in the morning the fisher had caught with his hame in the lake
a splendid fish, a pike, almost a shark, more than six
feet long, marked with black spots, the greedy mouth
spiked with predacious teeth. For the small fry round
about in the lake it had been certainly a gift of God to
be delivered from this tyrant. The fisher had to have a
regular struggle with the savage body of his prey before he crushed its head on the edge of his boat. It was
a lucky catch such as his trade seldom granted him.
Early next morning he would bring the succulent vic-
tual to market and sell it to advantage.

Such was his intention, and truly a good price was
he to get for his catch, indeed not even tomorrow but

today, and not in the distant village but here in his own house. For that very day the fisherman and his wife were to have guests again.

The two were standing as then, and often, towards evening, in front of their hut, looking out across country: the fisher, who now had an entirely grey beard, thinking with brooding pride of his splendid fish, like one who with more moroseness than joy holds fast infrequent fortune by the lock; his wife with her head bent on one side, weeping a little with inexpressive features. They spoke not a word. As then and now again it was turning autumn; September it was, with fallow light this evening over the hills sloping down to their shore. The light was due to the rain-cloud which at sunset darkened part of the sky and was near to discharging its rain.

Then afar on the winding forest path they saw riders, one behind the other, coming down to the vale.

For some time they spoke no word. Then the man in a hoarse voice said only:

"Riders."

"Ah, dear God," said the woman, folded her hands, and two bright tears rolled down her cheeks.

Then they were both quite silent and only watched without moving, fixedly, the approach of the strangers.

"Three riders and a vacant horse," the man said gruffly after a while.

"And a vacant horse," repeated the woman and clasped her hands tighter. She raised them higher in front of her face and added:

"Vacant and white."

Thus it was: two were riding, as there was room enough abreast, leaving the third behind. He was a servant, his mule was laden, it carried fat bags on each side. He led a fourth animal, unladen, with him by the bridle, and it was white, as well as its saddle and reins. The gentlemen in front of him also rode good, high-legged hinnies, well saddled and bridled. They were elderly gentlefolk, differing in height, one short, the other tall. They were wrapped in travelling-mantles with hoods. They pulled up close to the breathless pair, who only stared open-mouthed and forgot to bow down. The shorter of the two gentlemen gave them greeting and then asked, turning to the man:

"Friend, is this a solitary spot?"

"Your servant, yes, a place where nobody is," the other roused himself to say.

"Entirely solitary?" asked the tall one, and gave the fisher a long look, one corner of his mouth drooping heavy and devout.

"One cannot deny it, lord. This hut stands in the greatest possible loneness here by the lake."

"What is your trade?" asked the short one.

"I am a fisher," was the reply.

Then the two looked at each other and nodded. One raised his thick black brows, the other drew down still more piously the corner of his mouth.

"Hearken, greybeard," the shorter one said again, "don't conceal from us: is it perhaps here in the region of your secluded spot that there is a stone, a savage,

world-remote rocky seat or whatever you would call
such a place of retreat?"

"No, lord, such a place I do not know," he made answer to the question, and shook his head once for all as
he gave it.

"None at all hereabouts? You are a fisher, you probably fish in that sizable lake extending over there?"

"Yes, lord, I get my living there."

"And the lake has reefs, or cliffs, if you like, coming
out of the water, bare islands in short, one or other of
which one might call a desolate rock?"

"No, lord, by my soul, I should know the lake, but
I know of no rock-island in its waters."

"Why weeps your wife?" suddenly asked the tall
one and with his finger which bore a mounted seal ring
motioned at the fisher's wife.

"She mostly weeps," answered the man roughly.
"She is a weepy sort."

"Blessed are the meek," said the one with the ring.
Then he got down, as did likewise the shorter one,
from his beast; the latter, however, trod before the fisherman, laid his hand on his shoulder, and said:

"Amice, know that we purpose to be a burden upon
you, you and your tear-happy wife, for this night. We
gentlemen come from afar, even today, not to speak of
all the ground we have covered before that, for we
have been long on the road. Travel-tired and riding-
weary we are. Now evening is falling and rain threatens, yes, it is already raining a little. Will you give us
shelter in your lonely hut till early tomorrow? It shall

not be your loss." And as he spoke, the thickset man winked familiarly, as one who appeals to the common motive, the love of gain.

The fisherman was of one mind and again of another. The stranger's question about a stone was highly uncomfortable and made him suspicious of their presence. The wink promising profit, however, made him smile, darkly and self-consciously. He was another man, more pliant than once, that time when the naked rascal had come begging up to his hut. One catch, a good one came after another one today, and could probably be brought into profitable relation to it. Fiercely he held his good luck by the forelock.

"Humbly," he said, "are your honours entreated to condescend, however little this solitary hut is furnished fit for any visit, not to speak of such a visit. We are poor folk. If we even had the lean-to, the store-room that we used to have, we could put your animals in it, the greys and that white ass there. But the old shed fell in years ago. So your servant, as I see him doing, must make do the best he can, tie up the beasts and cover them against the rain, which, if I know the signs, won't be bad. But that should not be expected of you, nor that you should ride further by night, for there are wolves too. I have never sent away anyone from my door, lord or beggar, under such conditions. If only it were not for our great poverty and the meanness of this room, at which you look full of concern! Ours in the first place is the concern and the hesitation, for how shall we sleep you; how entertain you before that? For the entertainment, indeed, I know what to do, for today I caught a fish—I could have got a lot of money for it—a master fish it is and a tasty supper, whether the wife boil or bake it. But as for sleeping, there good counsel is dearer—even though the fish is not cheap—I am worried about that."

"Man," replied the shorter stranger, who had now put back his hood, showing thick, snow-white hair which charmingly became his pitch-black brows, "man, have no concern about us and how you will sleep us, for that is all one. It only seems to you, note that, that it is not all one. We are, certainly, gentlefolk; but under such peculiar circumstances that nothing and no situation can offend us, however contrary to our habits, for none, in whatever form, is worth talking about in comparison with the real and great one on whose account we have been sent out and at our time of life have taken this journey upon us. If you knew the trials which have been our lot since almost half a year ago we began our journey and which we bore without complaint, you would waste no thought on our bed for the night. A little straw here on the floor with a sheet over it we shall find a luxury, if your wife will prepare something like that. But if necessary we can even spend the night squatting here by the deal table, for it is all the same to us by comparison with the one great thing."

Thus the white-headed man. But when meanwhile his companion too had laid off his travelling-cloak and the clerical garb came into view beneath it, as also a little violet cap covering his fleecy grey hair, then the fisherfolk knelt straightway before him, seeking his blessing.

"Bless us, holy Father," implored the woman, wet-eyed. But the tall man shrank back at this address and warded it off with a sweeping gesture.

"Leave out the name, woman," he cried, "and name me not by that which only him becomes who cannot be far off—In nomine suo benedico vos." And with two fingers he described the sign of the cross above his hosts. As they arose, having been blessed, the man began again at once with his preparations and went back to his catch, the excellent fish, which he offered to sell to the gentlemen and serve it up for supper. But the lay gentleman answered him:

"Put all these things out of your mind, friend, and don't worry about us! We have brought what we need along with us. We have bread and wine, probably our servant will bring us a cold chicken-wing or some such thing when he has given the horses the feed we have likewise provided."

"Good, good," cried the fisherman. "But yet I'd like to see whether the pike doesn't look tempting to you as a main course, when I show him to you."

And he brought the fish in a tub, to the no small surprise of the strangers, who praised its size and fineness.

"On the market," said their host, "I would have got five florins for him."

"You shall have the double," promised the white-head, "and share with your wife the eating of it too, if she knows how to serve it up to us delicately prepared, baked, spiced, and with a good caper sauce. Can you engage to do that, woman?"

"Ah, noble sir," said she, "of capers I have scarcely heard, but there will be a bit of bacon to lard it and I can make a savoury stock which you will surely not fail to approve."

She promised more than she really thought she could do, but she was afraid of her husband, who was on fire to sell his fish above its price and would beat her if she proved incapable.

"Ten florins," cried the grasping man, "and it's a bargain! You travelling nobilities will have a dish for supper such as has hardly been offered to you in your travels. Now let me just wash and gut it so the cook can get to work on it."

The fisherman's wife remained standing by the guests, her hands crossed on her breast, while her husband busied himself at the hearth. Bread and wine the servant had set before them and they partook, pouring out some of the red wine in a travelling-cup for the woman to taste. She drank with relish and a by-your-leave, and it was probably so that the fire of the wine emboldened her curiosity, for she said:

"Great and weighty must the matter truly be, that has set you stately noblemen on the road and makes you indifferent to hardships you are not used to. I well understood that you came from far away and have covered great stretches of ground."

"That have we," confirmed the one with the white

hair and black eyebrows. "From so far we come as from
the land of Italy, where stands the new Jerusalem. But
not out of rashness, which would not beseem our age,
have we set out on our journey and sought throughout Christendom; no, but instead by direction from on
high."

"With reverence I hear it," answered the woman.
"And with reverence not meddlesomeness it is that I
ask what might you be searching for through Christendom?"

"That you will learn," said the shorter man, "together with all the world when the Word has fulfilled
itself in us: 'Seek and ye shall find.' Not much can fail
of it being fulfilled, and we can no longer be far
from our goal, according to our instructions. We have
crossed the cities and dominions of Italy, on horseback,
in wagons and litters, and thus approached the fearsome
Alps, in whose gorges the water foams down from
horrible rocks and where our path mounted climbing
through dampness and mist on long-foretold paths to
heights and slopes at whose desolation the soul is be-
numbed. There grows no tree or bush, in glassy light
the desert rubble spreads, whereon snow-covered peaks
look menacingly down and the pure arc of sky stretching over it seems desolate too. We breathed light, our
hearts were in our mouths, and by virtue of a sort of in-
toxication which overcame us and suited ill the awful-
ness of our surroundings, my companion, the clerical
gentleman there, quite contrary to his nature and physical constitution, began to expend himself in jests, for

which I reproved him because of the nighness of God."

"You cannot say," the taller one defended himself, "that my words were light."

"They could only be called so on account of their gushing abundance," responded the other, "and I speak of it only to give this good woman an idea of the monstrousness of the spheres whereinto our journey led us. But it went down thence too and, as we expected, we arrived in Germany, where men love usefulness and gain; sturdy men grub up woods into heath and meadow; distaff and shuttle support considerable towns, and learning flourishes in peaceful cloisters. We have lingered for naught but needful rest. Even renowned St. Gall could not tempt us to pause. Our mission brooked no delay. Westward and northward it urged us on, through many bishoprics, palatinates, and kingdoms, till we came to this country which borders on the North Sea and of which it is said that it was overspread with ravaging war, from which a firm-holding hand delivered it. Do you know of the firm-holding hand?"

"No," answered the woman, "we know naught of all that. Our hut stands too remote for wars and warcries to reach us."

"But after all there is something right about it," said the white-headed one, "it corresponds to our instructions. According to them we left the sounding sea at our backs and sought out the heights, the wastes and empty places of the land. Then the wilds addressed us

from the plains to the woods, and thence we strayed
onwards as our hearts bade us, up till the third day. We
struck into a foot-path where no hoof had ever stepped,
and the crooked grassy way led us to this tongue of
land in the lake and to your hut. Behold, here we are
and here we sit. And now drink once more, goodwife,
from my cup! Have a good pull to the health of your
guests. A good long one, so. And now tell us faithfully:
do you really know of no desolate stone or lonely rock-
perch somewhere hereabouts in the region of your bar-
renness?"

But the woman was afraid of her husband and answered:

"Your lordships have already asked the fisher and he
told you. Would he dare conceal it from you if he
knew of such a spot?"

"But why then do you tremble and weep?" asked the
tall man in his deep voice. For the fisher-woman could
not control her tears and her crossed hands shook on
her breast.

"My Father," she said, "that is only because it craves
me so to ask the lords a question—ever since you came
to the hut, yes, already when I saw you coming, from
far off, it urged me, poor female as I am, unspeakably."

"Ask!" said the priestly man.

"For whom, ah, for whomever," asked the woman,
"may the white ass be meant, the riderless one that you
lead along with you?"

"That," said the other, and dropped his voice still
deeper, "is intended for him whom to seek we have

been sent out from the new Jerusalem by guidance
from on high. For the Chosen One it is, whom we
search for through Christendom, whose place by all
the signs cannot be far off."

"Oh, my God!" said the woman, "then I will tell
you—"

But at the moment when she would begin, there
came a hoarse cry from where the fisherman was working over his fish—a cry of terror and sheer amaze, which
made the gentlemen start up and look towards the
fisher. But the woman turned abruptly, gestured with
outstretched arm towards the place whence the cry
came, and as though she knew what had revealed itself
there, she shouted as though in triumph:

"There, there! You've got it, you've got it!"

Thus she stood, her hand outstretched. But the gentlemen got up and over to the hearth, where the fisherman's terror-stricken voice was heard:

"There it is! I see it again and hold it, saved from
the bottom of the sea, God keep and preserve me!"

On the slimy board lay the fish, scaled and slit open;
while in his filthy hand the man held a thing, a key, he
was staring at it. "Woe is me, it is the very one and no
other! Saved out of the depths of the wave! In the belly
of the fish! The belly, I saw something strange about
it and cut it out, there it was, I have it in my hand, God
be merciful to me a sinner!"

And he tottered to the table, thrust his elbows on it,
and buried his filthy hands in his hair, together with his
find. The gentlemen approached him, while his wife

still stood as though in an ecstasy, with her hand outstretched towards the place whence her husband had
tottered.

"Friend," with deeper, milder voice now spoke Liberius, for it was he, he and Sextus Anicius Probus,
they were the strangers, now that at last I name our old
acquaintances by name, "friend," said the presbyter,
"speak to us and lighten your heart, wherein the find
in the fish's belly seems to have awakened the knowledge of old error! See in me your confessor! What is
it about the thing, the key in your hands?"

Then the blenched man straightened up and made his
confession, while his wife with clasped hands knelt beside him. Of the waylost wanderer in beggar's guise he
spoke, who many years before had come to the hut and
on whom he had heaped scorn and hatred, would not
even have granted him shelter without the intercession
of his wife. He had scourged him with vile words, for
he took him for a cheater, and all of them the man bore
in humility, with penitential meekness, and finally asked
him for some savage place where he might do penance
to the utmost, proportioned to his sins. To the grim
rock out in the water he had next morning brought
him and there exposed him, by his own wish indeed,
but out of spite, to make more bitter the hypocrisy,
and on top of that had put on him a leg-iron with a
lock, throwing the key of it out into the water, and
had sworn that if he ever saw it again and got it out of
the depths of the wave, then he would believe that the
man was a holy penitent and beg his pardon. "Accurst,

accurst," he groaned. "God has punished me and con-
founded me with a miracle after all this long time.
There, look at the key, swallowed by the fish, found in
the fish's guts, God's token illumining him, damning me
who mocked the holy man and condemned himself to
roast in hell; for pardon it is too late." And the fisher
thrust his elbows down on the table again and ploughed
with his hands through his hair.

But how thrilled were the two friends!

"Anima mea laudabit te," Liberius said with head
upraised, "et indicia tua me adjuvabunt!—Fisher," he
turned to the agitated man, "be of good cheer, for the
key was sent to you as a sign that you have sheltered
him to whom the power of the key shall be given and
the power to bind and to loose. He will loose thee and
pardon thee that thou didst not know him and that once
you did indeed according to his will but with hatred in
your heart. It is not too late for pardon. Tomorrow,
before daybreak, you must take us to the rock, ad pe-
tram, that we may bring him down, to seek whom we
have been sent forth, and your second trip shall free
you from the first one."

"Ah, poor dear honoured lordships, gentlemen,"
sighed the fisher. "What good will the trip be? I will of
course make it, and perhaps I shall have to make it to all
eternity, condemned everlastingly to row to and fro.
But how could you hope to find the saint there, where
I spitefully exposed him twenty years gone?"

"Seventeen," Probus corrected, "it is seventeen,
friend fisherman."

"Seventeen or twenty," he moaned. "What difference does that make? Don't ask that he has survived even one of them, yes, even a twelfth of one! I left him on the bare rock, in lacks any one of which was enough to murder every hope. If weather and wind did not kill him in short order, then hunger did, and that most likely even sooner than exposure. From his skeleton some bits, that is what we shall by chance find on top of the rock, and you gentlemen can take them back as relics to the new Jerusalem. But I cannot beg pardon of him or win redemption, but must to all eternity ferry to and fro between stone and strand in payment of my sin."

Then the gentlemen looked smiling at each other, shook their heads, and laughed a little with their shoulders.

"Man, you speak after your understanding," said the cleric then, and his lay friend added:

"Anxious and fearful one, look at your wife!"

For as she knelt there, her hands clasped under her chin, her heart was so full of faith and joy that it was plainly somewhat lighter round her head than elsewhere in the flickering light of the room.

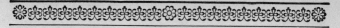

The Finding

THE FISH was not dressed and not consumed; I commend the fact that they all found it unseemly to lard and devour the bearer of the key and that the gentlemen contented themselves with bread and wine. In the fisher's poor soul would have been no room for grudge at the loss of the fish's price, full as it was of dread lest he must ferry for ever between stone and strand because he had mistaken the holy man. Yet he got his money after all, for his guests large-heartedly insisted on paying, one way or another, for what they had ordered, and thus in this minor point the man found himself content, however much distress of another sort weighed him down.

The sheen of her faith round his wife's head he regarded as her personal affair, entirely as the result of her fanaticism, which was no evidence against his conviction that one would find on the stone no trace whatever of the beggar or at most such remains as he shuddered to think of. Frightfully abased and chastened by the discovery of the key, he dreaded to visit again the place of his spiteful ill deed, dreaded too the disappointment which awaited the gentlemen after all their great efforts; for to hoist these elderly elegants up onto the rock would be no small thing, and then after such extended travels they would stand at a goal which could not possibly still have anything to offer them.

In my way I share the anxiety of this churlish man. For I well know, and you know with me, to whom I have told it all, what test was to confront the two men to whom the revelation and task had been assigned. Previsioned, as master of the tale, I could of course reassure myself that the test, as it were, was a jest, and everything ended well. And yet I await with some dismay the great embarrassment and confusion which was to face their confident hope.

The devout woman had laid the wide mattress of her double bed on the floor of the room for the messengers, and on it they had together an hour or so of impatient sleep, or else only one, more likely, lay on it while the other napped in a chair. But scarcely had dawn greyed when they stirred, asked the fisher for water to freshen themselves, ate some spoonfuls of porridge the woman brought them, and then would not longer put off the journey. On their mules they rode the short distance to the landing, led by the dour-faced fisherman carrying the ladder, also a pickaxe and some rope. The Roman servant, however, had to lead the white ass too, while the fisherman shook his head, and to wait for them at the landing. Some food, too, bread and wine, he brought, and worthy garb for him who would have need of it also lay on the white ass's back. These, as well as the provisions and the tools, were put into the boat. But Liberius, his mouth drooping at the corner, carried the key.

So the fisherman rowed them, sighing heavily the while, out on the quiet waters—an hour? Even two? They scarcely noticed. They peered forwards for the rock of the Lamb's word and at last it appeared on the empty waste, reddish-grey and bare, a flattened cone, quite tall—"kepha," as the cleric piously murmured, "petra," as he added, with folded hands. But Probus said, as they came near:

"I don't as yet see anything or anybody on the stone."

He stressed the word "yet," and yet his friend reproved him with a stern "Just keep on waiting."

"I am," answered the Anician. "But as yet no hut shows itself, nor any other sort of shelter, nor any figure of a man up there."

"With what and of what," said the fisherman gloomily in his beard, "would he have built himself a shelter?"

Liberius did not heed. "Row harder," he commanded, "come alongside the rock, that we may climb it without delay."

"Yes, climb up it," repeated his friend with emphasis, though he, the heavier person, looked forward with apprehension to the climb. In fact it was a thing easier said than done for people over fifty. The fisherman could get alongside and make fast; he could, in repeated tries, failures, and final fair success hook his ladder onto two points of rock within reach up above, so that, standing away from the not entirely vertical wall, it

afforded a swaying but tolerably secure ascent. But we
know that it fell far short of reaching up to the level
ground, and the job of getting his guests not only up
its rungs but across the further bare stretch of rock
looked to the fisherman in the reality not easier but
even harder than his imagination had seen it.

He tied his rope round all three of them together and
so arranged the ascent up the unsteady ladder that he
went first, Liberius followed him, and the Anician
brought up the rear. Hard indeed had the sinful man,
not strengthened by faith, to pull and to brake, even on
the ladder; still more when it left off and on the last
piece of the rock, up to its summit, no earlier foot or
step had made a mark at all. With his pickaxe he sometimes tried to make a step for his followers—it was no
more than an indication. They used it as well as they
could, panting, on hands and feet. Breathless, sweating
despite the cold, they got to the top one after the other,
crawled over the truncated level, stood up, forced their
eyes to look round—the fisher did it only dully, without expectation, the gentlemen eagerly, with eyes staring wide.

No more was there than from afar, from below, had
been to be seen: emptiness in the bare space they had
with such effort arrived at. Bewildering disappointment,
chagrin, the profoundest affliction overcame them. Had
the annunciation, the instructions received by both
equally, betrayed them both and led them by the nose?
Could the Lamb's words, confirmed to this point, turn
out in the end and at the very goal to be a lie? Involun-

tarily Probus and Liberius seized and pressed each other's hands.

That they did before—and at the same moment with the fisherman—they saw a thing, a living creature, scuttle away from the middle of the flat surface towards its edge; hardly larger it was than a hedgehog, now on all fours, now erect, now again letting itself down on its forelegs. Its course was like flight, but whither it moved there was no hiding-place. An object, however, lay there on the ledge, broken, covered with rust, the fisherman fixed his eyes on it.

"The leg-iron!" he shouted. But from the lips of the two friends came a suppressed cry:

"The creature!"

The hands of both as they held them trembled. With the other hand each crossed himself.

"Is this"—Liberius questioned the fisherman—"this creature running away of some kind known to you?"

"No, lord," the man replied. "This is the first time I've seen its like. There was no such thing on the rock when I brought the saint here."

"And what did you mean," Probus wanted to know, "by the cry you gave about the iron there?"

"That's the leg-iron," the man burst out, "rusted by the weather, that I put on the saint that time when I threw the key of it into the water—and the fish swallowed it. You gentlemen have got it here and there lies the iron, still locked, but not a fetter any more on anybody. The saint slipped it off. Perhaps he has gone up to heaven."

"Not thus did our instructions sound," replied the presbyter sadly. "He went up, who founded on the Rock His Church. It is bitter enough that we find the rock forsaken, after our most priceless instructions. Little does it help us to silence our grief with baseless conjectures."

"Vacant, you say," interjected Probus; "yet the word does not quite do justice to the truth. Utterly empty and without any trace of him we have been sent out to seek, we do not find the rock. There lies the iron he wore. He himself is not visible. But shall we, as Christians, make the invisible equivalent to the non-existent? Shall we waver in our faith and not rather remain convinced that behind the emptiness, the apparent nothingness, confirmation must hide? It is true: only by that one of God's creatures fleeing away there, near the iron, is life manifested in the place the Lamb has pointed out to us. It was not here when the Chosen One began his stay here, but now it is. Let us draw near it."

"It is very bristly," said Liberius with distaste.

"So it is," Probus agreed. "But more to fear than to ill nature can its behaviour be ascribed. We have nothing to fear from him—what if we had something to hope? Let us go to him!"

And as he still held him by the hand, he drew his friend, still resisting, to the edge of the plateau, towards the rusted iron and the creature sitting beside it. But how great was their amazement, the fisherman's as well, how it took away their breath and made them stand rooted, when the creature stretched out one of its short forelegs toward them against their approach and an indubitably human voice coming from its lips past the overhanging bristle struck on their ears:

"Away from me! Away from here! Disturb not the penance of God's greatest sinner!"

Transported the gentlemen looked at each other. Their hands clutched each other still more tightly. The prelate made with the key the sign of the cross. He said:

"You speak, you creature! Can one then conclude that you partake of humanity?"

"Outside of it am I," came the answer. "Away from the place revealed to me in order that by the utmost penance I may still perhaps reach God."

"Dear creature," Probus now interposed, "we would not contest your position. But know that we are ourselves sent hither by the most precious common vision and that we have been promised to find here him whom God has chosen."

"Here you will find only him whom God has chosen as the lowermost, uttermost sinner."

"That too," responded the Anician with urban courtesy, "is an interesting combination. But he whom we are sent to seek and fetch, him has He chosen for his Vicar, the Bishop of all the bishops, Shepherd of the people, the Pope in Rome. Learn that we are Romans, sons of the new Jerusalem, where the throne of the world stands vacant, because the opinion of the world became confused at the effort to fill it. But we, this priestly man and I, have been instructed in a double vision by a most moving Lamb, that God Himself has made the election, to whom it shall be given to bind and to loose, and that the Chosen may be found in a distant land, on a stone, on this stone, whereon he, so said the Lamb of God, had been living for seventeen years. We do not find him, we find only this iron, the key to which the sea gave back by means of a fish, and instead of the Chosen One we find you. We conjure you, do you know any news of him?"

"No further!" cried Liberius with suddenly mounting fear, as he seized the speaker by the arm. But now it happened that they saw two tears roll from the creature's eyes and down over its haunted, hairy face.

"You weep, dear creature," said Probus, who himself at the sight could scarcely keep back his tears. "More even than the gift of speech your tears are witness that you share in our humanity. By the blood of the Lamb, were you a man before your present shape was given you?"

"A man, if also outside humanity," came back the reply.

"And have you received baptism?"

"A godly man administered it to me, and christened me with his name."

"With what name?"

"Ask not!" cried Liberius at a pitch of dread, and sought to put his tall form between his friend and the creature. But the latter murmured:

"Gregorius."

"Horrible!" shrieked the ecclesiastic and fell on his knees, covering his face with both hands. His compan-

ion bent to him, towering now above him although so
much smaller in stature.

"Let us control ourselves, amice," said he. "This is
a great, I admit a bewildering but a most thrilling miracle, before which only resignation remains to our human intelligence."

"Devil's mockery and hellish delusion it is!" burst out
the other between his hands. "Fugamus! We are the
Devil's dupes! God has chosen no bristly beast of the
field for his bishop, though he tell us a hundred times
that his name is the Chosen One's. Away from here!
Away from this place of hellish hocus-pocus!"

He sprang up, and was about to dash off. Probus
held him fast by the robe. But behind them they heard
a deprecating voice:

"I once studied grammaticam, divinitatem, and le-
gem."

"You hear?" asked Probus. "Not only does it speak
and weep, it is completely equipped with knowledge
to loose and to bind. You would do well to give him
the key."

"Numquam!" cried the other, beside himself.

"Liberius," his companion pressed him gently, "remember the woman there in the hut, who in the garb
of the beggar knew the saint, and about whose head we
saw shining the sheen of her faith. Shall we be shamed
before her and doggedly refuse to recognize, in a lower
form, the Chosen One? Shall we go astray from the
precise promise of the Lamb?"

"There was," retorted Liberius, "from the beginning

something in our visions that did not accord, for you
asserted you saw the blood of the Lamb turn into roses,
whereas this manifestation was withheld from me."

"You interpreted that," responded Probus, "to mean
that as son and Prince of the Church you did not need
such a prop to your faith."

"That I am," cried Liberius. "A servant of the
Church, a guardian of her sacred honour. But you are
a layman and as such not competent to share my feelings. It is easy for you to indulge in credulity, while
my sense of being a representative writhes in shame. I
have been sent out with you, to fetch the Bishop of
bishops, Father of princes and kings, the ruler of the
globe, whom God elected. Shall I return home with a
spook, a sham not much bigger than a hedgehog in my
bosom, crown it with the tiara, seat it on the sedia gestatoria, and summon the city and the world to pay it
homage as Pope? Turks and infidels would cast scorn
on the Church. The Church—"

He stopped. Behind him they heard:

"Do not take offence at my form! Nourishment for
babes and resistance to heaven's weathers have reduced
it. Man's estate will return to me."

"Do you hear? Do you hear?" triumphed Probus.
"His appearance can be altered. But you, my friend,
turn out all too one-sidedly the aristocratic significance
of the Church and forget its popular side, of which
God gives here a powerful example. In the choice of its
head nothing counts which ranks us here below, not
blood nor stock nor origin, not even whether one has

been ordained as priest. The least and the humblest, let
him only have Christian baptism, and be neither heretic,
schismatic, nor suspected of simony, may become pope,
you know it. And you, figure of penitence, do you
know that man there, with the greying beard?"

"He brought me to this place."

"And did you wear this leg-iron?"

"I wore it until it fell off thanks to my shrinking
form. No iron was needed to hold me fast to my penance, for I held fast to it myself with my firm-holding
hand. To my sinfulness it was given to pull myself together beyond the average in every struggle."

"You seem ready to conform to the election?"

"There was no place for me among mankind. If
God's unfathomable mercy points me to the place above
you all, then will I take it, full of gratitude that I may
bind and loose."

"Cardinal Presbyter of Santa Anastasia sub Palatio,"
said Probus with authority, and stretched up to his so
much taller friend, "give this creature of God the key."

Then Liberius resisted no longer.

"Et tibi dabo claves regni cœlorum," he murmured
as he went down on one knee and offered to the penitent that which the fish had brought into the hut. With
the stunted little arms the recipient pressed the key to
his fuzzy breast. "Sweet parents," he said, "I will loose
you."

The Transformation

THEY decided that he who had brought him up here, the fishing-man, should carry the Chosen One down again in his arms to the boat. Very hard was the descent, almost harder than the climbing up had been; but they all got safely across the bare place to the ladder and down its rungs to the skiff, where they carefully deposited the bearer of the key upon the seat that ran round it; whereupon the fisher, rejoicing in the hope that he need not to all eternity ferry between stone and strand, laid to the oars with all his strength on the return journey.

With torturing anxiety did Liberius observe the penitent of the stone, and I question whether Probus's misgivings over the looks of the Pope as he sat there on the bench stood very much in the rear of his ecclesiastical friend's. His soul too was full of private scruples on the score of appearances, the more that he had taken on himself a great responsibility and in Christian self-examination must now ask himself whether the boldness of his attitude had not been conditioned by arrogance, that is by pride in the miracle of the roses, vouchsafed to him alone. And I do see that the uneasiness of the group reflects itself also upon the faces of those who are hearing the story. Only I myself, as the all-knowing narrator, am entirely blithe and unconcerned, since it lies plain to me in what easy and natural way this dilemma, the discrepancy between Gregor's misshapen dwarfish form and the elevation of the office to which he was called, resolved itself on the way, to the utmost satisfaction and soothing of the Roman aristocrats; and before the end of two hours there sat with them in the boat no longer a rough-haired, matted, calloused denizen of nature's kingdom, but a personable man, of his age near forty, well-shapen, with long black hair indeed, his face covered with a heavy growth of beard which yet could not quite obscure the agreeableness of his features.

How did the restoration come to pass? There could really be nothing simpler or give less difficulty to the understanding. After seventeen years of sucking at the breast of old mother earth he needed only that a higher form of nourishment should touch his lips to put back the suckling of the stone into the state of grown manhood. Very credible that this was known to his nature. "I am hungry and thirsty," he said after a few strokes of the oars; and chagrined that in their despondent mood they had not thought of hospitality, they offered him the white bread and the wine they had in the boat. He ate of the bread, drank of the wine, and from that moment on there began, at silent, constant, unhurried pace—I might say without much ado and, I assure you,

without the others who were witnesses being greatly
surprised or shocked—that change which restores to us
Grigorss, foster-son of the Abbot of Agonia Dei, victor in the battle with the dragon, now ripened to manhood by time, so that we need only wish for razors and
shears to remove, and that speedily, the heavy growth
that disguised his head, and make his familiar face, the
graver copy of Wiligis's and Sibylla's charming traits,
be visible again in all its purity.

As he was naked, they modestly handed him the garment of white wool with a short shoulder-cape which
they had brought with them, and also the little priestly
cap. Thus was he clad when they reached the shore and
the foot-bridge, and thus did he mount the white ass
with the white trappings which had waited there, together with the mounts of the gentlemen, in the care of
the Roman retainer. Thus too did he ride with those
who had fetched him, across the causey to the fisherman's hut, where the withered old wife knelt to receive him and as he dismounted bathed his feet with
her tears.

"You were kind to me, goodwife," said he, bending
to her, "when I visited this hut before. I have not forgotten how you brought me in out of the rain, and
waked me up that I might not miss the trip to my
stand."

"Ah, holy lord," she sobbed, "I merit not your remembrance or your praise, for God knows my sin.
When I protected you that day from the fisher's harsh
words, he taxed me with wantonness and fleshly feeling

for you and I denied the charge, falsely, as I now confess. For my eyes did really have to do with your limbs in the beggar's rags and with your noble features, and wantonness was at the bottom of the good I did you, depraved lost soul that I am!"

"That is a small matter," answered Gregorius, "and not worth talking about. Seldom is one wholly wrong in pointing out the sinful in the good, but God graciously looks at the good deed even though its root is in fleshliness. Absolvo te." These were his words. It was the first instance of the extraordinary clemency he was to display as Pope, so consoling to all men and only offensive to the draconians.

The woman was blissful. I suspect she derived from his absolution leave to feel still a little love for him in fleshly wise. But for him only one concern had weight: only in sleep had it left him, throughout the seventeen years of exposure on the rock, he put it before all else, even the journey to Rome, which the gentlemen were loth to delay, and the trimming of his hair and beard, for which office their chamberlain proposed himself. That concern was distress over his tablet, left forgotten among the rushes of his sleeping-place on the morning when he hastened after the fisher. Urgently he asked where it was.

"O holy sir," said the fisher, "according to my ungentle words I put you up for that night. The shed I put you in, in my blindness, was a rubbish-room. It stood up only twelve weeks after you went with me, then the wind blew it over and it fell to pieces. I burned the walls and the roof and where the little shed stood, look yourself, it is a vacant spot, it grows nothing but nettles and weeds. After so many years how should we find even a scrap of the thing you forgot? Alas, what use were it to search? Long since it rotted and was consumed, give up any hope to the contrary!"

"Think, man," Liberius sternly answered him, "remember you said the like when we asked you to row out to the rock. Nothing and nobody, so you complained, could we hope to find there any more. And how mightily has God convicted you of your little faith!"

"The Holy Father," Probus subjoined, "misses a jewel. Bring spade and hoe, we will go straightway and dig for him."

But Gregor gainsaid him.

"The tools to me alone," he commanded. "Then go into the hut. Only I will dig, and want no witness to my work."

"Your Sanctity," Liberius demurred, "may I observe that it would not befit the dignity of the Church if you were to work here with the spade and throw up the earth in the sweat of your brow. It is not the business even of us your envoys, but only of the fisher and our servant."

"I have spoken," answered Grigorss, and according to his will so it came about. With the sleeves of his robe rolled up he thrust his billet now here, now there into the gor where once he had lain and with his own hands burrowed kneeling in the earth, so that one might say

never did a man search with more fiery zeal for the
charter and record of his own sinful state. The nettles
stung his hands but he paid no heed and God rewarded
the stings, the struggle, and the sweat, for lo, out of
dung and mould it gleamed up at him and he drew out,
clean and bright as though fresh from the framer's hand,
even the ink undimmed, the infant's dower, his mother's anguished shrift, preserved for him as long by the
earth as once by the faithful Abbot, seventeen years
long.

He held it now in one hand and in the other the key
and to himself spoke the lines:

> "Shall I find my life's black story
> Turn to lustre in Thy glory?
> With what wonder do I see,
> Lord, Thy heavenly alchemy
> Clear the flesh's shame and pain
> Back to purity again,
> To the spouse and son of sinning
> Highly from the Highest winning
> Leave for earthly need where'er
> To open Paradise's door!"

The Very Great Pope

THE RINGING of bells, the surging and swelling of bells
supra urbem, above the whole city, in its airs overfilled
with sound! Who is ringing the bells? No one—save
the spirit of story-telling, in that he tells how, three
days before the entry of the Elect, they all began to
ring of themselves and did not cease to ring until before St. Peter his crowning was consummated. This is
historical fact—in all its miracle-beauty not quite the
purest joy for the populatio urbis. Three days and
nights long the bells of Rome were not to be stayed,
they rang with one accord, with the greatest vehemence
from all quarters; and to have all the time this monstrous droning and ding-donging in one's ears was asking not a little of human beings, the spirit of story-
telling is sure of that. It was a sort of blest affliction, a
sanctified scourge, for the cessation of which many
prayers mounted to Heaven from the less steadfast
souls. But Heaven, as I well understand, was of too
high a mood to give ear to such petty petitioning; for
it led the child of shame, his mother's spouse, his grand-
father's son-in-law, his father's father-in-law, mon-

strous brother of his own children, to St. Peter's seat and was, I well understand, so moved by its own incomprehensibility that the emotion converted itself into the self-acting, mighty swinging and clappering of all the bells of all the seven parishes. But from this dread visitation and from the great demand for cotton-wool, which as things were even in those times made dealers hold back the commodity to force up the price, from all this the populatio might gather that a Pope of extraordinary sanctity was drawing near.

He rode through Christendom on his white, purple-draped beast, his face cleansed of its beard, in manly beauty, and the number daily increased of those who followed him, for many heads of churches, counts, or simply such as were gripped by desire for pilgrimage and wish to be at the coronation and the homage joined his train on the way. The renown of a great penitent who had spent seventeen years on a rock and now was exalted by God to the throne of thrones ran before him, and everywhere on the roads lay in their hosts the sick and infirm, hoping to be cured by his touch or even only by his word or glance. History tells us that many were thus released from their sufferings—many, it may be, through a Christian death, if, that is, their infirmity had progressed too far when they dragged themselves from their beds and lay by the roadside. But others, who had touched the hem of his garment or even at a distance had shared in his blessing, threw away crutches and bandages and, praising God, proclaimed that they had never felt better in their lives.

Renowned Rome received him with jubilation—in part also, as is human, because now that he had got here the unruly bells would probably come to rest. He approached, so I am instructed, with his train, by the Via Nomentana, at whose fourteenth milestone the town of Nomentum lies, seat of a bishopric. As far as that had they carried the crosses and banners of the Roman basilicas to meet him, and all ranks of the people, clergy, nobility, the civic guilds with their banners, the troops of the militia, the school-children bearing palm and olive branches, he found ranged to welcome him. With their laudes mingled the distant brazen ringing, and the bells of Nomentum chimed in of their own accord. They told him of the miracle and he heartily rejoiced over the honour. As it was already growing dark, he spent the night in the Bishop's house and only next morning, in a long and tuneful train of pilgrims did he make his entry into the city. Not through the Porta Nomentana, we read, did he enter, but went a long way along under the walls and crossed the Milvian Bridge on his way to the Church of the Apostle. From many thousand wide-open mouths mounted to heaven the pæan:

> Rejoice ye people great and small
> Of Rome, Judea, and of Greece,
> Egyptians, Thracians, Persians, Scythians,
> A King rules over all!

That was he, the Abbot's foundling, the suckling of the stone, who was set as king over all the manifold needs of the globe and to whom, as he climbed the extent of marble steps to the portico of the Church of the Tomb, and a countless host of people covered the fountain square, the chorus of priests swelled out: "Benedictus qui venit in nomine Domini." Before all the folk, on the space before the entrance to the column-surrounded paradisus, he received from the hands of the archdeacon on his head the triple crown, the tiara, the pallium about his shoulders, the shepherd's crook in his hand, and on his finger the fisherman's ring. It is said that at that time, or even during his entry into the city, the bronze statues of St. Peter and St. Paul on their columns had joyously lifted high each his emblem, the one the sword of the earth, the other the key of heaven. Be that as it may, I neither deny it nor make it obligatory to give it credence. But Gregorius was dressed in many garments: the falda of white silk, the lace and linen alb, with golden cord round the hips, the shoulder-cape embroidered in gold and red, then in three mass-garments, one over the other, not including the stole, the maniple and girdle, all of white silk, gold-embroidered. They put on him the papal stockings, of heavy stuff and so stiff with gold embroidery as to be heavy as boots; they hung the glittering pontifical cross round his neck on a gold cord, shoved the fisherman's ring on his finger over the silk glove, and lastly they spread over his nine garments the weightiest one of all, like morning red and evening gold to behold, and for costly embroidery not able to flow at all. Then they set him upon the golden carrying-chair, and youths in scarlet silk bore him through the basilica, right round it, full as it was of the devout, to the last pagan marble piece of its pavement, whether extending broad and long under the high ceiling of the nave and from the distant apse blinding the eye with the brilliance of mosaics, or where beneath the same burden of ceiling it spreads its arms on both sides in double-columned halls.

To the high altar over the grave they bore him, there he celebrated his coronation mass, well knowing how to do it for that he had so early watched his foster-father in the cloister of God's Passion. Many bishops and archbishops sat round him, shining like stars, also others in plenty, lords, abbots, and judges. Pæan and ecstasy abounded, great and manifold. Afterwards, while the clamour of bells still went on, he was borne round the square of St. Peter and then by the traditional way—uphill and down, through the triumphal arches of the Emperors Theodosius, Valentinian, Gratian, Titus, and Vespasian and through the Region Parione, where at the palace of the Prefect Chromatius the Jews had stationed themselves and praised him with bowed heads; along the Sacra Via next the Colosseum and to his house, the Lateran.

Now let me tell you how it befell. Scarcely had he, in the soothing stillness which followed the final cessation of the bells, laid off the superfluity of his ceremonial garb, when he began to govern Christendom, to feed his flocks and dispense blessings upon the motley necessities of the earth. Gregorius of the Stone shortly showed himself a very great Pope, who performed

deeds such as the depictions on the bases of columns of
Roman churches, taken from elsewhere, ascribe to the
half-god Hercules. I know not what to choose first, to
praise him: that he saw to the imperative strengthening
of the Aurelian Wall, also fortified places like Radi-
cofani and the one called Orte, built churches, bridges,
squares, cloisters, hospitals, and an orphan asylum,
paved the atrium of St. Peter's with marble and decorated the fountain there with an ædicula of porphyry
columns—all this was the least he did. For not only did
he know how with his firm-holding hand to preserve
or to create the patrimonies of the Holy See, even in
Sardinia, the Cottian Alps, Calabria, and Sicily, but he
also made tractable the dynasts and defiant barons of
the lowlands, in that he made them decide, by a talking-
to or by stronger methods, to give up their castles in
order to receive them back again as fiefs of the Church,
so that from being free nobility they became people
and men of Peter.

Is even that anywhere near all? Far from it. So firm
was his mind that with pitiless severity he put down
the Manicheans, the Priscillians and Pelagians, the Mo-
nophysite heresy, the stiff-necked bishops of Illyria
and Gallia he made submit to the primacy of St. Peter,
and against those who got themselves paid for the ex-
penses of the ordination he went out in such a way
that this vice for a time almost disappeared from the
earth.

I am talking about his power; but it was not that
from which, more than all, his renown flowed; rather it

was his mildness and humility. He was the first to distinguish the honour and consecration of the priestly
office from the worthiness or unworthiness of its ad-
ministrators, and condemned ex cathedra the severity
of the African Donatists, who, like the grim Tertullian,
would have it that the priesthood was effective only in
hands of unspotted purity. For he said no one was worthy and he himself on account of his flesh most unworthy of his dignity and only through an election
which bordered on the arbitrary had been elevated to
it. That probably suited some rogues and lechers in
God's garden, since at the outset it protected the office
from all the contempt which human frailty might draw
down upon it.

His tolerance and compassion equalled the fixed purpose to which when needful he held; yes, his bold way
of enforcing the divine mercy, in cases where the Deity
would scarcely have come on it by Itself, aroused attention throughout Christendom. He indeed and no
other it was who prayed the Emperor Trajan out of
hell, because he had straightway procured justice for a
weeping widow whose only son had been murdered.
This did cause a scandal, and the story went that God
had let him know, very well, now it had happened and
the pagan was installed among the blest, but he would
better not dare ask the like a second time.

Be that as it may: Gregor's leaning to loose was all
his life greater than that to bind and from this disposi-
tion flowed the decisions and judgments which issued
from his judgment seat, arousing at first, often in the

Church itself as likewise among the people, an amazed hesitation, but in the end an inevitable admiration. Thus he decreed great latitude in the methods of enlightenment in distant and simple-minded countries. Where pagan temples still stood, they should not be torn down, only the idols removed and the walls sprinkled with holy water, that the simple folk might pray where they had always prayed, only now in the spirit of enlightenment. St. Peter's, he explained, was as they all knew built from top to bottom out of the material of the Circus of the detestable Emperor Caligula and so to speak consisted utterly and entirely in shame and infamy—hallowed only by the grave and by the spirit, in that one worshipped there. It all depended on the spirit. Where earlier primitive folk had slaughtered oxen to the demons, let them continue to slay and eat, only now to the honour of the one and only God.

How many and how varied were the questions that came before him!—and all of them he answered in memorable wise. They asked him whether the sick, without paying alms, might eat meat in Lent. They might, he gave answer; sometimes necessity came before the law. They asked him whether a bastard might become a bishop. He could, yes, he responded. Tradition forbade it, indeed, that was easy to know, for a man who had studied law; but if the illegitimate one was a true and religious man, and godly, and of firm-holding hand, if the circumstances were urgent and the electors united, then it would only be doing right to make an exception.—A monk in Geneva knew a little surgery

and cut about wherever he could. He cut out a peasant woman's goitre and told her to stop in bed. But
she worked instead and died. Might he go on as a
priest? Yes, pronounced Gregor. Of course it was not
quite acceptable for a man of God to do that sort of
work; yet he worked not out of greed but for humanity's sake, love of his art and horror of the goitre, and
he had given directions for treatment, the neglect of
which he could not help. So after he had performed
only a light penance he might again say mass.—Highly
exciting was the affair of the Moslem converts in the
land of Canaan, who in all sincerity, each with his four
wives and their children, came to the baptismal font.
Could these, in the name of God, become Christians?
This, so his chamberlain said, gave the Pope a sleepless
night. But then he bethought himself of Abraham and
the other forefathers who had lived, under the very
eyes of Jahwe, no differently from the Turks. He rose
from bed and dictated the answer to his scribe: In the
Gospel itself, to say nothing of the books of the Old
Testament, not a word is to be found that expressly
forbids polygamy. As plainly according to the laws of
their cult a plurality of wives was incumbent upon
heathen, then as Christians they should be allowed to
keep them, according to the example of the patriarchs.
It would be unwise to make the conversion harder for
them unless one must, and human conflicts would be
unavoidable if one laid upon them each to take one of
his wives with him into the new life, but to thrust the

others and their innocent babes back into the darkness, whereby the Church would suffer the loss of many souls. The mission was enjoined to act with this point of view in mind. Given in Rome, early morning, in the Lateran. Gregorius P.M. m.p.

What a sensation that made! It travelled as far as the Thracians and Scythians. If not for his severity against the Simonists, the heretics, and the stiff-necked recusants against the primacy they would have accused the Pope of laxity. And even so he gave ground for this accusation, by declaring once and for all that the baptism of a heretic converted to the Church was valid, because after all it was dispensed in the name of Christ, and refused second baptism, whereat several bishops of Africa and Asia were greatly exacerbated. An embassy from Carthage, come to protest against wrongful use of his absolute power, he refused to see, yes, he loosed the interdict against the unruly primacy of Africa in this affair. It would almost have come to a schism on this matter if Gregor had not shown just at that time by a perfect work of art in the way of a miracle, the kind that Moses performed before Pharaoh, that God was on his side. That is, by merely touching the chains worn by Peter, the Jerusalem and the Roman pieces, he made a whole of them so that they now formed a single chain of thirty-eight links. Hence the feast of the chain of St. Peter, which cannot be without root and origin and thus confirms the protocol of that act.

With it he either struck down or anticipated the

grumbling about slackness. And yet there were some
who asserted he would like to pardon unpardonable
sins like adultery and harlotry. That was not accurate.
He ordered for such malefactors right severe penance,
only not all too severe, that he loved not and was
against it. He himself had gone through extremest penance and been reduced by God to a horny, woolly little
creature and earth-suckling; but he was of the opinion,
and instructed all confessors and ecclesiastical judges to
share it, that one should lighten the sinner's load, that
remorse might be sweet to him. Justice is hard- and
horny-handed, while the world of the flesh needs indeed firmness, yet gentleness. If one so zealously pur-
sue the sinner, one may well bring more harm than
healing. Too rash a penance laid upon a seeker for grace
may make him lose heart, not bear it and again renounce God, spoilt as he is by the Devil, whose service he in reverse remorse takes up again. Accordingly
it is statesmanlike to make mercy go before justice,
since it creates the right measure in the life of the spirit,
by which means the sinner is saved and the good is constantly preserved, that the honour of God may wax
mightily in the Roman Empire.

Whom should not such teachings have rejoiced?
They rejoiced everybody, except some disciplinarians,
but an authority peculiar to his personality held them
in check. Also he was very beautiful to look upon, as
children of sin, for whatever reason, often are: a splendid man.

"He," says the saying, "is gladly hearkened to, whom

one loves." And he was loved, as far as Persia and Thracia, for they gladly heard him. Because of his amazing knowledge he was called the "apostolic oracle"; but for his lenity he was called "Doctor Mellifluus"—that is: "the teacher from whom honey flows."

Pattard

His mother, his aunt, his wife, these three had but one body among them, and that was now stricken in years, in hardship grown weak in strength and colour, so much had she clad herself in penitence and pains all this while and unremittingly drunk the water of humility. What her lover-son had laid upon her before he departed out of her land and went on his penitential pilgrimage, that she had wholly, with body and goods and patient soul, performed, many years long, more than twenty, and even so when he left she had been eight-and-thirty.

At that time he had been quite young, and would have, in riper years, probably made it milder for her, particularly as he could have told beforehand that Werimbald, her distant cousin, who after his disappearance became duke in Flaundres-Artoys, would make right harsh use of her forsakenness, her withdrawal from the things of this earth, her craving to drink the water of humility; that he would in every way diminish her widow's portion, so that the asylum which she was able to build on the highroad at the foot of the citadel

was of the very meanest, no better than a barrack,
where there was not even room enough for her to sleep
alone. So she slept among the sick and cripples whom
she gathered in from the highway or who knocked at
her wooden door, and to whom she was a grey angel
because she gave them a bed and fed them with gruel
and curds.

And there too she came to her straw sack to give
birth to her second little daughter, whom, like Herrad,
the first one, we might also call her grandchild. There
stood by her at her hour a woman, herself far advanced in pregnancy, who had conceived in sin from a
roving juggler with whom her husband had caught her,
and been driven out with the dung-fork; and when
only three days later the woman herself was brought to
bed, then Sibylla got up from hers to help in her turn
and delivered the woman of a boy. Gudula, this sinful
woman, stopped on with her and helped her to comfort the sick, to wash their wounds, to bathe and bind
them. Growing up, her daughters also helped, clad likewise in grey: Herrad red and white like an apple, whose
name was now Stultitia, her baptismal name being now
too proud, and she besides baptized by mistake; the second, too, called Humilitas without baptism and foreign
pale and brown again, with black eyes having a blue un-
dertone, very like her grandfather-uncle Wiligis and
thus also like her father-brother, on which account
Sibylla kept her much more strictly than Stultitia, who
moreover in looks fell outside the group.

But Gudula's boy, hers and the juggler's son, was

given in baptism the name of Pattard and wore it in
honour. For he became a stout, honest, faithful, handy
son of the asylum, even as a half-grown lad, and later
still more, versed in many skills, joiner and wood-
worker, candle-moulder, cobbler and oven-setter, bee-
keeper too, gardener, and such a carpenter that he
added to the building several new rooms and bed-
closets, that the mistress might take in more of the afflicted, isolate the leprous, and permit herself with her
daughters to sleep apart. Not only that, but he was
gifted to decorate most marvellously the inside walls
of the refuge. For from early on it had been his delight, not as any special one but along with the other
manual skills, to figure with charcoal, slate, and graph-
ite, wherever there was a wall-space that attracted him;
then to grind himself colours and mix them with water, white of egg, and honey, and therewith to present
to the eye man and beast, also higher beings like apostles and angels, with great convincingness and in natural colours. In such wise he had come far and further,
and when he was seventeen and had constructed the
new sleeping-kennels—a stocky fellow, swarthy, with
a thin face, bordered both sides with hair from his temples, so long that it looked like a beard—he rough-cast
the walls with wet plaster and in water-colour, with
the brush, painted on them the most amazing things: a
wounded and bleeding bishop with a halo, martyred by
soldiers; David, bringing home Goliath's head by the
hair, and looking as though nothing much had happened; the Lord Jesus, how He was baptized in the Jor-

dan, and again on the roof of a church being tempted
by a tailed Satan to jump off—and more of the like.
When that was done, again he grew cabbages, cobbled
shoes, never bothered his head when the ladies and
gentlemen from the castle, despite all their disgust at
sickness and festering sores, came down to the asylum
to see his pictures. But Duke Werimbald came not, having heard that the artist had lent to the Captain presid-
ing over the martyrdom of the Bishop a convincing
likeness to his own features.

Neither did these curious crowds get to see Sibylla,
although they peered about after her, and with reason.
For Grimald's child, who had considered no one save
her just as rare brother her equal in birth, was still, in
old age and her penitential garb, of regal though grief-
worn beauty. Grief-worn were her cheeks, and two
permanent furrows were graven between her brows,
but neither the years nor the deadly sins that weighed
her down nor all the stooping over sickbeds and bath-
tubs had had power to bow her form. Erect and com-
manding it was as at the time when Grigorss first approached her in the church of hard-pressed Bruges, and
proud her step, the nobility of the flesh strangely assert-
ing itself against the abasement of the soul by reason of
Christian consciousness of sin. Whether grey or white
her hair one could not see under the head-bands which
concealed even her brows. But the bitter tears of remorse and dread through so many years because of her
heaped-up, deadly sins could not destroy the special
beauty of her ivory face, this charm marked with the

pale sickle underneath the bands—which I will not try
to describe again since after all I am no Pattard and
cannot paint—for which, alas, they had had among
them all, brother and sister, son and mother, such mutual and exclusive feeling.

Only Dame Sibylla, the penitent, wore this beauty
now, in her age, in its marred form, for Wiligis was
gone, Grigorss had followed him and was probably
gone as well, though they had not brought her his body
back. But while sweet Wiligis was gone and sunk into
the earth through mere fineness of fibre, certainly Grigorss, her second spouse, had been the victim of his
own proud young manliness, for definitely the child
had overdone the penance and not given heed to himself, but let his beautiful body, that had shared wedded
bliss with her, be butchered by crooked sabres in the
Holy Land. Had thereby his soul escaped the fires of
hell? And Wiligis his? Who could tell her? Or even
how it stood with her own soul, covered as it was with
deadly sins as with festering wounds—whether she,
after drinking so long of the waters of humiliation, had
the smallest prospect of ever beholding God? Much,
when not bathing the sick, did she weep, kneeling hard
in anguished prayer for all three and their terribly tor-
tuous bond.

Then, when she was sixty, she heard that a very
great Pope had arisen in Rome, with the papal name of
Gregorius, who was a comforter of sinners and so good
a physician as never was for soul-bruises, of all who
ever carried the key, much sooner inclined to loose than

to bind. How should she not have heard of him? All
the world heard of him, the whole orbis terrarum Chris-
tianus, and to me it always seems as though he had always intended that along with the orbis she too should
hear. Had he not indeed become so great a Pope in order that his fame should penetrate everywhere and so
to her ear as well? At least, he had been so good a duke,
just because he so needed to on her account whom he
deceived. One must only need to more than the rest,
then one makes oneself a name among men.

So then the resolve ripened in the woman, in her old
age to make pilgrimage to Rome to the Holy Pontiff
and bring to his ears, whom it must at least interest, this
whole case of extreme and involved sinfulness, whose
central point she was, that she might at least receive
consolation and counsel from him. She told it to Gudula, her helper.

"Gudula," she said, "it is borne in upon me, and my
prayers have ripened it within me, that I will make a
pilgrimage to this Pope and in his ear confess my whole
unheard-of tale. There has probably never come before him such superfluity of sinfulness and it is fitting
he should hear of it. He alone can weigh this extravagant excess with the fullness of God's grace and measure whether the latter will be exceeded or whether
God's grace, even as excess, in turn is equal to it and
balances my sin. One cannot tell. Perhaps he will lift
his hands, curse me out of Christianity, and hand me
over to the burning pit. Then it is all over, and I know.
But perhaps I shall find peace in this confession—peace

here and a little blessedness there, even if only a limited
one—for me and those I loved."

Gudula listened, nodding her head, her hands in the
sleeves of her grey robe.

"I will take Stultitia and Humilitas with me too,"
went on Sibylla, "and set the innocent unblest fruits of
my deadly sin before his eyes, perhaps to receive the
boon of Christian baptism for Humilitas, despite the
manly prohibition of her father Grigorss. Pope Gregor
is said to be so magnanimous about baptism and has
granted it even to the many-wived Musselmans and all
their broods, as one hears everywhere. But you, so I
have decided, I will for the time set here over the asylum till I come back, damned or redeemed."

"Dear lady," answered Gudula, "you might take me
with you too that I may confess to our Lord Pope that
old sin of mine with the juggler and he may weigh its
weight against the grace of God."

"Ah, Gudula," answered her Sibylla, "the Pope
would smile at your confession and smile too at your
coming on that account before Peter's throne. That affair with the juggler was just a bagatelle, it was long
since atoned for and your son Pattard is certainly a
capital chap. He shall be my messenger when I write
to Rome. I am no princess now, and it is not fitting that
I write personally to the Pope. But I was a princess,
and I know how things should be done. I will write
to the nomenclator of His Holiness, his conseillor, I may
tell you, in matters of grace, mouthpiece for widows
and wards and all the oppressed, to whom one applies

when one has something to ask of the Pope. To him
I will write I stand at the centre of a story of abnormal
wickedness. By birth the grey-haired one, it shall be
said, stands high, but now for long a penitent, and im-
plores the favour of casting herself at the feet of the
Father of Christianity, to be granted to confess to his
ear the abomination of her life, which certainly is hard
and frightful to hear; one must be a man of great firmness to endure it and to believe that God can endure it.
Thus will I write to make curious the nomenclator and
perhaps the Pope too. Why are we women if we are
not allowed to use a little artfulness on such an occasion? In short, the letter is as good as finished in my
head, I only need to put it on parchment and Pattard
shall carry it to Rome. But I will make your affair come
in by the way, if the Pope grants me hearing. That he
will certainly be able to stand, even though it is really
relatively laughable."

"And Pattard?" she said to Gudula some months
later. "Where is he? Great is my impatience, and
makes the time longer than it is, but yet I reckon that
he must be back before long, be it with permission or
denial, but back he must surely come. My impatience,
Gudula, will turn into worry, not on my account but
on his and yours. For how should I stand with you if
something happened to him on the journey and we
never heard from him again because he was killed by
robbers or fell into an abyss? That would be more
frightful to me than if he brought a rejection back!"

"Just be patient, lady, and wait!" Gudula soothed

her, with her arms in her sleeves. "My Pattard, he'll
come out all right."

And really it turned out that in Rome Pattard had
fallen in with some other young folk who like him figured and painted in colour. He had made friends with
them and they had brought him to their master, to
whom they went to school for colour-grinding and
using the brush. He had him draw something, praised
him and gave him advice, and thus Pattard in all good
faith had lingered in the city although he had the Pope's
consent, given through the nomenclator, in his pocket.
He parted from Rome with reluctance, from his companions and their master, and thus was very glad that
Sibylla, when with many excuses for the delay he gave
her the confirmation, told him he should come back at
once when with Stultitia and Humilitas she set out for
Rome, and employ his experience as a help on the
journey. This he did, with much discretion, care, and
thoughtfulness, and brought mother and daughters happily through the already familiar stretches and perils so
that their feet struck not against a stone: through high
wastes and through sweet meadowlands down into the
city of cities and before the nomenclator, who directed
them to lodge in the nuns' cloister of Sergius and Bacchus, quite close to the Palace of the Lateran, for shelter and hospitality, and named to the suppliant the day
and hour, namely the very next day, when the Pope
would incline his ear and listen to her alone, in his innermost work-room.

The Audience

THE NUNS of Sergius and Bacchus received them friend-
lily, and the following day, before the appointed hour,
soon after early mass, the cubicularius, or chamberlain,
fetched the pilgrims from the cloister and led them to
the palace; there he delivered them, in the first hall to
the protoscriniarius, who passed them on to the vestiar-
ius, from whom the vice-dominus received them and
yielded them up to the primicerius of the defensorum
—and so on from room to room. Through many hands
they passed, and through ten stone halls it went with
them, who were bound for the innermost room,
guarded by Palatine halberdiers, guardanobili, portiers,
and red litter-bearers. In the largest room stood a throne;
past it two honorary chamberlains led them and at the
door gave them up to two privy chamberlains. Now
they were in the seventh, the private antechamber, and
there Stultitia and Humilitas remained, in the care of
two privy chaplains. Sibylla however walked on, led
by an elderly man, the curopalata, for the private antechamber was far from being next to the innermost one!
Another hall adjoined it, and next it still another, which

served no purpose save to create distance, and after that a small one with another throne, this too serving only to make space. But this one did have egress by an oaken door bearing the papal arms in marble above it, and kept right and left by scarlet-clad guards. To these the curopalata nodded his head and they opened both sides. The old man stepped back, but the woman paced past him and was in the innermost room.

The Father of the Christian world, in years at a guess forty-two (and I guess aright, for he had been ruling for five), sat on a red-gold seat at a table with a red leather top, covered with paper rolls among the writing-gear. He sat sidewise to her as she entered and even at the door bent low in the first deep curtsy, and he turned towards her his head, which was wrapped in a red velvet hood trimmed with ermine, reaching down to the nape of the neck and half over the ears. That is a handsome headgear, reserved for the Pope, and I very much like too the short mantle of the same material which he had about his shoulders over the white dalmatic—over that the pallium embroidered with crosses. Severe was his face in the hood, free of beard, the cheek-bones so white and strongly marked that it looked as though they were pushed forward by the clenching of the jaws; very gravely the upper lip, set rather far forwards from its beginning at the nose, rested on the lower one. But the dark eyes were bright with tears as they looked towards the penitent, though their gaze had not been extenuated thereby—and that is a rare and a fine thing, to gaze unflinchingly through tears.

She did not see it, for her eyes were piously cast down as she advanced making three low curtsies and at the end threw herself at his feet. With a movement almost too quick for dignity he raised her up, prevented her from kissing his cross-stamped morocco slippers, and gave her instead his ring to kiss. Then he motioned to a bench beside him, covered with red velvet; it had a sort of cushioned shelf on which to lay the hands. Thence she raised her eyes to God's vicar on earth and looked with reverence in his face. The old woman! She forgot to blink as she looked, forgot to look down, omitted, understand me, to twitch her lashes, which soon would have made her gaze not so much fixed as swimming, blurring its object, till it no longer fixes what it looks at, but seems to look into vague distance. No, she rather closed her eyes, passed the tips of her fingers lightly across her brow, and then looked down upon her folded hands.

"You have, dear lady and our daughter," began her confessor in a controlled voice, "made a long journey to us from your remote country, over which, as we hear, you were once ruler. Great must your longing be to open your heart to us and here to lay down its load. The hour for it is come. The Pope hears."

"Yes, Holy Father," answered she, "the hour is here, thanks to your compassion, of which I well know that it is only temporary and refers only to the listening, for how it will be after the hearing with yours and God's mercy—I tremble to think."

"The Pope hears," he repeated, and bent his ear,

partly covered as it was with the velvet cap, somewhat closer to her.

"God help me," she whispered, "to begin. Know, Holy Father, to my chastisement I preside, as was commanded me from a certain source, over an asylum for the dregs of the highway, and at my hand is my helper, Gudula by name, a grievous sinner. For twenty years ago she forgot herself entirely with a vagabond juggler and let herself be caught by her husband in the act so that in justified wrath he thrust her forth with a farm implement. So she came to me and joined her penance to mine and besought me to put in a good word for her redemption, which I undertake because God seems inclined to forgive her. For He blessed her with a son from the juggler, named Pattard, who is an excellent fellow and probably better than if he were from her husband. He is skilled at all trades, and paints with colours so naturally that I would like to ask you, Holy Father, whether he could not find a position at your court and paint your apartments and some chapels to the glory of God and in gratitude for his mother's redemption."

"Woman," said Gregor, and lifted his ear away from her, "have you come all this way only to confess this trifle? For after all that you wrote to our nomenclator, what passed between that woman and the juggler was a bagatelle compared to the sins allotted to you."

"That is only too true, Holy Father," she admitted. "And I have feared within myself you might in error praise me for unselfishly putting concern for my own salvation in the rear of that for a sinful sister and speaking first for her, even putting in for a job for her art-skilled Pattard. This interpretation would have been possible but you have rightly not brought it up. Not out of selflessness did I speak first of Gudula; I have only put her story first to gain time and because I am so terrified to tell my own and by confirming it to fill your ears with horrors."

"This ear and this heart," he replied, "are steadfast. Speak without pretexts. The Pope hears."

So then she told him in his ear, sometimes twisting her beautiful slender hands on the cushion, sometimes stopping altogether, the murmuring voice sometimes choked with sobs, all and everything, the whole intemperate tale, as I have told it to you, with exception of the twice seventeen years on the Norman isle and on the stone, wherein knowledge lacked her. Of her sweet brother she whispered and how they two considered only each other equal in fineness; of Grimald's knightliness, and how when he lay stiff in death the little owlets had screamed so fearfully round the tower and Hanegiff the faithful had howled up to the beams, but they had done it, anyhow, murderously, gorily, in bliss of equal birth. How they had gone on, and the body of the sister had been monstrously blessed with a brother-fruit. Of Herr Eisengrein and the harsh well-meaningness of his arrangements. Of Wiligis's departure and delicate death. Of her delivery in the water-burg under Frau Eisengrein's care and how they had

taken away the lovely boy and shut it in a little tun, so
that she scarce had time to furnish it somewhat for the
billowy voyage; with the tablet whereon stood his origins, loaves of bread with gold inside, and some good
stuffs from Eastern lands. Of the five swords she spoke,
which had pierced her heart, and of her falling-out
with God, to whom she had now no longer will to be
a woman, no woman at all, so that she scorned all wooers and thus brought her land to misery. Her old dream
also she confessed: how it had dreamed her she bore a
dragon, who tore her womb and flew away, only to
come back and squeeze itself again into her womb. And
so had it happened. For suddenly the child had become
a man, or rather a knightly youth with greatest claim
to manliness, and as her knight had tamed the wild
wooer with incredibly firm-holding hand. How she
then, she whispered, Holy Father, had taken the beloved, the only one whom she could and must love, for
spouse, and lived with him in wedded bliss for three
years long, also borne him a daughter, white and apple-
red, and later another, like herself and him. How by
the finding of the tablet, she sobbed, the identity of
child and spouse had been frightfully revealed and her
soul for horror had swounded, but only in play-acting-
wise, for on top the soul pretends and makes to-do
about the diabolical deception practised on it, but underneath, where truth abides in quietness, the identity
had been known at the first glance, and conscious-
unconscious she had taken her own child for husband,
because again he had been the only one equal in birth.

There it was: therewith was the uttermost thing confessed, for she would be unworthy of the papal ear if she had not confessed the guilefulness of her mind, holding nothing back. Now he might, red with anger, lift his hands clenched into fists and condemn her to hell-fire, rather that than for her before God and the Pope lyingly to keep back how secretly she had known all and how at the discovery her soul had only pretended.

She stopped. There was a silence. She said: "You have heard my voice long, Pope Gregorius. Shall I now hear yours again?"

She heard it again, if not full-toned, for he spoke low like the priest in the confessional:

"Great and extreme, woman, is your sin, and to the very bottom have you confessed it to the Pope. This thoroughness to the uttermost is greater penance than when according to your sin-husband's arrangement you washed the feet of beggars. You are expecting that I shall raise my hands and curse you. Has never anyone told you, who had studied God, that He accepts true repentance for all sins and that a human being, be his soul never so sick—if his eye only for an hour grows wet with rue, then he is saved?"

"Yes, I have heard," she replied, "and it is overwhelming to hear it again from the Pope. But not by myself will I or can I be saved, save only with him, my child and spouse. May it please your Holiness, how is it with him?"

"For the present," said he, "I ask you that. You have

never heard since that time what has become of him, whether he is living or dead?"

"Never, lord, have I heard from him. But as to whether he lives or is dead, of that I am convinced he is dead. For out of manhood he surely took upon himself so powerful a penance that he went too far. He did think that his sin overpassed mine, which I cannot admit. For if all his flesh and blood consisted in sin—his parents' sin—then he only in so far sinned that he in ignorance lay with his mother. But I with my brother conceived a spouse."

"The measure of the sinfulness," he responded, "is controvertible before God, the more so that thy child, in that place where the soul makes no pretence, likewise very well knew that it was his mother whom he loved."

"Father of Christendom, how heavily you tax him!"

"Not too heavily. The Pope will not deal with the youth more gently than you have dealt with yourself. A youth who sets out to find his mother and wins by conquest a wife who, however beautiful, could be his mother, must reckon with it that she might be his mother whom he marries. So much for his understanding. But to his blood the identity of wife and mother was familiar long before he learned the truth and play-acted about it."

"It is the Pope speaks. And yet I cannot believe it."

"Woman, he himself told us."

"What, what? So you have seen him before his death?"

"He is definitely alive."

"I cannot grasp it. Where, where is he?"

"Not far from here. Would you trust yourself to recognize him if God showed him to you?"

"Holiness, at the first glance!"

"And let me further ask: would it be very painful to see him again or would joy outweigh?"

"It would outweigh not only, it would be blessedly alone in the picture. Mercy, lord! Let me see him!"

"Then first see this."

And he drew out from under the papers on the table a thing which he handed to her: of ivory, framed, and written like a letter, the tablet. She held it in her hands.

"Where am I?" she said. "This is the thing of which I told you, that I gave to the babe in the little cask seventeen years gone, and again seventeen and three and five. God, oh my God, I hold it again—the third time! When I inscribed it with the infant's origins I held it, and again in the horrible hour when being shown by the wicked maid I drew it out of the drawer in my husband's room. What need for the sinful soul to guess how he might have come by the thing! The child, and the husband—the soul would have them far asunder and not grasp their identity. To the husband, so would the wife for long have it, the child gave this tablet. To you my husband gave it, lord, dearest Pope?"

"It is mine from the first. With it I landed, first on an island in the sea, then in the land of your fathers and mine. A new task, dearest, have I to set your soul, but

a merciful one: it is to grasp the three-in-oneness of
child, spouse, and Pope."

"My head reels."

"Understand, Sibylla, we are your son."

She bent smiling over her cushion, while her tears
ran down the cheeks ravaged by age and remorse. And
spoke between smiles and tears:

"That I have known for long."

"What?" said he. "So you recognized me in the
Pope's hood, after so many years?"

"Holiness, at the first glance. I know you always."

"And have, light-headed woman, only played with
us?"

"Since you would play with me yourself—"

"We thought to offer God an entertainment."

"And I played along with you. And yet it was no
play. For if three are one, even so the Pope is far from
child and spouse. To the chosen of the Lord have I
confessed from the depths of my soul."

"Mother!" he cried.

"Father!" cried she. "Father of my children, ever-
beloved child!"

And they hugged each other and wept together.

"Grigorss, poor darling," said she as she pressed his
head to her. "How ruthlessly you must have done penance, for God to have set you so far above us sinners!"

"No more of that," he responded. "My state was the
barest indeed, but the stars in heaven, the wind and
weather rang their changes, and added to that God
brought me low, made me a hibernating creature, so

then one does not feel it so much. But dear—dearest Mother thou—wert thou not astonied to find the son in the Pope?"

"Ah, Grigorss," she retorted, "the whole story is so beyond anything that the most astonishing thing in it astonishes no more. But how highly must we praise God's wisdom, that He, appeased by your diminishment raised you to be Pope! For now it is in your power to cancel the horror which still continues and annul our marriage. Only think that to this very day we are Christian man and wife!"

"Most revered," said he, "we will leave that to God and see whether or no He will ascribe validity to a work of the Devil like our marriage. It would be little fitting for me to pronounce the divorce and put our relation back on the footing of mother and son. For, everything considered, I would better not be your son either."

"But what, then, child, can we be to one another?"

"Brother and sister," he answered, "in love and grief, in repentance and in grace."

She mused.

"Brother and sister. And where is Wiligis's soul?"

"My father's soul? Woman, have you never heard that we succeeded in praying a pagan Emperor out of hell? Well then, no anxiousness over my dear uncle, whom I would so gladly have known in life, but whom one day we shall meet in paradise."

"Hail, child, to thy power of the key! You were so young when you went from me and denied your sec-

ond daughter baptism. Wouldst thou now, in thy maturity, as Pope refuse it to her?"

"Our daughters!" he cried. "Where are they?"

"I felt it, a little," she replied, "that you had not yet
asked about them. They are in the private antechamber."

"So far from here! They must bring them before us
at once."

It was done. Stultitia and Humilitas came in to them
in the innermost room and they too might not kiss the
slippers but only the ring.

"Dear nieces," said Gregorius, "thus we name you,
for your mother has found in the Pope a collateral kins-
man. We cordially rejoice with full heart to learn to
know you, in your differing kinds of loveliness."

To Sibylla he said:

"So you see, revered and beloved, and God be praised
for it, that Satan is not all-powerful and that he was un-
able to wreak his uttermost will till I had to do with
these as well and even had children by them, whereby
the relationship would have become a perfect sink of
iniquity. Everything has its limits—the world is finite."

Much more they spoke with each other, and as before, only under so much happier circumstances, Gregorius made his arrangements, since he was the man and
on top of that the Pope. For the present Sibylla and the
nieces were to lodge in the cloister of Sergius and Bacchus, but soon he would build her a cloister of her own,
where she as princess and abbess should preside in great
dignity. It came to pass just as he said and Stultitia re-

mained with her mother as Vice-Abbess, but Humilitas, after she had received Christian baptism, married Pattard, the figure-maker, since they had long been inclined to one another. Very far did the painter go in his sleight, held high rank in Rome, and might decorate many walls, in part because of his gift, in part because he had the Pope's niece to wife. This is called nepotism, but against it there is nothing to say, if it is justified by merit.

So they all dwelt together in happiness and each in his time died his death, each according as he had begun and in his turn. Sibylla died first, at eighty; older she lived not, for much early affliction and the harsh years of penance had probably shortened her life. Her brother-son, the Pope, outlived her almost a generation: he attained ninety years and as shepherd of the folk went ever higher, until at the end he excited the amazement of the orbis as apostolic oracle and Doctor Mellifluus. The others abode still a little here, the longest the children of Pattard and Humilitas, pleasing and happy folk, who were begot forwards and in the right direction and so lived. But however long, at last they too faded, like the summer leaf, and enriched the soil, whereon other, later mortals moved and flourished and faded. The world is finite and infinite only is the glory of God.

Clemens, who has thus brought the tale to the end, thanks you for your attention and gladly accepts your thanks for the pains he has spent. But let no one who has enjoyed the story draw a wrong moral from it and think that sin is a slight thing. Let him beware of saying to himself: "Well then, be thou a jolly sinner. If it turned out so well with this lot, how then shalt thou be lost?" That is devil's whispering. First spend seventeen years on a stone, reduced to a hedgehog, and bathe the afflicted for more than twenty, you will see if all that is a joke! But truly it is wise to divine in the sinner the chosen one, and wise that is too for the sinner himself. For the divining of his chosen state may make him worthy and his sinfulness fruitful so that it bears him up for high flights.

In recompense for warning and counsel I beg the favour that you include me in your prayers, that we all, with them of whom I told, may one day see each other in paradise.

Valete

THIS STORY *is based in the main on the verse epos* Gregorious vom Stein *by the Middle High German poet Hartmann von Aue* (c. 1165–1210), *who took his legend of chivalry from the French.*

A NOTE ABOUT THE AUTHOR

THOMAS MANN, born in 1875 into one of Lübeck's prominent merchant families, was only twenty-five when *Buddenbrooks* was published. His second great work of fiction, *The Magic Mountain*, was issued in 1924. Five years later he was awarded the Nobel Prize for Literature.

The chance request of an artist for an introduction to a portfolio of Joseph drawings was the genesis of his tetralogy, *Joseph and His Brothers*, the first volume of which was published in 1933. In that same year Mann left Munich—where he had made his home—and Germany, to settle for a time in Switzerland.

In 1941 Mann moved to Pacific Palisades, California. It was there that he wrote *Dr. Faustus* and *The Holy Sinner*. Three years later he became a citizen of the United States. In 1952 he moved to Kilchberg, a suburb of Zurich. There he wrote *Confessions of Felix Krull, Confidence Man*, the continuation of a fragmentary story that had been published more than thirty years earlier. He died in 1955, not long after a memorable three-day celebration of his eightieth birthday.